CW00852919

The Music Room

The Music Room

Jim Ellis

Copyright (C) 2018 Jim Ellis
Layout design and Copyright (C) 2018 Creativia
Published 2018 by Creativia
Cover art by Cover Mint
This book is a work of fiction. Names, characters, places, and incidents are the product
of the author's imagination or are used fictitiously. Any resemblance to actual events,
locales, or persons, living or dead, is purely coincidental.
All rights reserved. No part of this book may be reproduced or transmitted in any form
or by any means, electronic or mechanical, including photocopying, recording, or by
any information storage and retrieval system, without the author's permission.

Acknowledgements

Thanks to Cynthia Weiner, Libby Jacobs, and Miriam Santana for their support and encouragement; and a warm thank you to Maggie McClure for proof reading. A special thanks to my Good Lady, Jeannette.

Well, honour is the subject of my story.
I cannot tell what you and other men
Think of this life...

Shakespeare, *Julius Caesar*, act 1

Contents

Chapter 1

Apprentice Days

I was soon to be fifteen. I carried fantastic stories in my head. I held off the future dreaming of adventures in the Baltic Lands, imagined myself there fighting with Scots knights and mercenaries in the German service. And when I grew tired of that, I saw myself a Bronco Warrior, on the run with the last of the fighting Chiricahua. I was bored, but resigned to putting in the time until June. I wanted to be anywhere but St Mary's School. I dreaded what lay ahead when I left school: I wasn't going on the Baltic Crusade, or preparing to ambush the Cavalry; I was going down to Reid's foundry, a dirty noisy place where they built diesel engines for ships.

St Mary's was a school for boys, but on Sunday mornings at Mass I stared at the plump freckled girls. That helped shut out the soporific voice of the priest. Unexpectedly my life changed when I saw the new music teacher.

January 1954; the day school started after the Christmas holidays, the door of the music room clicked open and a lovely young woman came in. Her name was Isobel Clieshman. She was Springtime. I reckoned she was about twenty-three. She was lovelier than Hedy Lamarr or Joan Leslie, film stars I'd a crush on. Isobel Clieshman was real, and I wanted her to speak to me, but I'd have died had she. I felt so tender towards her; and guilty at the bulge in my pants.

There was hesitance in her walk; a movement of her sad eyes around the room. A look of regret that she had finished up in St Mary's and not some nice middle-class school in Glasgow.

To my class, she was 'The Proddy music teacher.' The verdict was 'Nae fuckin' tits.' For the wretched boys of St Mary's the pinnacle of female beauty was a fat arse and big knockers; a waspy belt pulled tight at the waist to give an hourglass shape. The boys lusted after Miss O'Hagen, a raven haired woman, run to fat. In her science class she talked about the body. She invited a boy to feel the pulse at her wrist; then squeezed her tit.

"The pulse beats in time to my heart."

The boys loved it. I was glad I had Isobel Clieshman all to myself.

I adored the delicate points of her small breasts, the long slender legs. She arrived at the untidy time of school life, the end of Fourth Year. We loafed at our desks, idle, and impatient to be away from St Mary's. The music teacher was so different from the young Catholic teaching assistants, faces scrubbed pink, fresh from convent training where the nuns had wasted their heads with stories of Baby Jesus, The Blessed Virgin, and All the Saints. Miss Clieshman stood out from the sober female teachers shrouded in thick wool twin sets, tweed skirts, and sensible shoes.

I wondered what malfunction of fate had brought Isobel Clieshman to St Mary's. It was a bleak Catholic Technical School existing to feed boys to the doomed shipyards, foundries, and sugar refineries of the town. Sometimes she seemed so lonely, staring into space. I called her Cliesh and she belonged to me.

Most of the teachers in St Mary's looked down on the pupils. But from the start Cliesh showed an interest in us. In those few months, she taught us that there was more to music than bawling out hymns and sea shanties. We were surprised when she asked us to bring our records from home. Cliesh wanted to know where we'd bought them, and we told her about Saturday afternoons searching for bargains.

Someone handed over a record of Cauliga by Hank Williams and the class sang along with it.

"Cauliga was a wooden Indian standing by the door..." It was good fun.

"Did anyone else bring a record?" Cliesh said.

I'd got to the point where I had to do something or go mad. Cliesh displaced my dreaming of Baltic Crusades and Chiricahua life on the frontier.

The evening before the music class searching for courage I'd walked The Cut, an aqueduct inserted on the hills above the town. I meant to lay my heart bare and to Hell with the taunts of the class hard men that I was nuts and sucking up; or the possibility that Cliesh might reprimand me, then have James Malone thrash me for impertinence. It was crazy one way love.

I stuck up my hand; a smart arse. "Bessie Smith, Miss."

She listened to the introduction of Careless Love; it was an old record, the lyric muffled. Cliesh caught the tune on the piano.

"Tim Ronsard, will you sing?"

"Yes, Miss."

The hard men tittered.

She played; I sang, voice pure.

"Love, oh love, oh careless love,

You fly to my head like wine,

You've ruined the life of many a poor man, and you nearly wrecked this life of mine...

Night and day I weep and moan..."

Cliesh fluffed a chord change and stopped the gramophone. She handed me the record, "Thank you, Tim. You've all been very good."

I caught her eye and she turned away. Cliesh dismissed the class a few minutes early.

The next class Cliesh played the orchestral suite from Carmen and The Flying Dutchman on the gramophone. She barely looked at me. Then she played a selection from the Siegfried Idyll on the piano; I had to look away.

She asked me to stay behind after class and put away the gramophone. I didn't want to leave. "I'll clean the black board, Miss?"

"All right."

I cleaned the blackboard slowly, perfectly.

"Where is your surname from, Tim?"

"Donegal, Miss."

"You've heard of Ronsard?"

"No, Miss."

"He was a French poet. Did you know your name was French?"

"No, Miss."

We stood at her desk close to the piano. She wore a finely tailored jacket and matching skirt of soft heather and mustard wool; a white silk blouse tied at the neck with a loose cascading bow. She glided across the floor, slender legs in sheer stockings, elegantly shod. That day her lips were red and full, eyes heightened with touches of blue, the eyelashes long, and black.

Cliesh told me about the French who'd fought with the Irish rebels against the English in the Rising of '98. The ships of the French Navy that landed General Humbert's Black Legion. After parole and repatriation some of the French stayed on.

"Perhaps you're a descendant of a Naval Officer, or a legionnaire."

"Oh, I wish that was true, Miss."

Cliesh smiled. She'd made me proud of my name.

I was stiff with desire after being so near her. I ran into the yard, ready for home. I was ambushed by the class hard men: McAllister, Burns and Montague. McAllister grabbed my shirtfront, his face close.

"Whit the fuck dae ye want wi' tha' Proddy bastard?"

His teeth had green stains and his breath stank; his neck around the shirt collar was stained with tide marks. McAllister grabbed hard between my legs "Ah! Ronsard wants tae hump the Proddy. Cunt's got a fuckin' hard on; an' her wi nae tits."

I pushed McAllister away. Burns came forward.

"Ronsard; whit kin' a fuckin' name is that? Cunt's a swank; 'mon we'll gie him a right fuckin' kickin'."

There was a scuffle. Montague pushed me to the ground. James Malone, Depute Headmaster, stopped us and sent me to clean up. "I'll deal with you later," he said.

I heard the drag of leather on cotton as Malone drew his Loch Gelly tawse hidden under the left shoulder of his jacket. The tawse: a quarter inch thick leather strap, two inches wide, and two tongues. Malone's was pliant and oily-soft from over-use. Leather cut air as he made a practice swing.

"Right, McAllister. Hands up. You're a waster, boy. You'll be in gaol soon."

I got away before Malone changed his mind and decided to thrash me too. I knew the drill. McAllister, hands crossed, right hand uppermost, waiting. The smack of leather on flesh as Malone gave him 'Six of the Best.' Pupils had a choice. They could take it on one hand; after three blows, change to left hand. McAllister's hands would be numb and useless for a couple of hours. The palms beaten raw, a spider web of blood blisters spreading across his wrists. I'd no time for McAllister and his mates. They were thugs, but I hated Malone when he punished pupils.

I hid in the School Library. I'd a key given me by James Malone when he asked me to run it. I locked the door, unlocked the kitchen to the rear of the library washing the drying blood from my face, nursing my black eye, and bruised lip. I shouldn't have been there so late on Friday afternoon.

Footsteps thudded on the wooden stairs. The heavy tread of a man, the fluttering clicks of a woman's heels as she tried to keep up. The door to the library opened, I heard James Malone's voice and he had Cliesh with him. I eased the kitchen door open. James Malone, back to me, spread his arms.

"Come in, Miss Clieshman. You have not seen our room full of books."

James Malone was a tough little man. He'd been under twenty when he won the Military Medal in France in the last month of the Great War. When he left the Army James Malone went to Glasgow University, winning a Double First in English and History. He dedicated his life to teaching. He was the cleverest teacher. A few of the staff respected him; many were in awe of him: the pupils feared him.

"Are you settling in?" James Malone said.

"Oh yes! I think so," Cliesh said.

"Good. We have a library, and, at long last, a music teacher."

Malone knew everything about St Mary's. He managed the school, patrolling the buildings and the grounds, gauging the mood of staff and pupils. He taught English and History. In the classroom, I often forgot that I feared him.

Before Cliesh came to the school, only James Malone showed any interest in us. His teaching was inspiring. He knew that a small group of Fourth-Year boys went to the cinema, and he would ask us about the films. Then he opened the door to the past. James Malone used The Grapes of Wrath to discuss the Great Depression, the New Deal, and American entry to the Second World War. When he knew that we'd just seen a Western, he'd describe the Frontier and Manifest Destiny. A dire film about Robin Hood and he told us about The Crusades and the peripatetic Scots knights and mercenaries hiring their swords to the Germans in the Baltic lands. I loved every minute of it.

"How is Fourth year doing?" Malone said. "It's a pity we do not have more time with them. They leave us when they are fifteen."

"Yes, it's sad," Cliesh said. They leave so young."

"Ronsard looks after the library. I trust him. Last year he ran off all the exam papers for the school on the Gestetner."

"Yes, I know."

"He's fond of you, and when he sees you he's glad and embarrassed. But he's just a boy; when he can't see you, he's miserable."

"Just what do you mean, Mr Malone?"

I cringed; there was a lump in my throat. My stomach shrank and the sweating started. I'd got her on James Malone's wrong side. Cliesh would hate me.

"Ah, Miss Clieshman. Don't be angry. You behave impeccably. It's hard for you, not among your own kind, and living away from home."

"Will that be all, Mr Malone?"

"No, Miss Clieshman. I worked to bring you to St Mary's and I'd like you to stay. Not everyone in the school approves of a Protestant teacher; they'd have you removed."

"I see."

I wanted to strangle the teachers who hated Cliesh.

"Stay a moment. Ronsard has an injured face. Don't ask him what happened."

I wanted James Malone to shut up.

"Was he fighting; is he all right?"

"Yes, but feeling sorry for himself."

"What happened?"

"He objected to rude remarks the class hard men made about you. They attacked him. He blacked an eye and split a lip before he was knocked to the ground. That's when I stopped them."

"That's awful, Mr Malone."

"Miss Clieshman, the Age of Chivalry is not dead. It lives on in Young Ronsard; you must give him your beautiful silk scarf and tie it to the strap of his satchel. He is Your Champion."

James Malone stifled a chuckle. It was hard to listen to him and Cliesh. The back of my shirt was wet. I blushed, face burning; felt a fool. My heart raced and thumped in my ears like a cannon on automatic. Cliesh and James Malone must hear it. I didn't give a shit about Malone, but how could I face Cliesh after this?

I stayed in the kitchen for another half hour to be sure they'd left the school. There would be trouble when my mother saw I'd been fighting. I walked home with an aching face and a sore heart.

The headmaster invited Cliesh to form a small choir to sing at the prize giving. I joined along with a few others. The weeks until the summer break merged as we rehearsed. The choir met most days and on some Sundays. I wanted to sing for her and see her.

Cliesh changed with the season. Summer was the time of her opening. She wore light dresses of delicate red and yellow, her hair flowing as she let it down, or, bound loosely with a wisp of silk. She was at ease, her features gentle and beautiful. It was joy to be near her.

Loving Cliesh made me careless. I dreamt about her every day. I was idle in the woodwork class, toying for weeks making a wooden crucifix, staring into space, and thinking about the clothes Cliesh wore, the tailored jackets and skirts, the sheer stockings, her shapely legs, and the elegant shoes, I went into forbidden territory and thought about her delicate breasts and more. Lust blotted out guilt.

A hard hand hit me twice on the back of the head.

"You're useless, Ronsard," the woodwork teacher said. "Plain lazy. Hands up."

The bastard gave me six of the best with his Loch Gelly. My hands were raw and numb. He wanted me to cry, but I kept staring at him, thinking fuck you.

"Get out of my sight," he said.

I walked home, suffering for love nursing my sore hands, rubbing life into numb fingers, bruised palms and wrists, whispering "I did this for her." I was crazy.

I sat at the kitchen table and wrote Cliesh in Gothic letters in my notebook. I drew a heart round her name, and pierced it with arrows. My mother picked up the notebook and shook her head.

"Who's that? I hope she's a Catholic. You're a soft lump, Tim Ronsard. You see and behave your self."

I tried not to think of leaving school at the end of June. I devoted myself to rehearsals.

The audience liked the songs. The enthusiasm for Handel's Where're you Walk was unexpected. Everyone loved I Met Her In The Garden Where The Praties Grow. The chorus stayed with me.

She was just the sort of creature, boys,
That nature did intend
To walk right through the world, me boys,
Without a Grecian Bend.
Nor did she wear a chignon,
I'd have you all to know.
And I met her in the garden
Where the praties grow.

I sang for Cliesh from my heart.

She shook hands with each one of her boys that last day and said farewell. I held onto her hand, and saw affection in her eyes. Cliesh's fondness crushed me; I'd wasted my love, my dreams broken glass. School days were over.

I left school and started work at Reid's foundry. My parents were very pleased. I was not. Discontent began in the Apprentice School.

Each morning I walked through the machine shop, deafened by screeching lathes, drilling, and milling machines and overhead whining crane motors. The stench of cut steel and cast iron flying from tool points; sparks shot off grinding wheels. I could barely stand the noise; the stink of machine suds spraying on hot metal jolting me awake. From day one, I hated Reid's.

The sole consolation at work was my friendship with Sam Minto. Sam was small and thickset, with a low centre of gravity. I was gangly, all arms and legs. We were awkward in our hand-me-down shabby adult clothes.

The School lasted three months. There were twelve apprentices. We spent our days inside a wire-mesh cage lit by blue arc lights, working at benches made from chequered engine plate, vices set on the edge. There was a lathe, two small drilling machines, a milling machine and an engraving machine on the floor. For one week each apprentice cleaned the urinals at the end of the workday. The place reeked of piss, disinfectant and lube oil.

The classroom was at the back of the School. We were instructed in basic engineering skills, elementary mathematics, using hand tools and calibrated tools. Instruction was crude. Apprentices bashed hands, lacerated knuckles, and mashed fingers hammering, chiselling, filing. The School was a grim chapter of bruised fingers, cut hands, chipped, filthy nails: in a week my fine hands and long fingers became coarse engineer's fists.

And the routine humiliation. Willie Cain, Supervisor, and Joe Tolly, Charge Hand, governed the School. Cain a small corpulent man in a three-piece suit and stained felt hat that was his badge of office. I dreaded his approach, puffing on Turkish cigarettes watching me work. Cain had been a star apprentice and he never missed an opportunity to preach the benefits of an apprenticeship in Reid's.

"Ye can achieve anything," he said.

Cain held up a small electric drilling machine and an automatic centre punch for our admiration. I can see Cain yet, gloating over his achievements. "Ah made these masel' when ah wis your age."

Cain had spent years working with boys. Outside the foundry he was a Captain in the Boys Brigade, a quasi-military organization for Calvinist boys. Cain should have inspired all apprentices, but had become a Career Protestant.

Tolly looked after hands on training. He was a sour wee man in a brown overall and a large flat cap. Often there was an overpowering smell of stale whisky from his breath. Sam and I figured the pair of them had been confined to the School to keep them from the real business of the foundry.

Cain and Tolly acted from deep conviction: they would do what was necessary to mould young minds. Most apprentices did not fight back. Boys averted their eyes, as Cain or Tolly berated some wretched apprentice for a minor infraction.

"See you, ya wee bastard. Ye should have been a fuckin' butcher. Then, ye could eat a' ye scrapped."

They threatened anyone caught looking. "Whit the fuck are ye lookin' at? Huv ye no' enough tae dae? Ah'll soon find ye somthin'."

Humiliation was routine in the classroom. Catholics and Protestants who were friends got the treatment. I was the token Catholic and Sam was the renegade who befriended me. We dreaded lessons in the use of the Micrometer and the Vernier gauge. Cain would light a Turkish cigarette.

"Ronsard! Can ye no' count? Whit the fuck did they teach' ye in St Mary's?"

Then he'd turn on Sam. "You, Minto! Yer a fuckin' disgrace; a right disappointment. Did ye no' go tae the Mount School? Keep back fae him and get on wi' yer work."

It was hard to cope with these onslaughts. Adolescents plagued by acne, clumsy movements, too many hormones and worst of all, sudden intense blushing.

Cain and Tolly believed that they could transform unpromising youths into useful employees. Often they were right. A few miserable boys resisted but surrendered in exchange for a measure of peace. I overheard Cain. "Aye, Joe. They'll know their stuff when we're done wi' them. We'll huv remade their heids."

"Aye; right enough, Boss."

Cain and Tolly couldn't manage apprentices. It had never dawned on them that a word of praise, a gesture of recognition, the faintest smoke signal of generosity might have altered things in their favour and brought all the apprentices to their side. Cain and Tolly were experts at remaking heads, and knew how to deal with hard cases.

Working for Cain and Tolly was misery, and there was no sympathy at home. Our parents felt that getting an apprenticeship at Reid's was a privilege. They had no idea what it was like in the Iron Cage. We learnt to rely on ourselves; Sam and I were the last two resisting.

I liked the Chiricahua Apache. I told Sam about their bravery and we tried to be like them, Bronco warriors, defiant and out of control. But our counter attacks were feeble.

When Cain and Tolly were working in the classroom we hurled two-foot long inch square files twenty feet into the roof space, burying the tang into the wooden supports. We told Tolly we had the shits and vanished into the disgusting jakes for ten minutes reading comic books.

Cain and Tolly used the job to punish us. There was no justice in that place. Had we been smart, we'd have conformed and Cain and Tolly might have lain off. But we were not smart. It went against the grain to conform and we fought on. Our strongest defence was dumb insolence and delay. Sam was last-but-one to finish the trades test. I was last. Sam ruined a valuable brass nameplate by cutting in a period not on the drawing. Tolly gushed his stale whisky breath over Sam's face.

"Fuck off, Minto! Yer bloody useless."

Sam shrugged and walked back to the workbench.

One morning Cain ambushed me. I was filing a brass nameplate to shape. Cain thrust a Turkish cigarette into the corner of his mouth and lit it. "That looks like a fuckin' sausage. Too bad ye canny eat the fuckin' thing." The master craftsman wrenched the file from my hand.

"Why don't ye' just finish it?" I said.

Cain's jaw dropped. He almost lost his cigarette, and he lost the place. "Another fuckin' word oot o' ye and yer suspended fur a week. Ah've a good mind tae sack ye."

He thumped me on the chest with the back of his right hand. Tolly looked on, a vicious grin spreading over his boozy old face. The threat of suspension or the sack subdued me; not that I gave a shit. It was the row at home that terrified me. My mother would take me apart and complain to my father. "Whit are we gonny dae wi him? He's right oot o' control."

And Tolly let us know who was boss. It was Sam's turn to clean the urinals. "A fuckin' disgrace. Dae them again," Tolly said.

I was waiting on Sam to finish. Tolly turned the screw on me. "You! Gi'e him a hand."

It was a wet night, and we missed our bus. It was a long walk home; we dragged our heels over black pavements, slouching in and out of circles of light from the street lamps. "Let's get that fucker, Cain and that cunt, Tolly," I said. Sam smiled.

I hadn't forgotten Cliesh, but I'd given up hope of ever seeing her again. How could a daft apprentice find her? Because of Cliesh I loved music. One night I came out of a cinema where I'd watched Carmen Jones. My head was full of the beautiful Dorothy Dandridge.

"Tim! Tim Ronsard."

My eyes locked onto Cliesh's eyes; Oh Sweet Jesus, just to see her. I felt my face reddening and looked away. She was lovelier now. I wanted to impress her, say something that would make her laugh, but I could hardly breathe.

"Hello, Miss Clieshman, how are you?"

Cliesh was dressed in a light wool coat, belted at the waist, a beige silk scarf knotted sailor fashion at her neck. She was statuesque in her elegant heels. I shook her gloved hand awkwardly.

"I'm fine, Tim. I'm so pleased to see you. Walk with me. Tell me how you've been getting on."

I told her that I was an apprentice in Reid's foundry and she picked up how unhappy I was. I made a few shy remarks about the film.

"I turn here, Miss."

"Come and have coffee, Tim. Come on Sunday afternoon. Let's say two o' clock?"

"That'd be nice, Miss."

The days dragged until the weekend. On Saturday I bought a cheap razor, soap and a brush for my first shave. I pressed my Sunday clothes and polished my shoes. On the Saturday night I walked the streets to save money. I wanted to bring her a small present.

Sunday morning I got out the new shaving kit.

"Will ye look at him shavin'. You're no goin' tae visit a teacher; you're meetin' some lassie." My mother didn't want me to grow up. I ignored her.

I appeared at Cliesh's door promptly. I was smart in suit and white shirt and one of my father's sober ties. But I was awkward standing at her door clutching a small box of chocolates wrapped in brown paper.

Smiling, Cliesh undid the wrapping. "Thank you, Tim. How thoughtful of you. I love Terry's chocolates."

We had tea, chatted pleasantly about school, and my apprenticeship. She glanced at the chipped, begrimed nails, the deep, unhealed nicks, and the cut finger joints; the ingrained dirt, and one nasty gash on the heel of my right hand.

I could've stayed until midnight, but had to be home by six.

"Will you come next Sunday, Tim?"

"Oh, yes. I'd like to come."

I took the long way home stopping at the old reservoir, staring into the dark water until Cliesh's face appeared. I'd never been happier.

I loved the Sunday afternoon visits to Cliesh: the bright coal fire; the copper and russet of autumn trees, visible from her windows; the late roses and Icelandic poppies bunched in vases on the sideboard. Her living room was comfortable. Stuffed sofas in front of an Adam fireplace, a copy. Heavy wallpaper brought the walls closer. A plaster cornice of duck eggs picked out in delicate blue. Mogul Miniatures of dancers and courtesans hung on the walls. The largest picture was a copy of Burmese Girls, by Russell Flint. The floor was dark varnished wood, a few oriental rugs placed advantageously, one of them a gorgeous Hatchli. In one corner there was an upright piano, a Petrof finished in deep polished rose wood. When she told me about the furnishings, the carpets, and the paintings, my love for her grew.

When my father was away at sea on the Irish boats there was a death chill between the Old Lady and me. She was sore that I hated working at Reid's, and she resented that I was growing away from her.

By mid-week I was fed up and Sunday, seeing Cliesh, was out of reach. To get to the cafe for a few hours I wound myself up to ask my mother for the price of a soft drink.

"Yer out far too much. Ye spend yer pocket money at the weekend. Dae you think I'm made o' money?"

I'd read and brood in my bedroom. But satisfied that she'd drawn blood she'd hand me a shilling or two to get rid of me, yelling as I went out the door. "See and get back here at a decent hour."

In the cafe, I'd nurse a Coke or an orange juice and think about Sunday.

I wanted to believe that Cliesh looked forward to the visits as much as I did. Did she grow fond of me? She seemed to dress to please me. I would wait for her to open the door listening for the faintest sound of her footsteps. Each time I longed to see her, catching her fragrance. The textures of that autumn were silk and wool: silk blouses, and scarves holding her hair back. Then I could see her small delicate ears. Cliesh loved simple wool dresses and skirts that showed off her slender legs. I could not keep my eyes from them and she caught me looking. I loved her beautiful legs.

They were innocent Sunday afternoons. We drank a small glass of Sherry. Then she played the piano. She was fond of Ravel, Debussy, and Poulenc. But her delight was Albeniz. She played selections from Iberia with spare, erotic passion.

Cliesh served afternoon tea; small cucumber sandwiches, or sardines on toast. She infused Darjeeling, Lapsang Suchon or the strong dark leaf from the Nilgris Hills. Near the end of the afternoon before I left, she brewed Kenyan, Java, or Columbian coffee. I loved that last half hour sitting with her, nursing a china cup and already looking forward to the next Sunday.

We often exchanged shy looks. When we talked she lowered her eyes suggesting innocence and invitation. Our hands touched as she offered plates, and glasses or cup and saucer. Sometimes, her long, cool tapered fingers, with the polished nails, would linger on mine.

She didn't know that I called her Cliesh. I'd not the nerve to call her Isobel. I managed to avoid calling her Miss Clieshman. When I had to I called her Miss.

Her clothes flattered her slim figure and small delicate breasts, the long slender legs; god, she was sexy. I desired her and felt guilty. She was so far above me and I adored her. One Sunday she sat beside me as we had afternoon tea.

"I like Sunday afternoons, Tim. I like being with you."

I nodded; not sure how to respond.

"Do you like coming to my rooms?"

"Yes."

"You know, Tim, it's not easy teaching music at St Mary's. The teachers; oh, some of them mean well. Polite and all, but they're not warm. I don't feel I belong."

The room was quiet, the coals in the grate hissing and cracking; wavering fingers of yellow flames casting shadows.

"I'm looking for another job. There must be schools that respect music. You know I give piano lessons?"

"Yes."

"I have a little money of my own. That helps."

She was making me miserable. I prayed. "Please, please don't let her leave."

"I loved the choir. You and the other boys, so open and friendly. You changed with me. It was so sweet, the way you sang."

"I liked the choir."

"What was I called in school; what was my name?"

"Miss Clieshman."

"Really?"

"They called you The Proddy; The Proddy music teacher."

The vexed look on her face; not that I meant to, but I'd cut her to the quick.

"And you, Tim. What did you call me when you thought about me?"

I shrugged; think about her? All day every day; I flushed a deep shade of pink, "Cliesh."

"Is that my special name ?"

"Yes."

"Tim, Tim, that's so lovely."

Westburn men kept tenderness out of their lives. They talked about humping, shagging, or fucking. But not love; not being in love. I'd never heard a woman speak of the heart. Perhaps when they're alone women talk about it. Love was scant in Westburn.

My love could have brought a photograph of Cliesh to life. But I was chained to the hard words of my people. I couldn't say what I felt for her. How could I tell Cliesh that I loved her?

Her fingers left warm tracks on my face. I was going crazy, a lump in my throat, swallowing, fighting tears. How could Cliesh ever love me, awkward, gangly, acne scars newly healed?

Cliesh dried my eyes. "Oh, Tim my sweet boy; I love you; I love you very much."

I knew it was all right. "I love you."

She smiled, radiant; sweet laughter. "I know, Tim; and I do love you."

The best words I'd ever heard.

We sat on the edge of her bed.

"It's my first time."

"I know, I know, Tim."

Then a lingering kiss, her tongue opening my lips.

"My shoes, Tim. Help me with my shoes."

I caught her smell on her new-worn shoes. I wanted her breath, her body, and her secrets. I came in her hand.

"Oh, Tim!"

I lay with Cliesh and she gave me what I longed for. We didn't undress. We lay together half-undone. Cliesh sensed my next shudder and her stockinged feet brought me closer, then she held me with warm, firm fingers, startling me.

"Touch me. Like this, Tim. Wait for me."

We crossed a frontier when we became lovers. Sundays changed. Cliesh eagerly opened her door and once inside her rooms, we kissed and touched. Some Sundays, we were so glad to see each other after a week apart, that we made love at once. After we'd drunk coffee, just before I had to leave, we made love, again, tenderly.

I was in love with Cliesh, but I never considered the risk she was taking, keeping those Sunday trysts. It wasn't illegal; she was twenty-four and I was sixteen. Discovery meant the end of Cliesh's career. And I'd finish up in the hands of the priests stoking my guilt. My mother would see to it.

I overheard my mother speak to my father. "He's goin' on a long time wi' that music teacher. Is he up to somethin'?"

My father grunted from behind his newspaper.

Cliesh knew how I felt about working in Reid's foundry. One Sunday she took both my hands, turning them over. "You have nice hands. Long fingers; I love that in a man. Are they sore?"

"Yes."

Cliesh smiled and pressed my hands, gently drawing her fingers across my ravaged nails.

"Wait."

She removed the top from a small jar and I caught the mild scent. Cliesh scooped out cream on her fingertips and gently worked the cream into cuts and nicks, loosening the grime in my nails. She cleaned my hands with a small towel and then began again.

"The second time helps the soreness."

The rubbing of my hands loosened more than grime. I wanted to talk about Reid's. I couldn't talk about Reid's at home, without a blistering row. I complained bitterly to Sam and he to me. But where we came from, what went on in that shit hole was simply a part of life. My stories of Reid's foundry appalled Cliesh.

Sunday afternoons passed blissfully. I felt so good being with Cliesh and I had little sense of what she might be giving up because of me.

I told her about going to the Jazz Club with Sam. I didn't tell her that we got drunk on the El D. "The quartet played My Funny Valentine. I thought about you. I wanted you to be there, Cliesh."

She drew back. I'd never seen her like this, flat, injured eyes, lips shrunk to a crimson slit. "I should think not! Riff raff and you drinking with that fellow, Sam. You went there with girls."

"There were no girls, Cliesh."

"You were drunk last night. There's wine on your breath."

Some Fridays Cliesh went to concerts in Glasgow. It was wonderful when she talked about the music she'd heard. I wanted to tell her that the song said how much I loved her. But, now I was raging.

"There wis nae riff raff there. Ah suppose ye go tae yer concerts wi' wan o' they swanky fellas ye met at the University."

Cliesh's gentle voice shifted to haughty Glasgow Kelvinside. "Why yes. Sometimes I do."

"Dis that make me yer Sunday ride?"

My head jerked at the force of the blow from her back handed cuff. I touched the marks left by her fingers and signet ring. All I cared for was slipping away.

"I'm so, so sorry. Please don't leave."

I stayed.

Something had happened to us. I'd made her jealous and I was in the grip of it myself. That was why we'd fought. It was risky for us meeting. We remained confined to her rooms on a Sunday. It was doubly hard for Cliesh. I should've thought about her life when I wasn't there. Drab week nights returning to a black hearth, a chill room: waiting on the kindling to catch; preparing a lonely evening meal. She might play the piano, practising. Perhaps a pupil would come in for a half hour lesson. Read a while. Holding back desire; failing, masturbating, until we could be together again. If only she had been younger or I had been older.

"There isn't anyone else," Cliesh said. "I go to the concerts alone. Sometimes, my mother is with me."

"You don't really think I would go out with a girl."

"I know you wouldn't."

We smiled and giggled through our tears and runny noses. I gave her my clean handkerchief. It was the sweetest reconciliation. We lay together a long time that afternoon.

That day made us closer. We were inside each other's thoughts and feelings. I'd never been as near to another person. When I felt low about Reid's, Cliesh listened and I revealed more about the place, the unrelenting harassment and petty humiliations.

"Why don't you leave, Tim? Do something else."

For Cliesh it was that simple, but I was from a family where the engineering apprenticeship was sacred. I shook my head.

"Speak to your father. Surely, he'd understand?"

"I've tried, but it ends up with my mother furious and there is another awful row. I've given up."

That day I told Cliesh about our revenge on Cain and Tolly.

Caprice and chance, and we upset the established order. One Friday as the apprentices cleaned the place up for the weekend. Sam grinned at me; impulsively, he squirted oil into the motor of Cain's precious drilling machine. Egged on by Sam, I opened the drawer holding the special tools and removed Cain's automatic centre punch. I pushed the point into a piece of case hardened steel. When the punch recoiled, its point had mushroomed, the spring broken. I returned the punch to the drawer.

Monday morning and slowly the school came to life: arc lights flickered on, switches clicked, motors turned and tools banged on work surfaces. Apprentices conversed quietly. Tolly switched on Cain's drilling machine. It burst into flames; smoke poured from its vents. The smell of burning rubber filled the School. Tolly reported it to Cain, and he was annoyed, but accepted it as an accident. Later, he sent an apprentice for the automatic centre punch.

"There's somethin' wrong wi' it, Mr. Cain."

Two things he valued destroyed in one day was no coincidence. Cain was shocked; he'd lost part of his youth. He had been got at. A wiser man would've taken stock; let his rage cool, then looked for the culprits.

Cain had Tolly gather the apprentices in the classroom. Cain stood at the front. The apprentices stared at him in his three-piece suit and stained felt hat. He lit a Turkish cigarette, drawing the smoke in deeply. He waited for the soothing effects of the nicotine. Then he exploded.

"Whit fuckin' bastard o' a boy burnt ma drillin' machine an' destroyed ma centre punch?"

Cain invited the culprit to own up. He'd help the boy responsible. No one believed that. I doubt that Cain believed it. Perhaps he considered individual interrogations, but that would have roused parents.

"Ah'll bring the police in tae investigate this," Cain said.

This was bluster and he must have dismissed it at once. Bringing the police in would show that he had lost control and undermine his now shaky authority. He lashed out again at the apprentices. "Fuck it! Ye a' know who did it. You, Nicol! Shearer. Who did it?"

Silence; the apprentices looked down at the toecaps of their industrial boots. It was an astonishing performance by Cain. This man who had spent a lifetime working with boys knew nothing of their honour code. No boy betrayed another. Cain's composure was collapsing; his authority was ruined.

Every apprentice in that classroom suspected Sam and me of the sabotage. While Cain thundered we were terrified of discovery, but we were learning to remain composed. Gradually, Cain's rage withered.

He dismissed us with a final threat. "Don't ye worry; Ah'll get the wee bastard that did this tae me."

The last week of the School passed slowly. The threat of discovery faded. We saw Cain and Tolly for what they had become: hollow men. Cain never discovered his tormentors. What else could he do but bury the memory?

At five o'clock I walked out the foundry gate with Sam. "Fuckin' automatic centre punch!" I said.

"Fuckin' drillin' machine!" Sam said.

I told Cliesh most of this. She rocked back and forth, laughing, her feet rising and resting on the heels of her shoes. "Oh, Tim! I shouldn't laugh. You've been very wicked, but they deserved it."

I'd never been happier than that time with Cliesh and the beautiful Sunday afternoons; and I was never as happy again for many years. I was in love; I felt safe.

The next Sunday Cliesh answered the door wrapped in her robe, her nightgown hanging above her slippers. Her beautiful chestnut hair was untidy, chalky face, eyes red. She'd been crying. "Come in, Tim."

There was no fire lit in the sitting room. I helped her back to bed, and made her comfortable. The bedroom was chilly.

"What's wrong, Cliesh?"

"I don't know, but I don't feel well."

I wanted to call her doctor, but she said no. She shivered under the bed clothes. I made her a cup of hot sweet tea, and she drank it greedily. There was a film of sweat on her brow, and I patted it dry with my handkerchief.

"My feet are cold," Cliesh said.

I went to the kitchen boiled a kettle and filled a hot water bottle, put it inside a woollen comforter. I lifted the bed clothes and rubbed heat into her freezing feet. I tucked the hot water bottle beside her feet.

"That's wonderful."

Cliesh burrowed into the blankets. I shivered in that unheated bedroom.

"I'll go and let you sleep."

"Oh Tim you're cold; but please stay a little while."

"I'll stay."

Cliesh moved restlessly and her face was anxious.

"What's wrong?"

"I worry so much. What's going to happen to us?"

There were teachers who, given the chance, would turn our love into a bad thing and finish Cliesh.

She reached for me with both arms, and I held her. It upset me to see Cliesh upset. I'd always looked up to her, expecting her to take charge if anything went wrong. I didn't know what to do.

"Tim; oh darling Tim."

"We haven't done anything wrong," I said. "It's not wrong for us to love each other."

"I was so lonely. You were so nice to me. When you left it was never the same. I was so happy to see you that night at the cinema."

She blew her nose.

"Tim, please forgive me, I never meant to fall in love with you, but I did. I'm too old for you. Oh, oh! If only I were younger or, you were older. How can you care for me? I'm all skin and bone."

Tears ran down her face, and she turned into the pillow. I turned her head. I found new words.

"Darling Cliesh, my love: you're slender and beautiful. I've loved you from the first day I saw you."

I folded my clothes on a chair and felt the goose bumps on my arms as the skin tightened. Cliesh raised the bed clothes and I was beside her and in her arms. She shuffled the hot water bottle onto my feet.

"Whatever happens, Tim, I'll always love you."

My mother was on the offensive. One night I lay awake thinking about Cliesh and how much I loved her. I felt so lucky and excited that she loved me. Just the thought of her, and my heart soared. I slept through the alarm and my mother hauled back the bed clothes. She was aghast at my board-stiff pajamas; her eyes bulged and her face turned crimson when I tried to cover my erection.

"Get up you, an' get ready for work. An' get tae confession on Saturday."

Later that week, I'd had a bad day at Reid's. I walked home tired and dirty. Things were much worse since I'd left the Apprentice School and moved to the Finishing Shop.

I was counting the days until Sunday; then I'd see Cliesh again. As I came through the front door, my Old Lady was waiting,

"Well; how did ye get on?"

"Fuckin' grim!"

It just slipped out. I'd made a bad mistake. But it was the response my Old Lady was looking for. It had been a grim day; now it was to get worse.

"Whit did ye say, Tim Ronsard?"

I didn't answer. But she had the hook in and tugged sharply.

She shook a book in my face. It was Hemingway's, The First Forty-nine. Cliesh had loaned it to me. The Old Lady had been prowling in my room. There was nothing to do; she'd opened letters of mine before.

"Nuthin' but damned filth," she said.

Up in Michigan. It had to be that story. I looked into the kitchen, the table was set for tea. My Old Man sat by the fire reading the paper, pretending this row was not happening. "Yer a changed boy since ye met that damned music teacher."

My gorge rose. I'd not let my mother insult Cliesh. "Aye; an' so what?"

Mothers know everything about their sons. They pinpoint the time they stop being Mum and become the Old Lady. That split second is the turning point when serious hostilities break out.

I imagined my love for Cliesh was a secret. I left trails a retired bloodhound could follow. My Old Lady was my keenest observer. I was sixteen. I was in love. Who can resist falling in love? My eagerness to go to Cliesh's rooms on Sunday afternoons, my heightened mood as the weekend approached. My mother couldn't fail to notice. I wonder what else she looked for to confirm her suspicions that I was in a state of mortal sin. I wouldn't have put it past her to examine the bedding and monitor nocturnal emissions. I was too relaxed, too happy. That day, she'd convinced herself that I was 'doing it' and it had to stop. My long, private war had just got much worse.

She raised her hand to slap my face. "Don't you speak tae me like that."

I caught her arm. "Don't you bloody dare."

My Mother hated it when I gave up clinging to her; and 'Ah love ye Mum' stopped. When she knew that the hugs and kisses, and more, were for someone else. But I thought she'd understand. Sometime when I was growing up, the compassion and understanding I thought we had, died.

"Will ye listen tae him and his bloody cheek," she said, turning to the Old Man. "Are ye goin' tae let him speak tae me like that?"

The Old Man rustled the newspaper.

She was in full flight now. "An' don't think yer too big tae huv yer ears clipped."

She tried again to slap me. Her face was poison. "Ah've seen her; yer bloody music teacher wi' her fancy hats and swanky ways. A right shit. No' fur the likes a' you. It's a good confession yer needin'.'"

My mouth dried, my stomach got smaller, blood draining, white faced. "Hats, is it? Ye widnae know a good hat if it landed on yer heid. Ye deserve the fuckin' Carmen Miranda prize."

The Old Lady was proud of her Sunday hats; the hats and the fox furs. They'd caused friction when she dragged me to Mass. I'd trail behind, then, to her fury, race ahead. Perhaps that was when the war really started.

"Pure wickedness, ye are. Ah'll get the priest tae ye."

"Go to Hell. Fuck the priest. You stay away from her."

Foundry talk.

The Old Man threw the paper on the floor. I squared up to him. I'd lose but I wasn't putting up with any more of this horror. My father pushed me aside and shook his head.

"For Christ's sake, be quiet the pair o' ye. Tim, behave. Show some respect. Leave off. Up In Michigan's a good story. Gi'e the boy some peace."

That shut her up.

"Get yer jacket, Tim. We're goin' oot," my father said.

My Old Man was quiet, but he put up with no nonsense. Suddenly I was wary of him. We left the house thumping down the stairs and landings of the tenement. Ten minutes later we were in the Clachan Bar, a favourite of his.

"Half an' a beer, Dougie; an' a half pint a light for him."

"But he's under age."

"Jist gie' it tae him, Dougie."

The drinks slid across the bar, and we moved back to a table. The Old Man raised his glass to me. I waited as he sipped the whisky, then chasing it with a good swallow of beer. He sighed, satisfied. I tipped my glass to him and took a sip of the bitter light ale.

"Whit's wrong, Tim?"

I looked at him, and then down at the table.

"Come on, son. Whit's up wi' ye?"

"I hate Reid's, an'I hate engineering. Ah want away from here. Ah could go to sea now."

I wasn't thinking straight when I said that.

"Go tae sea when yer twenty. Dae the last year a' yer time at sea."

I couldn't see it, but my parents were doing their best for me. I hadn't long left a technical school, and I wasn't a promising youth. I felt he just did not understand anything; my father had just sentenced me to four years.

"Ah go tae sea. Ah've been deep sea an' its nae bloody life on the deck or in the galley. As an engineer, ye'll be an officer."

"Ah'll join the Army when ah'm eighteen."

"Jesus Christ, Tim! Whit the hell is wrong wi ye? Army! Listen, son, Ah wis in the Navy fur two years in the War. Ah met enough bastards tae last two life times. Wastin' yer bloody life! Come on, son. Gie Reid's a try. Ye've only been there a few months. Finish yer time. It'll be there tae fa' back on. The world's yer oyster then."

He took sips of whisky and beer.

"Reid's. Is that a' that's wrong wi ye?"

I was on the verge of panic, and I was afraid of the Old Man.

"Ye've got yer mother worried sick wi' yer carryin' on. Books and singin'; songs Ah' never heard the like o'. Sunday is the only day o' the week fur ye. It's no' like ye, Tim."

My father understood much more about me than I could ever have imagined. "The music teacher; ye like goin' tae her rooms son, don't ye?"

"Ah do. She's great about music an' books, no' like school. She's nice."

"Ah've seen the music teacher, Tim; saw her once, near her rooms. She's a fine young woman. Ah can see why ye like her."

My father's tone of voice changed. He hadn't intended it, but there was a distant longing for something, or someone lost in his life. Perhaps he was thinking of my mother as a young girl. I'd seen the small black and white photographs. She'd been very pretty.

"Books and music, Tim. Is that a' there is tae it?"

"That's a'. Honest." I'd lied to my father and I was sick at myself. I couldn't have told him the truth. I was always underestimating my father. He pretended to believe me.

"Tim, whit is she, twenty-four? Yer sixteen, son; it's been good, Tim. She's helped ye wi' new things. She'll be leavin' soon. Ye said so yersel. She needs tae find another job."

I was at his mercy and I was ashamed at having squared up to him.

"When ye go tae see her on Sunday, tell her yer no' comin' back. Gi'e her back the book and tell her yer workin' hard at night school. Don't see her again, son. It's fur the best."

I wanted to fight back, but I didn't. I hated being at odds with my father. He was the link to sanity as my mother made war. I let him think I'd caved in. I would never give up Cliesh.

He put his hand on my shoulder. "Come on, son." We walked home in silence.

I was desperate as I walked to Cliesh's rooms. I was ready to do anything to be with her. I couldn't give her up. I hoped that Cliesh would get us out of this mess. She didn't answer the door. I stretched and stared in the window. The Petrof piano and the Hatchli had gone. Her pictures removed from the walls. My insides turned to water; my heart emptied. I denied that she'd left me; prayed she'd come to the door and explain the empty walls and the bare wooden floor.

The old woman who rented the rooms opened the door. "You're the boy who comes on Sunday?"

"Yes."

She handed me a cream envelope and shut the door. I looked into the empty room for the last time. I was beyond tears.

I went to the small park near the memorial to the Free French Navy. Cliesh wrote with ruby ink on cream paper. She'd gone away, found a job in the north-east. Had really wanted to explain it to me, but felt that a letter was best.

I read the last line again and again. I heard her voice. "Tim, darling Tim, you sang of me in the days when I was fair."

Chapter 2

Big Willa

Sam and me worked with the Reds during the apprentices' strike; warriors in the class war; picketing, fighting scabs, defying the police. Management separated us when the strike finished. I moved to the Fitting Shop.

At the mass meeting starting the strike I met Jake Burns, the Shop Steward from Reid's. Jake told the Reds that the timing of the strike was inept and the demands weak. They threatened to throw him out. Reid's apprentices formed a protective square around a drunk Jake and dared anyone to try. The Reds backed down and we got Jake out of the Good Shepherd's Hall.

The strike was exciting; a break from the monotony of Reid's. I was lifted by the police after scrapping on the picket line. The local paper carried a picture of the incident. I got off with a warning from the Sergeant. I kidded myself that we'd moved the class struggle on when management awarded a rise.

Sam drained his glass of India Pale Ale. "Ah'm oot a' this, Tim. Ah'm gettin' merrit tae Jean."

I was surprised. We were both eighteen. He'd been going out with Jean, a girl from Arran, come over to the mainland attending a catering course at the local college. She didn't like me.

"It'll be a quiet weddin'."

"Is she in the family way?"

"Naw. It's right fur us, Tim. Ye know fine Ah hate this fuckin' place as much as ye dae yersel'."

Sam's news and I thought of Cliesh and how much I missed her. Two years since she left. I knew her letter by heart and often whispered her last words bringing her closer. At times Cliesh was so near I reached out to touch her. I couldn't accept that I'd never see her again.

"You a' right, Tim? Ye look sick."

"Ah'm fine, Sam."

Jean's father had a small hotel on Arran. The mother was dead. Sam hit it off with the father. Jean loved Sam so he offered him a place in the business.

"Tim, Reid's is fuckin' grim. Ye need tae get away. If ye don't, ye'll g' aff yer fuckin' heid."

He was right. I'd miss Sam. We'd been through a lot together. When he left, I was very low.

I admired Jake Burns and remembered the way he'd told off the Reds the day the strike began. Some apprentices wanted to be his friend, but Jake kept his distance. He was too radical for the mainstream socialists and far too much of an individualist for the Communist Party. The Party apparatchiks booted him out for drunkenness. There was no denying it: Jake liked a drink.

Jake was about forty-two, middle height, slimly built, pronounced cheekbones and determined chin. A close clipped moustache decorated his upper lip. He cut his own hair, badly; it was ragged and patchy at the neck. Jake was a superb tradesman. He could tackle any job in the fitting shop. His union activities allowed him to flit along the edges of local left politics.

Jake was a hard negotiator; but he never wasted time on strikes. When the foundry was busy, he'd present management with demands for better rates of pay. Management would reject them. Jake would threaten a work to rule, limiting productivity. On cue, management would concede something. The union activity was a remnant of his idealism.

The old hands were content to take what Jake had won for them, but they did not like him. They feared his intelligence and determination. They worried Jake might destroy Reid's.

"Aye, a' right. So he kin get ye a few bob, some extra benefit," one Old Hand said. "But he's pure trouble. A Red. A' they fuckin' Communists, they're a' the same."

I liked Jake Burns; not that he would have cared. He was a loner. I never wanted to be a Communist, but I respected Jake's idealism. Jake always went his own way, and he was afraid of no man.

Jake never agreed to meet anyone, but it was no secret that he liked company when he was drinking. I ran into him one Friday night in the Empire Bar, a spit and sawdust shop on the end of the High Street.

Half cut, he urged me to get away. "Get tae fuck away. Clear oot o' Reid's afore it gets ye."

He buried his face in a pint of heavy beer. Belching, Jake wiped foam from his moustache as he lowered the pint glass to the bar.

"Ye never think aboot gettin' away, Jake?"

"Sure ah dae, but ah've got a wife and three weans tae think aboot. Hing aboot here, Ronsard, an' ye'll end up gettin' merrit, an then ye will be fucked."

Jake drank deeply from his pint. He was in a talkative mood. I wanted to find out more about him.

"Dae ye read much, Jake?"

"Aye, a' the time. Ah jist finished The Moon and Sixpence. Fuckin' great. The fella in it, jist up, and aff. Put everythin' behind him. Some times ah feel like daein' that."

Jake admired Alexander Strickland, Maugham's Gauguin-like hero and his escape to a new life.

"Listen, Ronsard. Ah've read aboot the class struggle. It used tae mean some-thin' tae folk here. Fur a while, Ah jist aboot gave ma fuckin' life tae it. Ah telt them a' aboot Marx and Engels, and Lenin, an' whit it means tae be fuckin' workin' class. Ye'd hear fuck all in school aboot the books ah read."

Jake took another long swallow from his pint. "Kursk, and Stalingrad; the Eastern Front. It wis the fuckin' Red Army and the Party that won the War. Kicked the fuck oot o' the German Army. That's true enough, Tim, but efter Hungary, ah hud enough o' the Party. Aye, an' they hud enough o' me."

Jake had never called me by my Christian name; he got me a pint.

"Thanks, Jake."

"Yer a' right, Tim, but yer a fuckin' dreamer. Leave Reid's, son. If ye stay, ye'll be miserable a' yer fuckin' days."

We drank the heavy beer in deep gulps, foam rings on the inside of the glass measuring the reductions of our thirst. Jake placed his hands on the bar and lent against it. "Ah'm gonny tell ye somethin'. Fuck knows why; ah huv nae talked aboot it in years. No' many o' the old hands know aboot it, so ye keep it tae yersel'. Right?"

"Sure, Jake."

Jake's glass was empty and I ordered another two beers. We sipped gingerly from the pint glasses.

"Ah wis a sodger in the International Brigade, 15th British Battalion. Ah went tae Spain in 1936. Ma time wis jist oot. When ah saw a' they newsreels an' the bombin' o' civilians, Ah volunteered. The Party organized it," Jake said.

I was surprised at this revelation. Jake had acted bravely. He belonged to an elite who'd garnered honour. He didn't have to go to Spain. He volunteered for the Brigades because of his idealism-the plight of civilians in Loyalist Spain had moved him-and he went to fight for the Spanish Republic.

"Whit wis it like?"

"Grim. Ah went tae Madrid. Mexican rifles wis a' we had; useless. The barrels used tae burst when ye fired. The grub; that wis worse. Ah et nuthin' but rice an' onions fur ages. Even the day, twenty years on, ah canny look at onions."

He dug into his inside-pocket and produced a battered wallet. Carefully inserting thumb and forefinger, extracted a photograph. "Ah kerry this tae remind me o' the time when ah thought ah could dae somethin'."

Jake shook his head; a thin smile creased his face. I looked at the small black and white photograph. A young man looked out from under a black beret set to the right, worn low on his brow. He had no moustache. Jake was a soldier all right: he held a rifle by his right side. He wore a military blouse over a dark shirt, baggy trousers caught at the knees by tight puttees that wound down to the tops of his heavy boots. Jake didn't look much older than me. A small leap of imagination and I saw myself in that photograph dressed like him.

The plight of civilians in Loyalist Spain had moved Jake. I'd seen old news reels of the Spanish Civil War, and being part of it scared me. But excitement smothered my fear and I hoped I'd have had the courage to follow Jake to Spain, and into the Brigades.

"Ah finished up a Sergeant. Ah wis at Jarama, Brunette, Teruel and the Ebro. Ah wis evacuated when the Brigades disbanded in 1938. Ah'm no' sorry ah went tae Spain, but we were fuckin' betrayed an' we lost. Ah'm gonny gie ye a book tae read, Tim; Homage Tae Catalonia. George Orwell wrote it. Read it, son; find oot a' aboot treachery and betrayal."

After Spain, Jake went back to engineering. He was a changed man, and dedicated himself to the class war. He tried to enlist in the British Army at the start of the War.

"Ah wanted tae huv another go at the Nazis and the Fascists. Ah saw first hand whit the bastards did in Spain. The Army said nuthin' doin'. Ah wis in a reserved occupation. Ah tried again in 1944. They were takin' anybody fur the Second Front an' the invasion of Europe. But they still said naw. Then, Tim, ah worked it oot. Ah wis a fuckin' Red an' they didnae want me; never mind that ah wis a real experienced sodger."

Jake shook his head. I could see that the rejection still hurt deeply.

"Tim, ye don't think Reid's is a' aboot workin' class solidarity an' the fuckin' brotherhood o' man. Ye could punch holes in that."

Jake didn't wait for a reply.

"Listen, Tim; whit it's really a' aboot is Protestants and Catholics at each other's throats. The old hands, fuckin' jinin' Reid's Masonic Lodge, stirrin' the shit. There's nae class struggle goin' on in Reid's. It's a' jist a fuckin' game played oot by a lot o' time servin' twats. Some times Ah feel like blowin' the place up."

Jake lifted his pint to drain it; changed his mind and rested his hand on the bar.

"Ah saw real class solidarity in Spain. Christ! We used tae clench wir right fist and shout, 'No Parsan!' Spain wis a' aboot the brotherhood a' man. Ah met folk fae everywhere: Poles an' Czechs, Germans, and Italians come tae fight Fascism. There wis some great Yanks fae the Abraham Lincoln Brigade; workin' men, ex Wobblies fae the IWW. Ah'm tellin' ye, Tim, it wis somethin'."

That night we became friends, or as friendly as Jake's solitary ways allowed. I hoped Jake had chosen me to tell his story. My respect and admiration for him soared. But I was sad for him too. Walking home I felt the weight of Jake's broken dreams.

Jake's war was over and he was trapped in Reid's. If only I could find within myself, a fraction of his courage and get out of Reid's. There was no escape to the International Brigade. I'd never find myself in engineering, and I made up my mind to find a way out of Reid's.

It was in the fitting shop that I met Big Fergie. He stood six feet two, his knees bent as he walked. Fergie was about thirty-eight with dark wavy hair, and his right eye socket was empty. On his right temple, there was a deep hole the size of a fore knuckle. Often, the empty eye socket pained him. On those days, he wore a black eye patch.

I had my overalls open to the waist. A black leather belt with steel buckle embossed with eagle and swastika held up my pants.

"Why are ye wearin' that belt, son?" Fergie said.

"It's a fuckin' German Army belt. Ma uncle took it aff a deid Gerry."

"Ah know whit it is. Ah wis in the Army. So, get yer arse tae the fuckin' stores. Ah want a number four drilling machine, a boring post and an air hose. Get it up tae the tap a' the engine. Right?"

I was wary of Fergie, and I stopped wearing the belt. I found out later that the belt, the Nazi badge on the buckle, offended him. He'd spent the war fighting Germans in North Africa and Europe.

During the five-year apprenticeship, we got one stint with a good journeyman. This was mine. But no one rated Fergie; he was one of the awkward squad. That's what the old hands called him. For the strike and other troubles I'd made, management was paying me off. I resented it at the time, but it was fair enough. I hated Reid's foundry.

I thought Fergie was a duff engineer. I wasn't so hot myself. I spent too much time getting up to mischief and dreaming of escape. The first few months working with Fergie, I sank into a brain deadening routine; fitting galvanized water-cooling pipes and copper lube oil pipes. Not for nothing was Fergie also known as the 'Pipe Major.' A little variety cured tedium for a few hours when we laid, drilled, and bolted chequered engine plate. We never got paid more than the measly average bonus rate.

"Fergie, fur fuck's sake! Why dae ye no' get at that fuckin' foreman an' get us some decent jobs?"

"Start usin' yer heid, son, instead o' yer gub. Then ye might work oot whit goes on in Reid's."

Fergie was married to a German. That put him beyond the pale. One of the old hands ambushed me. "Listen, Ronsard. Watch that fuckin' heid case yer workin' wi'. Got Big Willa wi' a Yank, or wis it a Russian? Shot her. Ah'm tellin' ye."

"Big Willa, is that Fergie's wife?"

"Aye."

"Is she big right enough?"

"How the fuck wid ah know? Ah've never seen her. Anyway, she's jist a fuckin' Hun."

"When'd he shoot her?"

"In Berlin jist efter the War. Scc that fuckin' eye o' his? Well, he shot it oot tryin' tae kill himself. That wis right efter he gied the sodger a doin'. The sodger that wis humpin' Willa. Then shot her. Ah'm tellin' ye, Ronsard! He tried tae fuckin' kill her. The Army gied him a year in the fuckin' jail."

What should I make of it? The Old Hands insisted it was true. But to me, at eighteen, the story seemed utterly preposterous.

"Whit'd he merry her fur?"

My informant shook his head. "Look, ye must have seen a' the pass oots he gets? Whit dae ye think that's fur?"

There was no denying it. Fergie often left the fitting shop during the day.

"He's tryin' tae catch her on the job wi' the milkman, or the coalman, the postman. Any cunt can get it fae Willa o' the Wehrmacht."

The foreman taunted Fergie when he asked for unpaid leave. "Tryin' tae catch the jockey, Fergie?"

Fergie stared at him, the good eye glinting. "Jist gimme the pass oot."

Events in the Fitting Shop revealed a few hidden truths about Reid's that would make it easier to break away.

The main engine broke down of a ship discharging sugar in the port. The owners were in a hurry to get her ready for sea. The fitting out squad was toiling in Sunderland, so management sent a foreman and a squad of old hands from the fitting shop to repair the Greek ship.

That left Fergie, myself and the awkward squad. For a while things improved in the Fitting Shop. A young foreman kept an eye on us. The place was tranquil. Daylight came through the glass roof panels, brightening the soaring cast iron columns supporting the roof. The part built engines, no engineers working on them, stark temples. I enjoyed the quiet with the old hands gone.

An unexpected rush was on. Management brought forward two engines. Fergie smiled at the worry of the young foreman, tackling rush jobs with the awkward squad. For the first time, I really paid attention to the job and learned about my trade.

We did OK, fitting turbo blowers to both engines; it was dangerous work. Skilled fitting, forty feet above the shop floor. A false move meant certain death on the concrete below. Then we fitted the fuel pumps.

I was using my head, anticipating the tools and equipment required. But, the important personal discovery was that I liked the responsibility. The first time I had the kit laid out at the job, Fergie's good eye shot up. He grunted approvingly.

One morning Fergie invited me to his break. That made me happy. We hid in a quiet corner under the bed plate. I drew boiling water for the tea and brewed up in the tea can.

"Here, Tim."

I caught the roll, egg yolk and fat staining the grease proof wrapping.

"When Ah wis in the Army, they called these egg banjos. The Chogies made them."

"Whit's a Chogie?"

"Punjabi Wallah; kept a wee shop at battalion HQ. Sold toothpaste an' soap, fags; made great rolls and sandwiches fur the Jocks."

Jocks; Scots troops. I could have become one by enlisting in the infantry. I'd be out of Reid's in a few weeks.

I'd deferred my call up until my apprenticeship finished. Most apprentices did so. After a bad day at Reid's I wanted the Government to conscript me immediately, send me to an infantry regiment and then Cyprus or Malaya fighting terrorists. But I might end up a cook stuck for two years in barracks. I couldn't make a decision. I'd no idea what I wanted.

It was good drinking sweet, milky tea and chewing egg rolls with Fergie.

"Good tea that, Tim. Jist like Army tea."

We worked hard and we made a lot of cash. The people remaining in the fitting shop were astonished at Fergie's skill. When I thought about it years later, I saw that want of opportunity was what held Fergie back. Right bastards, that lot in Reid's.

There was grace in our work, measuring, levelling, cutting proof marks, grinding, scraping, filing metal to fit, drilling and reaming holes for precision bolts, making things to shape, tightening nuts securing equipment. Fergie looked at me, the empty socket covered with the black eye patch, the good eye gleaming.

"A' right, son?"

"Sure, Fergie."

We were evening the score.

When the old hands returned pockets full of cash they'd scammed in bonus, they were furious, accusing us of taking their work and stealing their bonus. I overheard one of them.

"That wan eyed fucker, Fergie, an' that Fenian cunt, Ronsard. Pair a' bastards.

I gave the old hands the chance to make trouble and they got at Fergie through me. One Friday night I was in a dockside bar with some apprentices, and we got chatting to girls, operators in the canning factory.

A buxom pretty girl smiled at me. "Come tae the dancin' wi' me?"

I should've made an excuse and left the bar. But I'd drunk several pints of Draft Bass, a sour potent ale, drowning my sorrows and common sense, mourning my lost love. I was melancholy drunk.

"Ah've a girlfriend."

"Who's she then?"

"A music teacher."

"She's no' here, is she?"

"No."

After two years apart I was still crazy in love with Cliesh. I could only disappoint this girl. I couldn't do that.

My voice, the faraway look on my face and she knew I'd knocked her back.

She turned to her friends. "Hey, this yin's been gettin' his end away wi' a music teacher."

Coarse laughter. She faced me. "Ye think yer smart, but yer jist a fuckin' mug."

The girl turned her back on me.

Frank Pollock's apprentice heard everything.

The next week, one afternoon on the shop floor, Pollock nailed me.

"Whit's this aboot you an' a music teacher? Ah heard ye wir shaggin' her."

"Fuckin' shut it, Pollock."

"Piss off, ya fuckin' Pape shite. There's no' a good ride in ye."

"How the fuck wid ye know, ya tosser? You've got hair on the palm o' yer hand."

Stars and blue lights; then blackness. I surfaced and the right side of my face ached. I felt the swelling. I tried to get up and fell back. I lifted my head and saw that Pollock was flat out on the concrete. His mouth was bloody. Fergie stood over him, right forefinger raised.

"Don't move, Frank."

"Fuck ye, ya wan eyed bastard!"

Fergie's boot crunched Pollock's right hand. He shrieked and rolled over nursing his hand.

Fergie now had more time for me, our friendship made from skill and success on the rush jobs. But, I never dreamt he'd stiffen Frank Pollock on my behalf. He'd had enough of the old hands and their taunting. Fergie got me to my feet, taking me to the washroom. He soaked a clean rag in cold water and pressed it against the bruises on my face.

"Keep that against yer face Tim. It'll help the pain an' the swelling."

Fergie took the rag from me and gave it a fresh soaking applying it again to my face. "The music teacher, son; somebody ye liked?"

"Aye."

"Tim, how many times huv a telt ye. Use yer heid. Never tell them anything in this fuckin' place. Yer gonny huv tae explain yer black eye and yer sore face tae yer mother. Don't worry aboot that cunt, Pollock. He'll no' come near ye."

I'd have got a right kicking if Fergie hadn't stopped Pollock.

My father said little about my face. My mother went on the offensive. "Yer a damned disgrace, Tim Ronsard. Ah'm ashamed; a son o'mine wi' a face like that. Bloody well tell me whit happened."

I didn't answer her.

"Yer jist a damned hooligan. Get oot o' ma sight."

There was good news at home. My Uncle Harry, my mother's younger brother was coming home from Bari. Harry and his wife Sylvanna would stay with us for several days, but the children would stay with Sylvanna's Scots-Italian relatives. Word of the visit put my mother in a good mood, the first for a long time.

It was a warm damp April afternoon. My father had left that morning for another trip to Dublin on the Irish Boat. My mother would be out; and I didn't expect Harry and Sylvanna to be in the house. I went over the wall at Reid's. I'd had enough for one day. I was looking forward to playing Jazz records, and in the evening talking to Harry and Sylvanna.

I slipped in the front door. The bed creaking, the swish of bed clothes slipping to the floor; Harry and Sylvanna's hoarse whispering, brought Cliesh back to me when we made love. My hands shook. I remembered her curves and angles, the hollow of her back, her boy-girl body, her whispering that she loved me when her small delicate breasts came alive from my caresses. I hurt, missing her.

I cleaned up, and sat at the window watching the rain. An old seventy eight scratched away in the back ground; Jelly Roll Morton's Michigan Water Blues. Harry opened the living room door and sat in the chair opposite me. He was wrapped in a patterned silk dressing gown, and his hairy legs and bare feet stuck out in front.

"Home early, Tim?"

Harry had spoken nothing but Italian for ten years; there was nothing left of his Scots accent.

"I went over the wall."

"You could get fired."

"Ah could nae care less. It's grim in Reid's. Ah hate the fuckin' place."

Harry shook his head.

"How's Sylvanna. She a' right?"

"Sylvanna's fine, Tim. She's in bed sleeping."

Harry was a lucky man. Married to Sylvanna with three children. She was plump and sultry, and still in love with Harry.

"What's up; why so glum, Tim? Ten years ago you were a happy wee boy. Now your face is tripping you."

I shrugged. Talking about Sylvanna and I thought again about Cliesh. The longer we were apart the more I yearned for Cliesh and all her tender loving.

"You're happy in Bari?"

"We live in Mola di Bari. It's a nice town. Marrying Sylvanna's the best thing that ever happened to me."

Harry had a good life in Italy. Sylvanna's family owned land on the outskirts. Harry ran the family shop, selling cheeses, pulses, vegetables, olives and olive oil, wine, coffee; and cured hams.

"The Spring weather is gorgeous. Deep red poppies everywhere. I pick bunches for Sylvanna."

I pictured Cliesh packing a small vase with pale yellow Icelandic blooms. Poppies; and I was back to the Sunday I went to the banks of the Old Reservoir and gathered a good handful, wrapping them in tissue paper I'd taken from the house. And Cliesh making love when I gave her the bouquet.

"Italians are kind people. They love life. They like the British; from the War. I'm looking forward to going home."

While Harry and Sylvanna stayed with us there was no truce with my mother: she never let up in her long war with me.

"What's eating your mother?"

"Ask her, Harry. Ah huv nae a' clue, but Ah can tell ye its fuckin' miserable in here."

"Tim; cut the swearing. There's no need for it."

"Ye've got nae idea. Reid's a' fuckin' day and then her girny face and moanin' every time Ah come in. Sure, ye saw her last night at the table."

"Yes, I see what you mean."

I'd hoped for some relief with Harry being home; a lull in the guerrilla fighting for appearances' sake at least. At the evening meal, Harry asked about Reid's and I was non-committal. Then, Sylvanna kidded me about girlfriends.

"Ah huv the odd date; nuthin' serious."

"Come to Mola di Bari,Tim," Sylvanna said. "Nice girls there."

I loved her deep warm voice.

My mother erupted, driven by jealousy and rage. "Nice girls is it? There's nae pleasin' that one. An' there's nae pleasin' him at Reid's either. He dis nae like it. Ye think he'd be grateful at gettin' the chance tae serve his time. But no' him. He dis nae like the engineerin'. Never mind that it's good enough fur his faither. Ah don't know what the Hell he dis like."

Silence. My mother rose to clear the table. My father shook his head. Sylvanna was close to tears. Harry was livid. My mother went to the kitchen. I was hurting and so was Sylvanna.

"It's all right, Sylvanna. She was talking to me."

Harry put his arm round Sylvanna's shoulder. "Tim's right."

My mother came back to the table and launched into another attack. "Harry, ye don't know whit yer talking aboot. He's no' the boy ye used tae know."

"Right, that's enough!" My father said. "Harry and Sylvanna are guests here."

My mother ignored my father, turning at the kitchen door to hurl her richest insult. "Go tae Bari, or whit ever the Hell ye call it. Ye'd be wastin' yer time takin' him. He'd jist mope a' day. Him and his bloody music teacher. He's jist missin' a' that he wis gettin' fae her. She's nuthin' but a cow."

She'd humiliated me, and insulted Cliesh; called her a filthy demeaning thing. I hit back "Don't raise her name ever again, dae ye hear me? Ah'm jist no' huvin' it."

But there was no stopping my mother now. "A trollop, that music teacher. Ah'll say whit a please in here, an' ye can put up wi' it or no'. Jist as ye like." Her face was a mask of vindictive triumph.

I waited a few seconds and that confused her. I fixed her with a steady pointing finger. "If you ever say another word about her, I'm leaving here for good.

Now, shut up." My polite voice for after Mass when I addressed priests and Catholic matrons shook her. I pushed my chair back from the table and stood.

My mother covered her mouth with both hands. She was crying. "Where are ye going, Tim?"

"Out of here. I've had enought of you for one day."

I slammed the door; some homecoming, for my uncle and his wife. I walked the streets into the small hours.

"What happened last night was bad," Harry said. "You're not having a great time of it, Tim."

I pulled a face.

"I know about the music teacher. Your father told me about her when we went out for a drink the other night. You liked her, didn't you?"

"Ah loved her."

"I know, son, but there isn't anything you can do now. You've got to move on."

"I can't."

Why don't you come to Mola di Bari this summer; stay for a couple of weeks? You'll be happy there. Come and stay with us. It's a place to stay and settle down, to have a family and a home."

I fancied going to Italy, but I was far from ready to settle down. "That's great! Ah wish Ah could come, but Ah'm goin' tae Barcelona fur a couple o' weeks wi' some o' ma mates in Reid's. Deposit's paid. Ah canny come."

Harry shrugged in disappointment. "That's too bad, Tim. Next year then?"

"Yer on; Ah'll be there next year."

I was a child of the river. I'd early memories of British and American soldiers coming off troopships; the flight decks of carriers, hulking battleships, destroyers with raked masts, and funnels. By the time I was twelve after school and at weekends I was haunting the quays staring at ships and dreaming of abroad.

And the German prisoners of war. One day, walking with my mother near the Old Reservoir, a working party marched past three abreast, picks and shovels, sledgehammers resting on the right shoulder. Some dressed in field grey uniforms patched and worn. A few had jackboots. Many wore British battle dress with yellow patches and ammunition boots, their ankles bound with improvised puttees. The forage caps and service caps pulled over the brow or tugged to a rakish angle above the right eye said they were fighting men.

They hummed Lilli Marlene and swung their left arms across the front of greatcoats and tunics. Guards halted them at a cross road, and a grinning boy soldier thrust a bar of chocolate at my free hand, but my mother yanked me away before I could grasp the German's gift. When work was slack in Reid's I'd remember the German soldiers. Sure, they were enemies, but I never forgot their marching and quiet defiant singing.

One Sunday not long after Harry returned to Italy, I rose early and walked down the hill to the river confident that I would see a sugar boat at anchor waiting for a berth, or a Canadian Pacific liner on the hook, waiting for the tender bringing emigrants on board. But, what I longed for was a frigate or a cruiser lying in the Naval Anchorage. I loved the river; when I was eighteen it was the route out of Westburn.

I lingered on the Esplanade staring into the early morning fog covering the river, and heard the distant throb of engines. The raked bow and the forward gun turrets of a sleek, powerful cruiser emerged from the mist. The red white and blue horizontally stripped ensign flapping astern above her wake; I knew she was the De Ruyter. A tug moored her to a buoy.

I wanted to belong to the ship and get away from Westburn. I didn't worry that I couldn't speak Dutch. I'd have served in the galley, on deck, a wardroom steward. Joining the Dutch marines appealed to me. Anything but the engine room; that was too close to Reid's foundry.

The mist cleared, and De Ruyter's two escorting destroyers appeared line ahead, thin white bow waves, bright work twinkling. Muffled voices from the tannoy carried to the ashore as the ships dropped anchor and stopped engines.

Later that Sunday I saw Dutch sailors on liberty. Many of them were about my age. I liked the uniforms, especially the white hats with the gold Gothic letters on the hat bands, the ends trailing at the back. Had they asked I would've joined the Netherlands Navy and sailed away.

I heard a lot about equality and solidarity in Reid's. I didn't forget what Jake Burns said about the brotherhood of man. Reid's had its own rigid class structure, just as odious as the one outside the foundry gates.

Westburn, a small town with sharp class divisions. Sometimes the working class and the middle-class bumped into each other, but they did not mix. One time myself and a few apprentices gate crashed a dance at the rugby club. The rugby hearties and their women ignored us. We asked posh girls to dance. They shook heads, didn't speak. We left angry and humiliated.

During the apprentices' strike we picketed the drawing office trying to get the apprentice draughtsmen to join the strike. These nice middle-class boys in suits and shirts and ties pushed their way through the picket line. A phalanx of apprentice welders in heavy boots, pigskin jackets and tight berets barred the way into the offices.

"Get out of the way, scum," a big lad said.

A compact welder nutted him and fighting broke out. There were black eyes and cut lips on both sides when the police stopped the scrapping. That was the day I got lifted and warned by a Sergeant.

The antagonisms between the working class and middle-class spilled over into Reid's foundry. Drawing Office people had no time for the shop floor, and we hated them.

Fergie and me were reaming holes for fitted bolts to secure the cast iron guides for the connecting rods.

Fergie saw that a hole on the drawing was out of alignment. The young foreman sent word to the Drawing Office, and an aloof young draughtsman came down to the shop floor.

"What's the trouble here?"

"Fuckin' drawin's wrong, Mate," Fergie said.

The draughtsman ignored Fergie and looked at the foreman waiting for an answer. Fergie grabbed his shoulder. "Get your filthy hands off me."

Fergie tightened his grip. "Don't fuckin' look at him, talk tae me."

"It's wrong and you'd better fix it," the foreman said.

The draughtsman took the drawing away, corrected it, and an office boy brought it back.

The engineers wouldn't stand for the superior ways of office workers, but they had little regard for the feelings of those beneath them in the pecking order They had no option but to tolerate other skilled trades: plumbers, boiler-makers, welders, and burners, but they kept distance from them. The engineers tolerated the semi skilled; the machinists, the drillers, the slingers, and crane-men but talk about the job was barely cordial.

The engineers despised labourers who swept the floor and carried trades-men's tools. Some of them were Jakies fond of cheap wine. An old soak used to pour a half bottle of the stuff into his tea can and drink it with his buttered morning roll.

"Ye'd think he'd know better," Fergie said.

Frank Pollock watched the labourer brushing and cleaning round the bed-plate. Pudgie, a poor soul, his nerves wrecked on the North Atlantic Convoys.

"Hurry up, ya wee cunt," Pollock said. "We've tae start the fuckin' job the day."

I walked over. My gut was tight as I searched for courage. I sensed that my face was white with rage. I owed this bastard for punching me, knocking me out. "Job's clean. Leave him be."

"Fuck off, Ronsard. Mind yer ain business."

I grabbed the brush from Pudgie and struck Pollock a hard blow in the gut with the point of the handle. He fell onto his knees and bent over gasping. "Ah'm makin' it ma business, Pollock. Jist you an' me this time."

I waited, ready to boot him in the face. Pollock didn't get up. I gave the brush back to Pudgie, and he hurried away.

"Pollock wis askin' fur that," Fergie said.

Come the two weeks summer shutdown, and I was keyed up about the Spanish holiday. Four days on a train there and back: overnight to London, then Paris, and south to Peripignan, around the edge of the Pyrenees and finally, Barcelona. We'd been talking about it for weeks: drinking Sangria, San Miguel beer, the Vino. Meet nice Spanish girls. I had the bonus. My parents added to my bankroll. I was half way through the apprenticeship. This trip might sweeten me enough to complete the rest of it.

Friday night; we were traveling on the Sunday.

"Fancy a bevy the night, Tim?"

"Sure, Fergie."

"Good. Ah'll meet ye in the Glengoyne Bar at seven o' clock."

The bar was all mirrors and dark wood, a mahogany gantry and sawdust on the floor.

"Tim. O'er here." Fergie was wedged in at the corner of the bar. He looked different in his dark blue blazer and grey slacks. "Yer lookin' good, son. The Spanish lassies'll be waitin' on ye."

Two shots of whisky and two half pints of dark ale slid across the bar. "Good holiday, son." We slugged the whisky and chased it with swallows of ale. It was going to be a long night.

"Ye never met ma wife, did ye?"

"Naw, Ah huv not."

"Her name's Ute. She's aboot this height. An' she's bonny, wi' fair hair."

He raised his right hand palm down to indicate her height. There was a look of great tenderness on Fergie's face. It wasn't the drink talking.

"Wis she in the Wehrmacht?"

"Aye. She wis a nurse."

Ute was from Danzig in East Prussia. She had spent most of the war nursing German soldiers wounded on the Russian Front. In the long retreat from the advancing Russian Armies she'd escaped to the West, to Hamburg in the British Zone.

"Whit mob wur ye in, Fergie?"

"Infantry: Ninth and Tenth Seaforths, Fifty first Highland Division. Ah went tae North Africa, Sicily, and Italy. Then Normandy and Germany. Ah thought aboot becomin' a Regular efter the War."

The Fifty-first was a crack formation. Harry had an attachment to the Division for a while.

"Did ye ever get tae Berlin?"

"Naw. Ah wis stationed near Hamburg."

Fergie had lost his eye on the shooting range. A peacetime conscript carelessly discharged his rifle. The 0.303 round ricocheted and hit Fergie in the eye. His Army career was over. The Army awarded him a small pension. While recovering in hospital, he'd met Ute. They'd fallen in love, got married and he brought her back to Scotland.

Fergie's warm words, the way he and Ute met, the gestures when he talked about her, and I longed for Cliesh. I wanted to tell him about Cliesh and how much I loved her.

"We've got a boy a' eleven and a wee lassie. She's eight an' looks like Ute. Ute disnae keep well; asthma. That's why Ah get a' they pass oots. Ah huv tae see that she's a' right."

I wanted to believe Fergie and dismiss the stories put about by the old hands in Reid's. They'd spent the War in the foundry in reserved occupations.

"Mebbe ye'd like tae meet Ute?"

"Ah certainly wid."

"OK, Tim. We'll g'up tae the hoose the night."

"That be a' right?"

"Sure. Ute likes company. Ah've telt her aboot ye. She'll no' mind."

I hoped he was right. Another two shots of whisky and two half pints slid across the bar. I'd lost count of how many I'd had. Fergie was well oiled and I was close to guttered.

"Two fur the road, Tim." We drank the last drinks.

We came through the front door armed with hot fish and chips folded first in white paper and then two wrappings of newspaper.

Ute came forward at once. "So you're, Tim? I'm very happy to meet you. Fergus has told me about you."

Ute's offered hand was cool and firm. She was a pale, blonde, elfin beauty. I couldn't tell if she was asthmatic. Eleven years in Scotland had not removed her accent, and no rough Scots had entered her speech.

I thought we'd eat the fish and chips from the paper wrappings. That's what drunks do. But Ute took the parcel from Fergie and put the food in the oven. On the wall, framed in dark wood, I saw a garish Ecce Homo. I remembered the stoup on the lobby wall when we came in.

"Ah converted when Ah merrit Ute. Ah wis never particular aboot religion, an' Ute wis." Fergie laughed. "Ah'm a Tim, son."

I was one of the token Catholics working in Reid's foundry. Most of us had Irish ancestors; we were quietly detested. To the old hands, Catholics were 'Fuckin' Fienians;' 'Teague Bastards.' Religion: Scotland's spoonful of bile.

Now I knew why they hated Fergie, and, why I was his apprentice. He had 'Turned.' I felt closer to Fergie and Ute.

Ute laid the table, buttered bread and made strong tea. We dined properly and sobered up. Jacob and Erika, the children, crept from their beds, wakened by the noise. The boy, sitting by Ute and the daughter, perched on Fergie's knee. Shyly, they ate from the small plates Ute gave them.

Fergie and Ute shared quiet affection in that small tenement flat. Fergie's black eye patch did not seem out of place; it didn't matter to Ute, Jacob and Erika. Here, there were no taunts, and no pain. This was Fergie's refuge. I remembered the blissful hours I'd spent with Cliesh in her rooms.

Ute made filtered coffee. "You like coffee, Tim?"

I sniffed appreciatively. "Ah do, Ute."

"Who gave ye coffee like this; the music teacher? Fergie said.

"She did."

It was a shrewd guess. The taste and the aroma of the coffee took me back to Cliesh's rooms and how happy I had been with her. I'd heard nothing from her in two years. I missed her.

"Ah better get up the road," I said.

Fergie stood, his arm around Ute, her head resting on his chest. "Take care o' yersel when yer doon there, Tim."

"Come and see us when you get back from Barcelona," Ute said.

I walked home, chilled, the effects of the drink and food wearing off. I thought about the men in the crowded bar. The stench of smoke, stale beer, and sweat; drunks forgetting their hopeless lives for an hour or two. I had to get away.

I wanted something better for Fergie and Ute, and for Jacob and Erika. And I wanted it too. Fergie belonged in another age. I remembered James Malone's teaching of history, and imagined Fergie, a wandering Scots mercenary, myself his assistant, hiring our swords in the Baltic Lands. Fergie, made a Teutonic Knight, meeting the Lady Ute in remote Courland, wooing and wedding her and living happily on their small fiefdom. And I advanced to his Squire, seeking the hand of Cliesh.

I didn't go whoring in Barcelona. I was scared of catching the pox. Whores were the only women paying us any attention. The decent girls kept their distance.

I got drunk several times and, as we lay on the small municipal beach, I had plenty of time to think. I was swooping from one thought to another, as I surfaced from mild hangovers. I thought about Cliesh. I just wanted to see her. But this time, common sense refused to budge and I accepted that she had gone. For a long time I forced Cliesh out of mind.

I had to put my mother behind me. I couldn't handle her; not right now. I'd had enough of her.

I had to put another thing behind me. I wasn't going to waste my life in Reid's foundry.

I was looking for something where I could excel; and I wanted to test myself, just like Jake Burns and Fergie.

The train stopped late at night in Perpignan, and we got off to stretch our legs and find a hot drink. I walked to the back of the platform to look at the recruiting poster stuck to the wall. It was a collage of pictures of the Foreign Legion.

I smiled at the image of a bearded legionnaire playing an accordion at a Christmas celebration. But I looked seriously at the photograph of a colour party, and behind them a double rank of legionnaires parading in front of a desert fort. There was a photograph of a Sergeant standing at the bottom of a rock strewn hill. Above him an old fort, ruined battlements and a crumbling watch tower.

But what got my attention was the portrait of two legionnaires not much older than myself. They grinned at the camera, dashing, tough and competent in camouflage dress and green berets with the winged dagger badge above the right eye. They had silver parachute wings displayed on the right breast. I stared until my eyes watered. The poster offered a new life of adventure and comradeship in the Legion Etrangere. I remembered Dien Bien Phu. I knew the French were fighting in Algeria.

I removed the poster from the wall, folded it, and tucked it inside my windbreaker. When I was alone in the hotel room, I took it out from my case. An idea about what I might do took shape. I'd found the strength to take responsibility for myself. I wasn't going home. I hoped my father would understand.

Two days before the end of the holiday, I bought a train ticket to Marseilles. I went to Fort St Nicholas, the depot of the Foreign Legion. There were thirty volunteers. They took eight of us, and we signed a contract for five years. I followed the Scots Guards of old into the French service. Three weeks later we were shipped to Algeria. I took a deep breath as I stepped ashore in Oran, and saw the Legion Sergeants waiting to herd us into the trucks.

Chapter 3

Soldier's Pay

I got off the train from Barcelona in the early morning, sore from sleeping upright in my seat. The sun chased away my stiffness as I walked from the main station in Marseilles. A Gendarme gave me directions, then touched my shoulder. He spoke a little English.

"You're a respectable young man. The Legion is full of criminals and misfits. Whatever it is that's wrong, go home and make it right." I thanked him and moved on.

I strode through the quiet streets, but I was nervous and uncertain about my decision to enlist in the Legion. At the Quai de Belges I headed for the Quai de Rive Neuve and where it became the Boulevard Charles Livon, on the right stood Bas Fort Saint Nicolas, sharing command of the narrows of Vieux Port with Fort Saint Jean on the other side.

At the entrance to the Fort I nearly turned back; the sweat trickled down my back. I told the Corporal manning the gate that I wanted to join the Foreign Legion. He stared past my right shoulder, motioning with his hand that I should wait.

The Corporal returned and beckoned me to follow him. I went through the wrought iron gates, under the metal arch embossed with the legend: Legion Etrangere.

In the Office of Engagement, a veteran Sergeant sat behind a desk. He had a good look at me. "Yes?" He was an Italian.

"I've come to join the Foreign Legion."

"Why?"

I felt ridiculous speaking to this decorated veteran, old enough to be my father. "I want to be a soldier, in Algeria."

"Go back to Scotland. Join the British Army. You're not ready. Five years in the Legion is long and hard. Forget all about it."

"I'm eighteen. I've thought about it and I'm old enough to join."

"It's a hard life."

"I've come of my own free will."

The Sergeant shrugged. "Wait here."

Later, a legionnaire took me deeper into the fort to a small hall with benches round the walls. There were thirty people waiting, shabby, tough looking men from all over Europe. Whispered conversations in strange tongues filtered through the smoky air. There were no Scots, no one from Britain. I shrank into my jeans and wool jerkin.

I was afraid but rejected leaving, knowing I'd be taunted if I went back to Reid's foundry. Worse would be the fierce rows at home. My mother telling me I was an ungrateful brat.

A Legion Officer and two doctors came to the room. We stripped to underwear for medical tests. I'd lost any sense of time. Later, the officer appeared again, accompanied by a German Sergeant. They wanted eight of us - two Greeks, two Germans, a Pole and a Dutchman and me - we signed a contract for five years. The officer said there was no going back.

I spent three weeks in the Fort. A Sergeant took away personal possessions. I exchanged the clothes I stood in for Army-green denims and rough boots. My heart sank as I handed over my passport, a book about Barcelona and a small overnight bag. I was left with shaving kit, tooth paste and a tooth brush. Stripping away my past had begun. I'd signed a contract for five years with half-baked ideas about what it meant to be a legionnaire. I'd deluded myself that I was a latecomer to the traditions of the Scots mercenaries hiring their swords throughout Europe. I must have been off my head. I never saw a sword in the Fort.

I got used to dawn musters, but loathed washing in cold water. I wore the shabby denim uniform, feet aching, being crammed all day into ill-fitting boots. I swept the yard several times a day; cleaned the jakes of excrement caked to the sides of the traps; tried to forget the stink of urine. One morning I honked up my breakfast and had to clean up the puke.

Time dragged on the train journey from Barcelona to Marseilles. I imagined a jolly camaraderie of foreigners working under the tough but kindly Sergeants. By some mysterious process, we'd become soldiers. Mealtimes at the Fort demolished this nonsense. Everyone was hungry, for the Sergeants and Corporals worked us hard. The food was good but there was never enough of it and fights erupted over the shares. I managed to sneak untouched scraps of nourishment as the hard cases, former soldiers, the pimps and petty criminals, traded punches.

I was scared shitless most days, for the NCOs did nothing to protect younger recruits from the hard men who joined. A sorting out was going on - preparation for basic training in Algeria. Some men did not cope, and the Legion got rid of them. I was the youngest volunteer - and I was usually ignored - but I was learning to behave Legion fashion.

I obeyed orders and stayed out of trouble. I saw what happened to those who didn't. Minor offences meant push ups, or push ups avec musique - clapping the hands between push ups-or given a kick up the backside. NCOs knocked tardy recruits to the ground and kicked them until they rose, and struck them again. Once I saw a man's front tooth punched out. I didn't want to lose any teeth.

I was obedient and that would have surprised anyone who knew me in Reid's foundry. I survived but I was cuffed several times by a Corporal for minor offences, picking up a black eye and bruised ribs.

During parades the Sergeants drummed home the message: we had volunteered for an elite corps. No one had asked us to come to the Legion. Legionnaires existed to uphold the values of the Corps, and to die for France.

"You have no identity, you are dreamers serving France," a Sergeant said. "You belong to the Legion." Legio Patria Nostra: the Legion had replaced my country; it would become my family. It was a sobering message. Would I ever take Legio Patria Nostra, for myself; feel the Sergeant's pride in the Corps? I was far from sure.

We stood two ranks clad in our shabby denims and rough boots. A pair of Corporals moved through the ranks inspecting us. "Head up," he said pushing my chin up with his fingers. "Attention! Arms straight, palms open, fingers together." He lined my hands up just behind my trouser seams. A Captain stood in front.

"The Legion gives a man respect, and love, tough love," he said. "For many this is the last chance. Many of you have nowhere else to go. The Legion is a small family, a band of brothers. There is always a brother at your side, and on your side. The legionnaire is never alone."

Love; what the Hell was he on about? I glanced at the hard men, the petty criminals and rogues surrounding me. They stared straight ahead, mirth tugging at the corners of their mouths.

"It is difficult to teach brotherhood," the Captain said. "You know nothing, and understand nothing. Some of you don't know how to wash," and he pointed a finger. "Many of you stink. But you will learn through discipline."

In this hermetic place solitude and loneliness might drive a man to desert or to suicide. But about halfway through the time at the Fort I made a new friend. He approached me at dusk as I stood on the battlements of the Fort.

"You're from Scotland?"

"How did you know?"

He held out his hand. "I'm Aristedies Spillyades; from Paphos in Cyprus. I had a Scots teacher and recognized your accent."

Aristiedes was about my age and build, with a dark complexion, a head of thick black curly hair, a warm smile, and an eager manner. I liked the look of him. I was glad someone in the Fort displayed a spark of humanity. Aristiedes smiled and we exchanged firm handshakes.

"I'm Tim Ronsard. I'm from Westburn, in the West of Scotland."

The Legion arranged a change of name for volunteers. Men who wanted to disappear and escape wives and families or the law leapt at the offer. Legio Patria Nostra replaced old loyalties. We'd decided against anonymity, and our friendship made life bearable. We ate together, sometimes we worked together, and in the evenings we talked on the battlements. But the Legion would soon absorb Aristiedes and me.

Aristedies had volunteered, to get away from the bombings and assassinations of the guerrilla war against the British on Cyprus. He'd fled to a bleak place. "I was under pressure to become involved. The British Army was hard on us. I wanted no part of it. But I didn't want anyone to think I was a coward, and I joined the Legion."

I told him about my life in Scotland, and I mentioned Cliesh.

"You joined the Legion over a woman?"

"It was Reid's foundry that drove me out."

French Army Intelligence Service interrogated us, breaking up the dreary routine of chores. They photographed us and took our fingerprints. Security procedures were impressive. They knew everything about me: St Mary's School, the engineering apprenticeship in Reid's foundry. That my father was a sea going engineer and where my mother was born. The Intelligence Service was making sure that we were not wanted by Interpol. A few volunteers disappeared.

After three weeks at the Fort we boarded a trooper in Marseilles. When she docked at Oran I wanted to forget about the squalor of the ship, and the misery of seasickness.

We spent a week in Sidi bel Abbes working on the rock pile smashing boulders to coarse chips with a fourteen-pound hammer. A Corporal armed with a machine pistol guarded us. The labouring made us fitter, preparing us for basic training. The journeys through Sidi bel Abbes, to the rock pile broke up the routine of hard labour. The Legion paid us about two pounds a week.

From the back of a truck, I saw my first garrison town, the cheap restaurants, and bars catering for the legionnaires. But daily trips revealed more. The French had built an attractive modern town; many fine public buildings constructed of honey coloured sandstone. The bandstand in the town square, with fine white, latticed ironwork and a gently pitched roof supported by cast iron columns. Legionnaires and their women sitting in the cafes under the trees, drinking wine or beer and listening to the music of the Legion Band. I tried to picture Cliesh sitting there with me. But it wouldn't hold. She'd see me, a hard case, a legionnaire. I was now so far away from her.

The Arab quarter was different: the shrouded women, the men in baggy trousers and hooded djebellas, pointy slippers of yellow leather, poking out below the hem. The smell of grilling kebabs and lamb followed the truck from stops at road junctions. The little shops with Arab men sitting in the door-ways framed by dark interiors, sipping glasses of mint tea. Goats herded past the trucks by small boys ignoring the hooting car horns and yells of drivers wanting them to clear the road.

"Reminds me of Turkish villages," Aristedies said.

Recruits could not go out on pass while processing for basic training was underway, before being sent to Mascara or Saida. In the evening, we went to the foyer, the open mess where the recruits congregated to drink beer and talk.

I was the only Scot. The majority of the recruits were Germans, and the rest came from Spain, Italy, France, and Belgium. After a few bottles of Kronenbourg the men sang French and German songs.

I liked the German marching songs, but it felt strange, singing along with the old enemy. I thought Germans were bad until I met Ute. Later I found that many of my German comrades were honourable men and brave soldiers. I was learning to take people as I found them.

A German Sergeant, a tough former Luftwaffe paratrooper who'd fought at Casino, was in the foyer, checking on us. He began singing Rot Scheint die Sonne, the anthem of the Fallschirmjäger, marking time with his hand. The German recruits led the men into the chorus. Aristiedes and me kept quiet. It didn't feel right singing that song.

The Sergeant came over. "Sing. It's a good marching song. You're going to be legionnaires." We sang. When the song finished, he pushed us to the centre of the foyer. In a few seconds he had us singing Erika, a rousing German march popular with the recruits.

The Legion assessed our aptitude and intelligence. Legion Security made further checks. A Major questioned me about my name. "You have a French name. Is your father French?"

"No, Sir. My father is Scots."

"How did you acquire a French name?"

"My family came from Ireland to Scotland, Sir."

"Go on."

"The French sent ships and Marshal Humbert's Black Legion to Ireland to fight with the United Irishmen against the English in the rising of 1798. One of my teachers thought I might be descended from a French sailor or legionnaire who remained in Ireland, Sir."

"And you want to serve France and the Legion?"

"Yes. Sir"

As I marched out of the Major's office I remembered the day that Cliesh had made me proud of my name. I had to stop thinking about her or my heart would break.

We got off the trucks at Saida, gathered our kit, and prepared to march to our new quarters. I saw a section of marching infantry, in olive green fatigues. Eighteen men in columns of three, at the front a Sergeant and two Corporals, faces expressionless under the brims of their black kepis. They carried machine pistols at the waist slung from the right shoulder. Behind them, three legionnaires carrying the section's light machine guns. Under the MAS rifle muzzles, a compact phalanx of white kepis, red and green epaulettes, swayed to the slow Legion march.

"You think we'll ever look like that, Aristiedes?"

"God knows, Tim. I hope so."

I remembered James Malone mocking our belief that Scots were the best soldiers in the world. He said that there were men from elsewhere who were better. Malone prodded the air with his finger, and quoted the British General, Alan Brooke. Fragments came back.

"Out of ... the falling snow flakes ... I shall never forget. The grandest assembly of real fighting men ... marching with their heads up ... owned the world, lean hard looking men, carrying their arms ... marching with perfect precision."

Alan Brooke referred to the Foreign Legion. I had a surge of confidence. "We'll be like that when we're done, Aristiedes."

The barracks is where the Legion brotherhood begins. At Saida I had my head shaved again. We were known as Zeroes. That meant that we knew nothing. But, the Legion would teach and discipline us.

After a few days, I liked getting up at 5.00 AM. A quick wash and shave, breakfast. A bowl of coffee or chocolate with bread, butter, and jam. We ate quickly. I learned the French way, to shake hands with everyone first thing in the morning or the first time I met them that day. Then we swept around the barracks or worked in the kitchen. By 8.30 AM we showered and changed and prepared for the snack, usually a piece of baguette and a wedge of pate.

We learned the French language and to sing in French. A Sergeant walked us through the Legion songs beating time with his hand; teaching us to pronounce the words and sing slowly in a deep voice.

There was much hard work. We cleaned and painted the barracks. Then we learned to order our kit. Thirteen uniforms for summer and winter and they had to be arranged for inspection by the Sergeant. The kit immaculate and symmetrical, boots lined up under the bed, room cleaned, and toilets speckless. Otherwise, the Sergeant went berserk, and threw kit out the window.

One miscreant's kit went out the window, and he lost the place. "Fuck you. Outside right now," this big Canadian said to the Sergeant, a power pack standing about five feet seven, a former NCO, Panzer Grenadiers. He removed his badge of rank.

I heard the crunch of bone as a head butt broke the Canadian's nose. Instinctively his hands went up covering his face and blood seeped out from between his fingers. The Sergeant landed a volley of punches on his torso. As the Canadian bent over, the Sergeant booted him in the groin and he collapsed on the floor whimpering.

"Any more heroes?" The Sergeant said, looking round the section. Silence. "Get him to the infirmary."

I adapted to Legion ways. Basic training was hard but made us fit. Jumping, running with a pack on the back. Stepping from the back of a legionnaire, foot on his pack to the top of a wall and vaulting into a pit, and dragging ourselves out of it. Tackling the obstacle course with a heavy pack. Jumping and rolling on the ground wearing a gas mask. Crawling under wires with a sack on your back or pushing the bag in front crawling under the wire. Crawling with the rifle cradled. Climbing up a wet and wooded slope using a rope. Rope climbs, hand over hand, sit ups, push ups.

Every morning at dawn we ran. The Corporals drove us over five miles, gradually increasing the distance to nine miles. Laggards got a boot up the rear end. And we marched six days a week, five miles out to a point on the map, usually a hill top where we stood easy and listened to NCOs for three or four hours. Then we marched back for the mid day meal. Then we'd march back to the hill for more lessons, and march five miles back to the barracks. After few weeks of this routine I forgot about tired legs and aching feet. I was fit and full of energy.

I learned to march far carrying a heavy load, and to find the will and energy to fight when I got there. The NCOs drummed into us that it was simply a question of mind over matter. We drilled and marched smartly, but we were not Her Majesty's Infantry from the elite Brigade of Guards. I liked shooting with the MAT 49 machine pistol and the MAS 49'56 semi automatic rifle. They were terrific weapons. Soon, I was putting a magazine of rounds from the rifle into the centre target at about four hundred yards.

About halfway through basic training, we marched in from exercise carrying full pack and rifle. Two hundred men paced out the slow swagger of the Legion, eighty-eight steps a minute, through the streets of Saida. A small band waited for us, and we followed behind for the last half-mile to the barracks. One of the Spanish Sergeants formerly of the Spanish Foreign Legion, gave the order and the band struck up Le Kepi Blanc. Our voices were strong. I liked singing; it transformed us from a rabble and made us a unit.

I remembered Cliesh's choir. How lovely she was at the school prize giving. I'd never met anyone like her. She was so feminine; the elegant clothes, the sheer stockings and fine shoes. I pictured how she walked. I'd no idea where she was now, and we were so far apart. I doubted I'd ever see her again.

But I cheered up when I glanced at Aristiedes marching by my side. We exchanged a grin. I gazed ahead to the men marching in front of me and I knew we looked good, just like that section as we marched carrying MAS rifles. A crowd watched us and there was applause from the Pied Noirs as we passed. I was chuffed with my hard, lean soldier's body, and the uniforms that made us part of the family: Legio Patria Nostra. It was the best day yet.

We halted on the parade ground, and the band marched away. Commandant Besson appeared with the Senior Sergeant, and addressed us. He was a veteran Legion officer, who'd lost his left arm in Indo China. His uniform was old fashioned. But he looked fit and fresh under an unfashionable officer's tall kepi. He had a good look at every man, inspecting the ranks, his swagger stick swinging from his gloved right hand, the point grazing the calves of his gleaming leather gaiters. The heel tips of his highly polished dress boots clicked on the parade ground. I liked the look of him; the loss of the arm enhanced his authority.

Commandant Besson was a tough, efficient, and fair officer. There was nothing old fashioned about his training methods. But he was a fanatic for the Legion.

"The dead bring fame to the Legion," he said. "Their blood brings new force and new life to the Legion."

Kepi Blancs were handed out, and he reminded us of Honour and Legio Patria Nostra. "You are soldiers. You are being trained to kill," he said. "You belong to the Legion."

I dressed for our visit to Saida. We looked good and I was proud of my new life. I remembered fragments of the Honour Code. To serve France faithfully with honour; every legionnaire my brother in arms, irrespective of nationally, race or creed … the sacred mission; that I would never abandon our dead or wounded; nor under any circumstances surrender my arms.

I had a few beers with Aristiedes in several bars as we gaped at the brothels and the soldiers in cheap restaurants. We were self-conscious in our smart walking out uniform. It was our first time on pass since basic training began.

Later, half shot we headed for the Rose of Saida, keeper of the sweetest tarts. A Corporal said her whores were lovely. I was thinking of the love Cliesh and I had for each other.

We passed a tattooist's and looked at the display in the window. Eagles and entwined serpents; hearts pierced by arrows. Regimental badges, battle flags. Like the tattoos we'd seen on veterans.

"Let's get to the Rose before it fills," I said.

"A minute, Tim,"Aristiedes said. "Look; there, in the corner."

I looked in the window and saw the card; 'Legio Patria Nostra.'

"Let's celebrate, Tim. Only four years and nine months left!"

"Is that all?"

We both burst out laughing.

"Tim. What do you say?"

"I'm game."

When we got to Rose's we had a new decoration. On my left forearm, tattooed in blue letters, framed in red and green, the colours of the Legion: 'Legio Patria Nostra.' We were a pair of daft boys.

Neither of us had bagged off. We were new to the pleasures of the bordello. I'd no idea what to expect on my first visit to a knocking shop. We waited in a shabby room, the atmosphere cold and impersonal. Two tired girls with sore feet hobbled in on high heels. They wore underwear and stockings, under a short robe left half open. We haggled about the price; had we French Letters? We had - the MO issued them to legionnaires going on pass.

We went to separate rooms, and the girl kicked off her shoes, yanked down her knickers, and lay back on a grubby single bed. There were no embraces or whispered endearments and no kisses. She wanted me in and out to make way for the next randy soldier. I could have been fucking a keyhole. She lay rigid under me, turning her head away, her hard eyes glinted in the half-light. I grabbed her hand as she reached for a packet of cigarettes.

"Fuck that," I said. "I paid for your time."

She snorted as I pinned her shoulders to that sordid little bed and had my money's worth. Why had I bagged off; what was I looking for when I went to the Rose: tenderness reminding me of Cliesh? What I got was a cheap ride.

I sat with Aristiedes in a bar; we sipped our beers waiting for the truck back to the barracks. I thought about the days of tender loving with Cliesh. I ached for her, longed for her body, for the sound of her voice. I would have given anything just to see her again. How could I, stuck in Algeria and obliged to go to whatever corner of the globe the Legion sent me?

"Some ride," Aristiedes said.

"Right; some fucking ride," I said.

After that I kept to the military stews. The girls were clean, and it would have been bad luck to get the clap or the pox.

After four months of basic training I'd become an Infantryman, a footslogger.

I'd serve honourably in any Legion Regiment. But I dreaded anything to do with engineering; that would remind me of Reid's foundry. I hoped for the Infantry. Aristiedes and I were delighted when we were posted to the elite Second Parachute Regiment-2 REP.

At Phillipville, I watched the trucks packed with paratroops rolling through the barracks gate. They were tired but looked good in their apple green berets. The Regiment was returning for two weeks in barracks after four months of operations against the Fell, the military wing of the FLN fighting for Algerian independence. We were waiting in the training cadre for a posting to one of the companies. I would be glad to get away from the training cadre. That night, Aristiedes had the Guard. I had a pass, and went to a nearby bar. I wanted an hour or two on my own. I had an aerogramme and went first to a quiet café and wrote to my parents.

Dear Mum and Dad,

I'm fit and well. I hope you got the message from Bob who was with me in Barcelona that I was joining the French Foreign Legion for five years. I've not been able to write before now.

I'm with the Legion's Second Parachute Regiment. You can write to me at the Legion Post Office.

Please try to understand, I was unhappy working at engineering and could never have settled in Reid's foundry. I'm happy in this new life, and I've made a good friend in Aristedies Spilyades from Cyprus.

Some weeks later I got letters from home. My father wrote,

"You've taken a wrong turn, son, but it's your decision and I respect it. Make a success of your service. I wish you well in the Legion."

I'd upset my father, but I still had his respect.

My mother sent her own personal message.

"It's a wicked thing you did, Tim Ronsard, cutting yourself off, giving up your apprenticeship to join a rabble and stuck in Algeria. You're a right disappointment. You were never the same son to me after you met that music teacher. I curse her for she has ruined you."

I'd already lost Cliesh and now my mother's love had gone. I was furious at her bile, but it was no surprise. Relations between us these past two years were bitter. I kept these letters hidden in my kit.

Later that evening I was in a bar popular with legionnaires. I sat in a quiet corner nursing a beer, taking stock of the last few months and wondering about the future. I was proud of the new parachute wings. I'd completed the parachute course lasting six weeks; the final test, six jumps, one of them at night. I touched the silver wings pinned to my right breast and smiled.

I was lean and fit after basic training, and the harsh regime and bad food imposed by the NCOs at the Regimental training farm. It was hard, but I'd thrived.

We were up at 5.30 AM, and ran fourteen miles cross-country; we had to run faster each day. Hand over hand climbing the rope; push ups and sit ups. The regime got harder: five-mile jog, in full kit; sprints up to 100 yards carrying a legionnaire.

Unarmed combat, on hard ground: two men finished up in hospital; one with a broken collarbone and the other with a broken ankle. At practice I was paired with Aristedies, and we went through the motions, trying hard not to hurt each other. The Corporal pulled us apart. He was an American hard case who'd been in Korea with the Marines.

"Fuckin' Girl Scouts," he said, bashing Aristedies about, tripping him, hurling him to the ground. He paired me with a big Danish legionnaire.

He was forty pounds heavier. I was scared, but after two hard throws that winded me I was angry. The Dane grabbed me, and I booted him in the groin, but he just scowled, picked me half up and butted me on the right brow. I felt the eye closing and the pain was bad. But, I managed to punch him in the adam's apple. He dropped me and just about choked. I got behind him and scissored his legs, bringing him down heavily. I banged his face off the gravel.

The Corporal held my hand up. Faraway I heard his rasping voice. "Legionnaires adapt, improvise, and overcome." He sent us both to the infirmary. I was learning not to get walked on, and to look after myself.

We learned field craft in the hills, practising navigation and map reading, planning, and spotting ambushes. I gave serious thought to the Fell, the enemy-how they organized, set booby traps, living and moving in the field. But we lost half a dozen men: deserters, failing the course, sickness, and injuries; and prison.

Regular Army parachutists trained us at a well organized camp near Algiers. There was decent food, cinemas, comfortable foyers. The NCOs emphasized safe parachuting -falling, jumping with the stop chute. I leaped from twenty-five feet, and felt relief as I swung in the stop chute harness inches from the ground.

Waiting to board the plane for the first jump brought mood swings - elation, afraid that I'd die when the 'chute failed to open. I was close to shitting myself. The instructors checked harnesses and safety 'chutes, correcting mistakes. I was calm when the section boarded the plane.

The plane levelled off at one thousand feet above the drop zone, the red warning came on and we stood, hooking up static lines to the rail and shuffled towards the open door of the aircraft. The green light and the instructor slapped the first man on the shoulder, and he was gone. The second man hesitated, and then he too disappeared. The third man refused to jump and was hauled to the side. He was sent back to Saida.

I was fourth. Unexpectedly, I was confident and barely felt the instructor's hand on my shoulder. I threw myself out the aircraft door and fell into stillness. Two white canopies drifted behind the plane and far below. There was a crack; my chute opened, and I was wrenched up; elated, I descended under the white canopy.

That first jump, men sprained an ankle, broke a leg, crushed vertebrae. By the fifth jump, the section cleared the plane in under ten seconds. On the last jump, there was one Roman Candle; the parachute of a French Regular failed to open fully and for some reason, he didn't get the emergency 'chute open. He struck the ground and died.

Nothing I'd done in Reid's foundry compared to the sense of accomplishment I felt on passing out of basic training and successfully completing the parachute course. Not the excitement of the strike or the new sense of competence I gained when working with Fergie.

I had been around other men for an age. I looked round the bar. It was good to sit alone and relax. I saw a tall, well built, and immaculately turned out Sergeant come into the bar. Off duty Sergeants don't pay much attention to legionnaires, and I was surprised when he came over to the table. I stood at attention, a knee jerk reaction.

"Sit down. I hear you jump well," he said. "We don't get many Scots in the Legion."

He ordered two beers. "I'm Dieter Westhaus. Mind if I sit down?"

"Please," I said.

We sipped our beers. Why the Hell was he talking to me? I was surprised at his fluent English and Scots accent. With his deep tan and cropped fair hair, he might have been a member of the Afrika Korps.

"You're surprised by my accent?"

"Yes Sergeant."

Sergeant Westhaus was from Hamburg; he'd volunteered for the German Airborne shortly after his seventeenth birthday. "I gave up high school. I was patriotic. My father was furious. He wanted me to go to the University and become an engineer. But, it was not what I wanted. My father was a foreman engineer in Blhom and Voss."

I ordered two more beers.

"Keep your money," he said. "I'll get them."

Sergeant Westhaus must have read my file. He knew all about Reid's foundry, and where I was from.

"I need a couple of good infantrymen" he said. "One of mine is leaving. I have another in hospital so I'm having you and your Cypriot friend join my section."

Dieter Westhaus fought the British in the Riechswald in 1945. The Germans resisted fiercely, but Scots troops of the 51st Highland Division beat them. Seaforth Highlanders captured Dieter.

"They called us Para Boys. Treated us as adversaries. I liked that."

Dieter went to Britain, finishing up in Scotland in a POW camp. He worked on new buildings, repairing war damage; and he was unsure about returning to Germany when the British Government repatriated him in nineteen forty eight. His parents were dead, killed in the fire bombing of Hamburg.

"I liked Scotland. I was well treated. I learned about what went on in Germany while I had been fighting. The British showed us film from Belsen. Going home did not appeal to me after I heard about the murder of the Jews. I was ashamed of my country. I considered staying in Scotland. Some of my comrades stayed on. I often wonder how my life might have turned out."

He laughed his deep musical laugh, which I came to like. "I was young. I wanted adventure. I'd no ties. University no longer appealed to me. So, I joined the Legion and vanished."

I'd kept my name, but I realized that I too had vanished into the Legion. The Corps was now my family and my country. I'd grasped the meaning of Legio Patria Nostra.

Dieter served in Vietnam, fighting the Viet Minh. He fought at Hoa Binh: three months of Hell, from December '51 until February '52. A grumbling appendix meant evacuation from combat, and his malaria flared up. After convalescence, Dieter arrived in Algeria and joined 2 REP. He had been with the Regiment since the beginning in 1955.

I was lucky; Dieter liked Scots. Gradually I mastered the arts of soldiering serving in his section.

The Well was my first operational outing. The section was to reconnoitre a friendly village that had requested a patrol. Dieter had logged that immediately.

"Something odd there, Sir," Dieter said.

"I don't think so, Sergeant. Just routine."

Dieter persisted. "Sir, it's a secure friendly village. Why did they request a patrol? We should be careful."

Lieutenant Armand new, fresh from St Cyr. The Legion attracted the top graduates. But Armand was lazy and irritable. Since he'd taken command, we'd looked to Dieter to lead.

"Seal off the village, Sergeant, and I'll take a strong patrol into the village."

Two heavily armed Dodge 6x6 trucks went in; eight men. I was with one of the vehicles blocking the village. I lay in ambush and watched, covering the legionnaire manning the machine gun mounted in the rear of the truck. We'd been there ten minutes when I heard the explosion and saw the black smoke mushroom over the buildings and slowly disperse in the warm air. Dieter ordered us in over the RT.

The village square was a charnel house. The round coping stone of the well had gone. Lieutenant Armand's head, beret in place was a few feet from his torso, thick blood oozed from the base of his neck, soaking the sand. One of his arms had disappeared. Two legionnaires killed by the blast lay farther back.

A Fell band terrorized the village, threatening the headman; compelling him to lure a Legion patrol close to the booby trapped well. The Fell was long gone when the bomb went off. The Intelligence Services took him and his sons for interrogation. We dynamited his house and left it a smoking pile of rubble. The wailing and ululations of the women echoed through the village as we left carrying our dead in the back of a Dodge.

Four months on operations and two weeks back in barracks was our routine. I'd been with 2 REP for a year. We'd been out for three months operating against Fell bands. They were an elusive foe. It was my third time out. There had been fighting but so far I had not seen the enemy up close. Sometimes, way to the front, shadowy figures might be glimpsed; then nothing. I'd fired the 7.5 MAS semi automatic rifle several times. Once on the ranges a Sergeant said, "Being hit will bring tears to your eyes. Then it'll kill you."

I was resting against a tree, after a bloody skirmish. We'd laid out the dead bodies of Fell for the Intelligence Officer. He was turning a cadaver over with his boot searching the uniform.

Twenty Fell located in the Aures Mountains, and we'd killed them. Helicopters, firing rockets, cannons, and machine guns had slaughtered some of them as they attempted to get round our flanks. The survivors were crowded forward towards our line by the helicopters. I looked at a dead man I'd shot in the head, as he dodged and weaved away from our line. There was hair and fabric from his forage cap burnt to the edges of a neat hole at the base of his skull. I helped Aristiedes lay him on his back. There was no face just a mess of bloody flesh, shattered teeth and bone fragments. Brains and mucus spattered his tunic. I managed not to vomit, sucked up enough saliva to clear my throat and spat out the mess.

"Spillyadis, Ronsard! Over here," Dieter said.

He waved us to a solitary Fell corpse. A rocket propelled grenade that failed to explode embedded in his chest; the warhead was unstable, the flesh riddled with pin head burns from the propellant. Two thirds of his torso hung open exposing his broiled intestines; we vomited.

"Sandbag him; if that grenade goes off, it'll kill someone. Don't move him," Dieter said.

We stacked four sandbags covering the corpse smothering any explosion. I had a bad taste and drank from my water bottle.

"Better him than you. Remember the well," Dieter said. "This bastard could have been one of the bombers. You think he'd give a fuck if he'd killed you? He'd cut off your knackers and stuff them in your mouth."

That day the Fell had attacked with rifles and mortars and I was afraid, but I'd not run or shit in my pants. I heard the helicopters coming to lift us. I removed the green beret, wiped off the sweat on my head and face. I tightened the ribbons at the back. Aristiedes was doing the same. I felt better.

The move to Dieter's section had been a good one. He ran a tight outfit and I was learning my trade. He showed me no favours and I did not want any. But there was a problem, a Swiss Corporal from Basle, who forced his attentions on young legionnaires. Someone should've shot him out on operations.

"Watch Roche; an evil bastard," Dieter said. "He carries a stiletto."

I was friendly with a cook. I worked hard when I had kitchen chores. He taught me to cook, and I'd make snacks for the section. I liked these sessions, eating together, drinking beer and wine.

That night I'd cooked pieces of chicken with garlic, onions, and tomatoes in a cast iron pan. We had beer and wine. A Spaniard had joined the section. I wanted to bring him in.

"Join us?"

"Thanks," he said.

Roche pushed his way into the tent and invited the young Spaniard to the foyer. The foyer and a few beers; then threats with the knife and a blow job.

"He wants fuck all to do with you, Roche," I said.

"It's Corporal Roche. You want trouble Ronsard?"

Roche could charge me; get me in custody, beat me up. But he'd not pulled rank.

"Leave," I said. "You don't belong here."

I turned to serve the food while it was hot. A stupid move.

"Tim, for fuck's sake," Aristiedes said.

I saw the switchblade curving a shiny arc. I got my head round far enough and dodged the blade aimed at my eye, but Roche slashed open my brow and cheek.

I hit Roche square on the face with the pan splashing him with hot oil, covering him in sauteed chicken. He dropped the blade and rubbed his eyes. Broken teeth shot from his mouth; blood ran down his chin. I drove the edge of the pan into his shins. As he went down I smashed him in the head with the underside of the pan sending his beret flying. He was out cold.

I was berserk; blood covered my face and ran onto my shirt. I felt like killing Roche but Aristiedes and the Spaniard dragged me off. Dieter pushed into the tent.

"We were outside, Sergeant, over at the kitchen," Aristiedes said. "We came back, and caught Corporal Roche searching legionnaire Ronsard's kit. Roche went after his eye with a knife."

"Stealing?" Dieter said.

My comrades swore that Roche was stealing. You don't steal in the Legion. If caught, thieves are punished. I reckoned Dieter knew what had happened with Roche. He looked at the Spaniard. He examined my eye.

"You'll scar; don't be careless again," Dieter said. "Get Ronsard to the medics. Bring Roche to my office. Then clean up this mess."

The infirmary attendant stitched me roughly and left a jagged line of puckered flesh discoloured by trapped bruised blood running from my brow and well down my cheek. My eye was hooded, and I looked hard. Next morning the Company Commander demoted Roche to the ranks and sent him to the Penal Battalion at Colomb Bechar. I got eight days in prison for fighting - and I had my sore face. I felt clean when I got out. I'd paid my dues, and was marked as a tough guy. I liked that.

Aristiedes, ahead of me, wading through snow drifts. The Company climbing to the frosty cornice topping the ridge. Silhouettes: berets, greatcoats skirting legs, the hump of packs, and the weak sun glinting off the metal of MAS rifles. I was the last man, watching for signs of a Fell band.

Dieter watched from the right of the line. He seldom lost men and felt personally responsible for bringing his boys back safely. I was confident that little could happen to us.

I cleared the snow cornice, rejoining the rear of the section labouring through deep snow covering the dead ground. An easy ridge lay ahead and then a high, wooded plateau. The window of good weather was giving way to a storm. We found an empty cave the Fell had abandoned. Empty tins and warm ashes piled in a recess on the floor.

"That was done without anaesthetic," Dieter said.

He jerked his head towards the ledge on the cave wall. An arm amputated above the elbow lay beside a hacksaw blade, annealed blue by a sterilizing flame; a piece of wood chewed by teeth marks, beside bloody rags.

The wind howled across the cave mouth, tendrils of spindrift whipping up a curtain of snow through the freezing air. Outside, the Lieutenant deployed the men: scouts in arrow formation to the front. The main body behind in a well spaced line. I was with Aristiedes in the rear. The snow storm broke, hiding the men ahead. We walked straight into an ambush.

It was a professional job. The front, taking heavy fire; to the right, the burp of a machine pistol. I heard the cries of wounded men. The Lieutenant ordered an advance.

Dieter quickly regained the initiative, directing a Corporal, four men and a light machine gun team to the left, out flanking the Fell, breaking up their line.

Light machine guns in the main position fired on a fixed line at the front of the Fell line. Dieter got the man firing the machine pistol with a grenade. On the left the Corporal poured automatic fire into the Fell.

Should the Fell retreat we'd pursue them and re-establish contact. They might break to the right or left and try to fight their way out. Firing stopped, and six of them in a ragged line came out of the spindrift. Grenades exploded, rifles and automatic weapons opened up firing short bursts.

"Cease fire; cease fire," the Lieutenant said.

The wind shrieked. Dieter snaked through the low undergrowth towards us. "Ronsard, Spilyadis, check our rear."

We found nothing. Dieter gave the all clear, but one Fell got through. He came out of low brush, took aim and hit Aristiedes in the chest, sending him spinning. The Fell's rifle jammed; he worked the bolt, cleared it and aimed at Dieter. I shot him twice in the torso, and he went down. I crawled to Dieter.

"Make sure he's dead," Dieter said.

The Fell was alive. He groaned clutching his chest and stomach wounds. He raised his arms to surrender. I shot him in the heart. We seldom took prisoners.

"I'm sorry, Tim," Dieter said.

Aristiedes' mouth gaped, and his teeth showed; he was dead. Revenge wouldn't bring Aristiedes back, but I was glad I'd shot the bastard that killed him.

We had two dead and three wounded. A helicopter came in to take them out. We stripped the Fell of weapons and useful equipment, and left them for the vultures to pick their bones clean. Dieter and the Lieutenant waved me and another man over.

"Get the dead and wounded onto the helicopter," the Lieutenant said.

I took Aristiedes' watch. I wanted a keepsake. I had a good look at him wanting to fix his face in my memory. Then I wrapped him in his ground sheet, and fastened it. The friend of the other dead legionnaire did the same, and we laid them on the floor of the helicopter; its interior was bleak and functional dull grey metal. Grey quilted cladding covered the sides above the bench hiding the wiring: a flying morgue.

We got the wounded onto the chopper. One man had leg wounds and lay unconscious. The two walking wounded were in shock. One cradled his arm, bound across his torso by bloody bandages. The other stroked his wounded shoulder with his free hand. They were full of morphine. We fastened the unconscious man into a stretcher. The walking wounded were strapped upright on the bench. The MO painted an M with Gentian on their foreheads; the doctors needed to know that they were drugged with morphine. The MO pinched the cigarettes hanging from between the lips. These two would be out of it for a while.

The whirring rotor; the helicopter was ready to lift off. Rigor mortis had not set in yet to stiffen the dead. I couldn't remember which bundle was Aristiedes, and I was far from ready for him to be taken away. The helicopter vibrated, and wind blowing into the interior moved the bodies. The first surge of grief came, and I prayed that Aristiedes' head would emerge from his waterproof shroud. "Tim, get me to hell out of this," he'd say.

A strong hand grabbed my collar. "Out, Ronsard. I don't need another man killed," Dieter said. "You saved my life back there. Thanks."

We formed up and marched to the rendezvous point with the trucks taking us back to the base camp. I whispered a prayer for Aristiedes' mother. God help her when she heard that her son had died for France.

The Regiment honoured the dead, and I was part of the escort at the burial: bugles and rifle volleys fired over the graves. The Commanding Officer delivered a powerful eulogy: Honour and Legio Patria Nostra. I just managed to keep a hard face. I got a medal.

I needed time to mourn. But right after the funerals I went to Corporals' School: six months of brutal training. I'd learn to give orders and make decisions. When I was out against the Fell I wanted to bring my boys back safely.

The day I got back from the Corporals' Course, Dieter invited me to the Sergeant's Mess. We were drinking Kronenbourg. I was feeling good. I'd passed in the top five. But I was sad too: Aristedies should have been with me.

"Good to have you back, Tim."

"Glad to be back, Dieter. I wish Aristedies was here."

"Yes," Dieter said. "He was a good man."

I felt the loss of my friend. I gulped down half a bottle of beer to get rid of the lump in my throat.

"I expected you to pass higher in the class," Dieter said.

That hurt. I could've passed higher, but I didn't want the attention that went with being top of the class. Putting up with the scrutiny of senior NCOs and officers would distract me from establishing myself as a new Corporal. I shrugged.

"I was twenty-four when I made Corporal," Dieter said. "You're twenty one." He was being kind. Dieter had made Corporal Chief in two years, and it had taken me three years to reach Corporal.

"How's the section?" I said.

"Everything is fine in the section, but there is trouble elsewhere; you remember Dalderuup?"

Dalderuup, was a Corporal when I joined the Regiment; a hard case from Holland, but running to seed. He claimed he was an officer in the KNIL, the Koninklijk Nederlands Indisch Leger, an outfit similar to the Legion. He'd joined the Legion when the KNIL disbanded in 1950. The Company Commander demoted him for drunkenness. Dalderuup nursed a huge chip on his shoulder.

"What's he been up to now?" I said.

"A pissing contest with the Sergeant, who beats him when he's untidy, half-drunk, or just plain insubordinate. He's been inside a couple of times. He's heading for the Penal Battalion."

Dieter avoided violence. Instead, offenders got hard exercises, extra drill, restricted diet and the agonizing Canard: walking duck fashion, carrying a rucksack filled with rocks, straps replaced by steel wires, wearing a steel helmet with the lining removed.

I got down to becoming a competent NCO, and prepared to deploy against the Fell: discipline, drill, route marches.

One morning my authority was challenged. Khun, a young German, paraded unshaven and hungover. I thrust my face about one inch from his.

"No shave?"

"No, Corporal."

"Fifty push ups."

When he reached the forty, I made it harder.

"Faster, avec musique. Get your razor and shave." He dry shaved, nicking his face several times.

I set a fast pace, and the section was first back in barracks from the route march. The men hauled Khun along when he was close to collapse. They got him into his best uniform and he paraded in front of me.

"You volunteered for this. No one asked you to come to the Legion. You're going to behave; do your job?"

"Yes, Corporal."

I dismissed him.

That evening I had a beer with Dieter. "Exercise and drill?" he said.

"Does the job," I said.

A few days later, Dalderuup was late for parade and the Sergeant bawled him out. He challenged the Sergeant to fight.

"Fuckin' toy soldier," Dalderuup said.

The Sergeant punched him twice on the Adam's apple. Dalderuup staggered, wheezing, and clutching his throat. The Sergeant held him by the shirt front and butted him. Dalderuup's face was a bloody mess. He lashed out striking air. The Sergeant scraped the inside edge of his boot down Dalderuup's denim pants, stripping the skin below the knee. The Sergeant let him collapse.

"Four days inside," the Sergeant said. "Two hours of drill at double time with full pack, and rifle in the morning. Two hours of Canard in the afternoon, restricted diet and sleep in a slit trench." Dalderuup asked for it.

I forgot about Dalderuup and continued preparations to deploy to the Morice Line, a barrier of electrified wire, mines, and radar sensors. We hung dead animals on the wire, cats, dogs, and small donkeys to scare off the Fell crossing from Tunisia into Algeria.

Dalderuup deserted with a machine pistol two days after the Regiment moved to the Morice Line. If the Fell got him, they'd kill him, and keep his weapon. If the locals caught him they'd hand him over for the reward.

Three days later word came that Dalderuup was hiding in a village to the west, near the lake of Chott Melrhir. He must have tried to cross over into Tunisia, heading for Ghfsa and the Mediterranean, hoping to find a ship.

Dalderuup failed to get across the frontier, and had turned west. Local Arabs saw him. He'd fired the machine pistol wounding a man. The Gendarme watched him until a Legion patrol picked him up.

"Let's go, Tim." Dieter said.

I stood easy in front of the Lieutenant.

"Take a truck and three men,"the Lieutenant said. "Draw supplies for two days. Bring him in, Ronsard."

I walked with Dieter to the section.

The Captain suggested you for the job," Dieter said. I was being tried out.

The patrol looked good: smart and experienced, green berets Winged Hand-and-Dagger badge above the right ear, camouflaged Tenue Leopard fatigues, brown combat boots over polished with black, white cotton scarf folded in a slip loop. We packed the Dodge 6x6 truck. I added an assault pump action shot gun. We drove forty miles in silence. I navigated; I had to bring the patrol back safe.

We arrived at a desolate place. "What are you going to do?" the Gendarmerie Sergeant said.

"This is Legion business. Keep the Arabs quiet; stay out of the way."

Dalderuup hid in a hut on broken ground, at the edge of the village. The shutter of the solitary window hung by one hinge. A legionnaire checked the rear of the building. "No door or windows, Corporal."

We spread out, covering the front of the hut. "Dalderuup. Throw out your weapon; walk out the door slowly, hands on your head," I yelled.

"That you, Ronsard, ya Scotch cunt? A fuckin' boy doing a man's job. Come and get me."

"Come out now, Dalderuup."

He appeared for a second at the window and shot at us. We had good cover. Dalderuup narrowed the gap between the shutter and the edge of the frame and the muzzle of the machine pistol poked out.

"You think he'll surrender, Corporal?" a legionnaire said.

"Get the shotgun. Load it with solid shot and knock out the door and shutter. Wait for my order. Cover the other side of the window. When the shutter and the door go in, two teargas grenades into the room, one through the door, and the other through the window."

One legionnaire gave covering fire with a machine pistol, forcing Dalderuup to take cover. l moved forward using ground cover, signalling when in position. I gave the order. The shotgun boomed twice, blowing the door flat into the hut;

the shutter disintegrated. The grenade launcher fired twice; tear gas billowing round the edge of the door and open window. We moved forward and stopped. Dalderuup would be out soon.

I took aim with the sniper's rifle. He staggered out choking and coughing, eyes streaming. The machine pistol pointed in our direction. I had him in the telescopic sight. One round near the heart and he shot back against the wall of the hut. I put the second round in his forehead, and he crashed into the dust. No one had asked Dalderuup to come to the Legion.

"Cover me," I said.

I went forward; rifle trained on him. He was dead. I waved the patrol forward.

"Good shooting, Corporal." The legionnaire spat in the dust beside Dalderuup's corpse. We wrapped Dalderuup's body in a tarpaulin and threw it in the back of the Dodge.

Back at the camp, I had the corpse laid on the ground and drew back the tarpaulin to below the waist. Dalderuup's chest was bloody; dried blood on his forehead. Blood leaked at the edges of his back and from behind his head. His bowels had voided and piss stained the tarpaulin.

I reported to Dieter. "Dalderuup's dead. He's out there. All the men are back."

The Lieutenant, the Captain, and the Lieutenant of Dalderuup's section came. The men of the Company assembled.

"Take a good look," the Captain said. "This is what happens when deserters take a weapon. Good job, Corporal. Get rid of that corpse. Make a full report in the morning."

The dismissed men hung around staring at Dalderuup. A man spat on him and another kicked him.

"That's enough," I said. "Take him away."

I gave Dieter the report the next morning and he passed it along the chain of command. We walked to the perimeter of the base to cool off. "Good job yesterday, Tim. It had to be done."

We turned and walked back to his quarters. "Tonight, make something, and we'll have a few beers," Dieter said.

I liked Andre Sobell. He was a nice kid from Belgium, a Walloon. He was like me when I was nineteen. When I made Sergeant at the start of my fifth year he was in the section. Sobell was a good soldier. He'd make Corporal soon.

Sobell was crazy about a girl in the military brothel, and she was keen on him. Maria was about twenty. I nicknamed her Our Lady of Phillipeville. Sometimes

I called her Mary Magdalene. She was from Colombia and had come to Algeria from the Canaries for quick cash and a return home.

It's tough loving a pretty whore. The Legion forbade marriage for legionnaires until they'd served seven years. Sobell had several years still to serve. If he made Sergeant before he'd served seven years he could marry. But had they been able to marry, life in the Legion would have made it very difficult for them. Anyway, Maria would go home when she'd made enough money.

It was hard on operations against the Fell in the Aures Mountains, the Nematchas, the Grand Kabylie, or down to the Morroccan border. Up to four months in the field; men killed and wounded. At the Regimental base back in Philipville Sobell couldn't wait to see Maria. I'd try to get him a pass the first night he was back.

The Regiment's departure to the Nematchas was brought forward. We were leaving in two days. I'd not had a pass and neither had Dieter.

"We can go out tonight," Dieter said. "I fixed it with the Sergeant Chief."

"I gave Sobell a pass," I said.

"The pretty little thing in the brothel?"

"Yes. He's in love with her."

"You getting soft in the head, Ronsard?"

We left the barracks late, and ate in a simple restaurant. The Pied Noir couple that owned it liked us. They served good steaks, fried potatoes, and a generous salad. We shared a litre of local red wine with the food. I was content. It was getting on for ten thirty when we went to a bar before returning to barracks. I've forgotten the name of the bars I frequented in Phillipeville; but not Le Chat Noir. I remembered it because I saw Sobel and his girl there. And how they obviously felt about each other reminded me that I loved Cliesh.

Sobel was embarrassed when he saw us. He wanted to be alone with his girl. We didn't care that she was a whore. Sobel was lucky to be in love.

Maria was lovely: petite, with dark, heavy hair framing her face. The hardness of her trade hadn't marked her face. I was sorry that she'd chosen a hard life.

We saluted them with our glasses. The girl lowered her eyes and Sobell nodded briefly. Unease spread over Sobel's face as we went over to their table, worried that we might muscle in and turn their tryst to misery. I realized then how little he knew either of us. Sobell stood up, very formal and presented us to his girl.

"Maria, Sergeant Westhaus, and Sergeant Ronsard."

I doubt that she expected us to be polite: Dieter offering his hand. It hung in front of Maria; she smiled and pressed his hand; Dieter bowed and stepped back. I shook her hand when she turned to me.

They drank Vin Rouge, a rough wine. Sobell was broke and too proud to accept anything from the girl. Dieter went to the bar and brought back a bottle of decent claret and four glasses. We sipped the wine. Sobell had the pass until roll call the next morning. I backed up to the bar and beckoned Sobell.

"You taking your girl to a decent room?"

He shrugged, blushing with embarrassment. I stood in front of him and forced an untidy ball of francs into his hand.

"I can't take this Sergeant Ronsard."

"It's a fucking loan, Sobell. Pay me back sometime."

We went back to the bar and drank Kronenbourg.

"You're a regular Cupid, Tim," Dieter said.

Later, I lay awake. Sobell was lucky to have Maria's love. I hoped that he'd believe their affair was worth the pain he'd feel when she went back to Columbia. I missed Cliesh, but it had been so long since we'd been together and the hurt of not being with her had diminished. But, I'd have suffered all that misery again if I could see her, even for just one day.

March 1962 and the French were withdrawing to sovereign bases; the Legion's long war with the Fell was ending.

Five hard years at war since I'd joined and the Legion Regiments had done much of the fighting. 2 REP had played its part in the 'Challe Steam Roller' and killed thousands of Fell. We stayed in sectors for up to two months pursuing every contact. We never lost the initiative: Commanders rapidly assembled intervention forces. The Regiment on trucks, and helicopters, assisted by ground trackers, and air reconnaissance, swept away bands of insurgents. It was the work of professional soldiers.

We gave the Fell a rough time, but we lost men. It was hard soldiering. We overcame the harsh terrain, the extremes of heat, and cold. The brutal ambushes and skirmishes fought, often in thick cover. The High Command said casualties were negligible, but seeing a steady trickle of men from your outfit killed and wounded by the Fell made for a hard and bitter war.

But I didn't regret joining the Legion. I liked being a soldier; not just an ordinary soldier but one belonging to a unique Corps. I'd changed from a skinny recruit weighing one hundred and thirty-two pounds to Sergeant in an elite regiment, weighing a lean one hundred and fifty pounds. I'd found my calling.

We drank beer in a bar near the base taking stock of the past and considering the future now that the war with the Fell was over.

"My guess is the French will get out of their Algerian bases eventually," Dieter said. "The Pied Noirs with any savvy are leaving before the FLN take over."

"It's hard giving up what we won," I said.

We worried about our place in the Corps. 1 REP had disbanded. The regiment had mutinied and sided with the Generals in the Putsch of 1962. They blew up their barracks and on the trucks taking them away, sang Je Regrette Rien.

"We're legionnaires," Dieter said.

"You think 2 REP will disband?"

"I don't think so. But the Legion will shrink, and I don't want squeezed out."

Dieter looked glum and I was depressed too. We needed cheering up.

"We beat the Fell," Dieter said, grinning. "We're warriors, just like the Three Hundred Spartans. Ours is a higher calling. That's why we defeated the Fell. I always knew that we could win."

The Legion was part of the true Army of France, the paratroops. Not the army of parades and ceremonies, but the fighting divisions and regiments, commanded by officers who led by example, who lived rough with their men. Leaders who made us masters of the battlefield and better guerrilla fighters than our enemy.

"Politicians," I said. "They let us down. They gave up."

"That's true," Dieter said. "The French sleep in their beds because we fought. They have no idea what it's like here in Algeria. We kept them safe. But we don't play politics."

"You remember the day on the ridges?" I said.

A November day 1960; we slogged up a mountain to about six thousand feet struggling for breath in the thin air. A forward party surprised a group of Fell and exchanged fire. We lost several men. A swarm of armoured Pirate helicopters darkened the sky; fast moving blobs, casting shadows on the mountainside as they came in low sweeping back and forth across the ridge raking the Fell with machine gun fire.

Two companies, elite Legion paratroops, the Regiment, in camouflage fatigues, the Tenure Leopard, green berets bright in the clear air moving in an open line, superbly fit, with deep reserves of endurance, surging up a steep approach to the heights. I was proud to be part of it.

I felt vulnerable as the Fell bullets thudded into the ground and a burst of automatic fire sent rock splinters flying past my head. Legionnaires dashed forward, taking cover in dead ground and behind boulders then zig zagging forward. We burst through a ragged scattering of stunted bushes. Our rifles and machine guns crashed like distant thunder and ricochets sang off boulders. I had my rifle on automatic, firing into Fell slit trenches.

"You bombed dugouts with grenades," I said.

Dieter shrugged. "So I did. We killed fifty-three Fell."

"No prisoners, " I said.

The regiment had done well that day.

"After Algeria, Tim, we're the future," Dieter said.

"How much time left in your contract? "Dieter said.

"About six months, but I'm thinking I'll sign another contract for a year."

"Good. Do it tomorrow. The Officers will respect your commitment. My contract will take me to about twenty years."

"You're ripe for the pension."

"Not yet,Tim."

Dieter waved to the barman; two beers appeared.

2 REP was moving from Phillipeville to Telergma, and the men would build a new camp near Bou Sfer. Demoralizing work for elite troops causing drunkenness and insubordination; punishment. Men would desert.

We often talked about why men joined the Corps.

"An American in the Regiment; he was proud of the Legion," Dieter said. "He told me belonging to an elite unit is like being dead already. I think he'd given up on life; got himself killed, just before you joined.

"The Fallschirmjager was an elite, but I didn't volunteer to get killed. I was a POW. I was unsettled when the war finished. I didn't want to go back to Germany. I wanted to be a professional soldier; I joined the Legion."

"I didn't volunteer to get killed."

We drank more beer. "Tell me again, Tim. Why did you join?"

"To get away from Westburn."

"And to forget the woman?"

"Yes."

But I'd not forgotten Cliesh. "Tim, darling Tim, you sang of me in the days when I was fair."

The last line written in the letter she'd left me. "Men without women, eh?" I said.

Dieter laughed. "You were lucky to have known her."

The Kronenbourg was going down well. "How long since you've been out of Algeria, Tim?"

"About five years."

"Must be about seven or eight years since I came back from Indo China."

Dieter wanted out for a while; so did I. "We do a good job on the building work," Dieter said. "We can apply for leave."

"I can't build anything," I said.

"Scots taught me to build. I'll keep you right."

"Good."

"We could go to Paris," Dieter said. "Let's put in for thirty days leave."

It would be a great leave if I could only meet Cliesh again, but she was stuck in Scotland. But there would be girls in Paris, maybe nice girls.

Chapter 4

Meeting Again

We came off the ship in Marseilles after the overnight crossing from Oran. It was June, 1962. I'd shared a cabin with Dieter. We'd spent too much time in the bar drinking Ricard and had slept for a few hours. But we showered, and felt fresh for going ashore.

"Tim, I'm feeling good," Dieter said as we walked out of the docks to find a taxi. We were well turned out in walking out uniform, medal ribbons on left breast and on the right, the coveted silver parachute wings. Black kepi, the eyes shaded by Ray Bans.

"Me too," I said.

We'd shaken off the effects of the pastis by the time we reached the station and headed for the platform and the Paris express. More than five years since I'd been out of Algeria.

There was some time to kill before the train departed. We had bowls of black coffee and croissants in the station cafe. Loud voices came from a table at the far end of the bar. Three drunk Royal Marines from the British carrier anchored in the harbour. They stopped at our table.

"Fuckin' Foreign Legion?" The Sergeant said. Rum tainted his breath, and threads of puke hung on his uniform.

"West Coast?" Dieter said.

Three drunk Marines in Marseilles make trouble and one of them is a Scot from Westburn. I shrugged.

"That's right, Westburn," the Sergeant said. "You're a Jock?"

"German."

"A fuckin' Nazi," a Corporal said through blubbery lips distorted by drink.

French units usually stayed clear of us. The Legion's reputation held them back. But this trio couldn't mind their own business.

"You're pissed," I said. "Why don't you leave now and we'll forget all about it."

"Try makin' us," the Sergeant said, swaying, eyes going in and out of focus.

The other Corporal, less drunk than his two friends, turned on me, "Ah suppose you're the fuckin' Jock Beau Geste."

I stood. Dieter swept off the Ray Bans as he got to his feet. "Another time. We've a train to catch."

"Yez are full o'wind and piss the pair o' ye." The Sergeant said. "Time ye joined a real fuckin' army. Fightin' Arabs is yer fuckin' limit."

We stared, and they blinked first. The waiter came over and ushered them out the door. A fight here and we might finish up in the hands of the MPs and that would be our leave ruined. But the drunk Corporal turned at the entrance, hawked, clearing his throat and spat on the carpet.

Dieter stubbed out his Gitane and cracked his knuckles. "Let's remind them who we are."

I slipped the waiter ten francs. "Keep an eye on our kit?"

"Yes, Sir."

We followed them into the pissoir. It was empty, just three Royal Marines' NCOs, caps pushed back, pissing. We came up behind them. I took a Corporal on the right, spun him round, and punched him on the jaw knocking him out. Dieter delivered a rabbit punch to the Sergeant, hauled him round and butted him full on. He was out cold, blood gushing from his ruined nose.

I had the Corporal who spat at us by the throat. His reeking breath enveloped my face "Now you know who we are." I gave him a thick ear and pushed him into the urinal.

We made the Paris Express with a couple of minutes to spare. Hammering the Royal Marines got some of the Algerian War out of me and Dieter, for he dozed off, and I let the past get rid of the rest.

It was good to be back in Europe, and I dug into memory: getting out of Reid's foundry, coming from Barcelona, and joining the Legion. I'd exchanged letters with my father, but my mother had cut me off. And Cliesh; I missed her, but she was gone for good.

The countryside flashed past the window, and I settled down. Dieter slept, moving with the motion of the train. We were an unlikely pair; a German and a

Scot. I rolled with the swaying carriage. I shut my eyes; the regular drum rolls of the wheels sent me to sleep looking forward to our leave.

At Fort St Nogent, Vincennes on the outskirts of Paris, the Legion takes care of its own. We had a bed, good food, and wine. Nearby was a Metro station with trains to Paris. We meant to spend our entire leave in the City.

We visited the Marais on our first day. People looked at us. The dirty war with the OAS spilled over from Algeria, but Parisians were not used to seeing Legion NCOs. Pied Noirs, settling in Paris, glad to be out of Algeria bought us drinks. We got loaded on Ricard.

Back in the Fort, we undressed and lay down. Dieter smoked another Gitane. "How are we going to get through this leave?" I said. "My liver will disintegrate."

"Let's bag off tomorrow," Dieter said.

An ancient Corporal came into the room. His turnout was immaculate; he must have been in the Legion since about 1930. "Sergeant Ronsard?" he said.

"I'm Ronsard."

"Woman called; left a message. Sergeant Ronsard, would he call her?"

He handed me a slip of paper. "Did she leave a name?"

"No. I didn't ask and I didn't say you were here."

"OK. Thanks."

Who could possibly want to speak to me in Paris? One of the Pied Noir women?

"Call her now," Dieter said. "Maybe your luck has changed."

I dialled the number. Two rings and a woman answered, "Hello."

"Sergeant Ronsard speaking."

"It's Cliesh. Is it really you, Tim?" Her genteel Scots accent, voice hesitant but so precious to me after eight years. I remembered her words of love. I fought to keep my legs steady. All the love I had for her filled me, and I wanted to tell her. But all I managed was, "I'm Sergeant Ronsard."

"Tim, it's Isobel, Isobel Clieshman. Don't you remember me?"

I hung on for an eternity. She started explaining: had been in the Marais. Saw me in the cafe; had not been sure it was me and decided to leave a message at the Fort. "I'm glad you got the message."

"Ah, yes," I said. "I remember now." My stomach was churning, and I was in bad shape. I wanted to say to her, "Is it really you, Cliesh?" I said I'd meet her the next afternoon at the café in the Marais.

"You look terrible," Dieter said. "Was it a ghost?"

I sat on the edge of my bed. "It was Cliesh. I can't believe it. I'm meeting her tomorrow afternoon."

"It's good you're going. Relax, sleep well. We'll talk in the morning if you want to."

I rose early and hid my anxieties, shining my shoes, pressing my uniform; I could've been going on guard. I showered, over-brushed my teeth and rinsed my mouth and gargled my throat. Finally, I shaved carefully.

"Ronsard, you're a nervous wreck. What the Hell is wrong with you?" Dieter said. "It's a date. We're in Paris. You're not going on guard. Calm down." He handed me his half-full bottle of cologne. "Smell nice for her, she'll like that."

I had a last look in the mirror, straightening my green tie. What would Cliesh make of me: cropped hair, gaunt face, and hollow cheeks, the blue-black scar tissue, proud as a vein forced out from my flesh and running down from my left eye onto my cheek to the edge of my mouth. I would find out soon enough. I put on the Ray Bans and the Black Kepi.

"You really like her?" Dieter said.

"Yes, I do."

"And she's a nice girl, so just take it easy. Don't do anything rash. OK?"

"Right." I walked out the Fort swallowing several times. When I got to the Metro station I had calmed down.

I sat at the back of the cafe terrace. I'd removed the black kepi and the Ray Bans. I sipped Ricard, enjoying the cold liquorice taste. Cliesh hadn't arrived; perhaps she was having doubts and wouldn't come. I wanted to see her, and to be near her again. I tried to forget the way she left me.

I recognized her walk the moment she entered the Place des Vosges. It was a long approach to the cafe, and gradually my eyes filled with her. Cliesh wore a washed blue silk dress, hair caught up in a matching wisp of silk; the sheerest stockings and fine, black shoes with Louis heels and eye catching ankle straps. Tight fitting black leather gloves and a slim leather handbag matched her shoes.

Was she calm beneath her immaculate appearance; or was she like me, a nervous wreck? I got up to meet her. We stopped arms length apart. Her face was working, then it crumpled and she smiled through her tears. My throat was tight. We embraced and Cliesh was sobbing, and my eyes stung.

"Dearest Tim. It's wonderful to see you."

I kissed her gently and found words I'd lost. "Darling Cliesh; dearest Cliesh."

"Tim, oh Tim, I'm so sorry, making a fool of myself. Please excuse me."

She vanished into the café. A man looked over and stared. I glared at him, and jerked my head back. He placed a note beside the bill and left.

Cliesh came back to the table her eyes repaired. But, this loving moment couldn't bridge the last eight years; awkwardness kept us apart.

She sipped her dry white wine. "Oh Tim, your poor face. What happened?"

She'd removed her gloves, and I liked her long fingers with the polished nails lingering on the ugly blue and inky scar on my face.

"I had an an accident a few years ago."

"Your hair was longer and soft; now it's so short."

"Goes with the job."

We were farther apart. I ordered more drinks. Our talk was banal.

"You're well, Tim?"

"Pretty well, Isobel."

"Shall you be here long?"

I explained that I had thirty days leave. We'd stay in the city, but might go south.

"I've lived in Paris for two years."

I liked Paris and so did Dieter. A good place to live. We were elated being out of Algeria: a couple of soldiers on the town. We'd walked from the Arc de Triomphe down the Champs Elysees; the Legion had paraded there. Rested in the Jardin des Tuileries, drank Ricard. I'd hazy memories of Sacre Coeur and lunch in the vicinity. By the time we got to the Place des Vosges where Cliesh saw me, we were sobering up before heading for the dives of Pigalle.

"Nice town, Isobel."

"Yes it is."

Cliesh smiled, her voice warm. She was everything I remembered. I'd never stopped loving her; and part of me wanted to tell her. But I'd called her Isobel, knowing she loved being called Cliesh. I nursed a grudge at the way she'd left me.

"Have you seen Victor Hugo's house?" Cliesh said. "That's it over on the corner. There are nice buildings in the Place des Vosges."

"Good weather in Paris this year, Isobel?"

"Yes. It's been quite hot."

"Hot in Algeria too."

Cliesh smiled again; she was so lovely. But my stupid grudge left me marooned. She was quiet, and I was edgy. "My first visit to France, apart from three weeks in Marseilles when I joined the Legion."

She inclined her head. I looked at my watch; that shook Cliesh. She thought I'd leave. "It's coming on to four o'clock." Cliesh said. "It's a lovely afternoon. Why don't we go to the Luxembourg Gardens?"

"OK."

"We could stroll and talk." Cliesh twisted and untwisted her fine gloves. I reached across and laid my hand on her hands.

"You'll spoil your gloves. Is something wrong?"

"No, no. Well … It's just … just that I thought we could have dinner and I made an arrangement, at a nice family place near where I live. I said I'd let her know if we're not coming. I mean if you'd rather not, that's OK."

No woman had ever given so much thought to me. Not the whores I'd visited in North Africa, nor any of the Pied Noir women I'd managed to pick up. Cliesh was so kind and good, and I'd made her feel awkward.

"Of course I want to come. It's so nice. I was going to say something about dinner."

"Oh good. I'm so glad. You'll like it. The owner used to sing and dance professionally. She was very beautiful. She's a dear friend. Her name is La Divine."

We took a taxi to the Place de l'Odeon, and walked along the Rue de Vaugirard. We admired the frontage of the Palais du Luxembourg turning into the Gardens from the Rue Guynemer. We watched the chess players and the card games.

Cliesh smiled a lot. I adored her beauty and poise, her smooth haircut, her elegant shoes, the carefully applied lipstick and makeup, but after five years in Algeria, they felt a little intimidating. I was randy and wondered if she wore fine lingerie under her beautiful dress. Our hands touched, and our footsteps crunched into the gravel.

"I'm glad my shoes have low heels. We're walking a lot."

I took her elbow and guided her to a chair beside the Fountain des Medicis. The fountain hissed and splashed, little waves lapping the edge of the pool. It was very soothing. We were close again. It was early evening, still light and quite warm.

"Tim, I'm hungry."

"Me too. Do we need a taxi?"

"Yes; its near Les Halles."

Cleish was lovely in that easy light before dusk. The city was beautiful. The taxi took us across Boulevard Saint Germain. At the Quai de Conti, we crossed the Seine at Pont Neuf. Soon, we were at Le Coq D'Or, La Divine's place. The front of the shop was painted deep green; the name, printed in gold letters across the top of the window. It was a combination of Bar Tabac and restaurant. To the side was the dining area, with soft lighting. The tables had red chequered tablecloths. There was a zinc-covered bar, the small marble top tables with the straight back chairs, cushioned seats round the walls. It was the place tourists search for and never find. La Divine was behind the bar, she'd been watching for us and waved to Cliesh as we came through the door.

"Isobel, dinner is nearly ready."

La Divine came round the bar walking stiffly in elegant shoes; she had good legs. Guardedly she extended her hand and had a good look at me. I liked her on sight. She had been very beautiful, but some hard drinking had taken its toll of her face. Crows feet round her eyes, crinkled against smoke drifting up from the Gauloise hanging from the corner of her mouth.

"So you're Tim. I'm La Divine."

"Hello, La Divine. I'm happy to meet you."

"The drinks are on me," La Divine said.

Cliesh drank dry white wine and I had a Ricard. We drank and talked with her for half an hour before dinner. I was having a great time. This was no drinking bout, picking a fight and smashing the place up. That had happened often enough in Algeria.

It was wonderful to see Cliesh among people who liked her. She was so happy and I knew again that eight years had made no difference to how I felt about her; I loved her.

I worried if I'd see her again after tonight; and if I did, what then? I was going back to Africa when my leave was up. Cliesh introduced me to her many friends as they came over and I could not take in all their names. They bought us drinks. One man paid for the wine with our meal.

"You know a lot of people," I said.

I saw now how much all this meant to her. She was so anxious that I would like everything. I could have wept with gratitude.

"I'm so glad you brought me here," I said.

"Hmm," Cliesh said. I thought no one was looking at us, and I laced my fingers through hers; the sweetest pain. She pressed my hand to her lips. "Oh Tim, Tim …"

A woman called, and Cliesh released my hand and turned to talk to her.

"She loves you, Tim," La Divine said. "I've never seen her like this. You make her so happy; be good to her."

"Yes," I said. I promised myself that I'd be good to Cliesh.

We dined well: rillettes, garnished with salad; a magnificent cassoulet; a basket of good bread; burgundy to drink. How wonderful to share food with the woman you love.

I'd adored the afternoon teas with Cliesh at her rooms back in Scotland when I'd fallen in love with her. Our dinner was more intimate: hands touching; I brushed my fingers against her stockings. She smiled and held my hand.

La Divine sat with us after the fruit and cheese. She brought a bottle of Burgundy and a glass for herself. She poured three good measures. "A present," she said.

La Divine had purchased the Bar Tabac with savings from her days as a dancer and singer. Cliesh gave her grandson piano lessons. That was how they met and became friends. Cliesh posted her notices near the bar and clients had made contact. La Divine was a good friend and a kind woman; my liking for her was stronger. The radio was on; Piaf singing Mon Legionnaire.

"I love Piaf. When Marcel Cerdan died in the plane crash, I was heart broken. He was the love of her life," La Divine said. La Divine had drunk enough to make her sentimental. Then, in a deep smoky voice she sang along with Piaf. I joined in.

"Oh, I'm glad you still sing," Cliesh said.

"We sing in the Legion."

We left to tearful farewells from La Divine. "Bring him back, Isobel. Come to see me before you go back to Algeria. Both of you come again. I'll make dinner myself."

We stood on the pavement outside Le Coq D'Or. "Would you like to see my apartment? Have coffee? I have nice cognac," Cliesh said.

"Yes."

"It's not grand where I stay, Tim. I hope you like it." Cliesh worried that I would like where she stayed. I'd spent the last five years in barracks or in the field. I'd been with whores. The Pied Noirs hated us, then they liked us, but I'd never been inside a Pied Noir house.

"I'd like that very much."

"Let's walk, it's not far."

A balmy evening, the street quiet; we strolled and held hands tightly."Glad you came, Tim?"

"Yes. I'm glad you found me."

Cliesh had come on holiday to Paris and fell in love with the city. The troubles with the OAS spilling across the Mediterranean had not put her off. She was making a modest living as a muscian and teacher. The money she had from her father tided her over the odd fallow period.

"I'm less well off here, but the city is wonderful." Cliesh said. "There is so much to see and do. I like the neighbourhood; there are good people and enough of them love music. I love French life. I might become a French citizen. I'm happy here."

"After serving five years, Legionnaires can have a French passport. I've thought about it."

Paris suited Cliesh. She flowered here. Now, there was a chic feminin- ity about her. Cliesh had a new presence. She adored flitting between the anonymity of the city and the intimacy of her quarter. Cliesh thrived where people respected music; she was a part of a musical underworld that flour- ished in people's houses, at private recitals, teaching the piano to the sons and daughters of her neighbours.

"Before I saw you I'd the strangest sensation," Cliesh said. "I knew that some- thing would happen."

That morning she'd worked with a boy of fourteen. He would soon need an- other teacher to develop his technique and his powers of interpretation. They'd played the Evocacion, from Iberia.

"I played it again when he left the apartment. It made me nostalgic for West- burn." She smiled. "I walked to the Marais, and the feeling was stronger. Iberia always reminds me of lost love. Then I saw you."

"Iberia does that to me."

"Really?"

"Yes."

The evening was so pleasant and we dallied. Cliesh asked me about the Le- gion.

"I'd had enough of Reid's. I was impulsive; I had to get away."

I'd never met anyone who planned to join. My five years service wasn't a story stretching from Marseilles to the present.

"My first contact was grim." It was a tale of incidents; shrapnel fragments surfacing on an old wound.

"Why not leave, right away?"

I'd been forced into Reid's foundry; but I'd volunteered for the Legion. "I'd come too far to go back to Westburn and Reid's foundry."

"Then what?"

"The Legion took over; shabby working uniform, dull, menial work; food, OK. Three weeks later we went to Oran in a troop ship"

"Was it awful for you? You were just eighteen."

"I settled quickly to the routine."

"Is it really so tough?"

"It's disciplined, but it's fair. I've done OK. I'm a Sergeant in the Second Parachute Regiment."

I tried to please her. "I told an Intelligence officer about the teacher that made me proud of my French name."

"Was it me?"

"Who else?"

Cliesh smiled. She kissed the proud scar on my face. Her lips resting on my disfigurement touched my heart, and I knew that Cliesh loved me.

"Let's go up to my apartment."

The apartment was simply furnished. Walls and ceilings painted brilliant white; woodwork a bright white gloss. Cliesh had brought some of her things from Scotland: furniture, pictures, carpets. The Petrof piano of polished rose wood released a flood of bitter sweet memories. We'd made love on the matching stool. These things that meant so much should have made us closer, poisoned me; I nursed my grudge at the way she'd left me.

"Nice room."

"Thank you."

I sipped cognac from a fine glass.

"You're hot, Tim. Take off your jacket. I'll make coffee."

I folded back the cuffs of my shirt to the elbow. Cliesh poured coffee.

"What's that?"

I glanced at the tattoo on my left forearm: LEGIO PATRIA NOSTRA in dark blue, bordered by red, and green.

"A drunken mistake."

"Is the Legion your family, Tim?"

"What else? I've been in more than five years."

The grudge burnt inside me. "Why did you leave without seeing me?"

Cliesh stared at her shoes.

"You left me that letter."

"I'm so so sorry, Tim. I couldn't tell you I was leaving. Tim, I've missed you. You know I had to leave. Please tell me you understand."

"You couldn't face me for your own sake."

Cliesh was close to tears. "Please Tim, let's not quarrel. I'm just glad I found you again. Let me play for you."

"Let's have a Legion song."

She was crying and tears wet the front of her dress.

"You walked out on me. I wasn't good enough for you. Now you're looking for a bit of rough with a soldier. The scars, the tattoo; everything. That's what I am. I belong to the Legion."

"Tim, please."

"Fuck you. I wish I'd never met you."

"You'd better go, Tim Ronsard."

"Sure, Isobel." The scar on my face throbbed, that conductor of old bad blood shooting poison into my black soul. With the back of my hand, I swept the brandy glass and the coffee cups and saucers off the table, shattering them on the floor. My hand came down, the palm swinging past her face. Cliesh shrieked, terrified.

We stared at each other across the few feet of space. Shame overwhelmed me, and I turned away. I could not hold her eye. I grabbed my uniform jacket and the black kepi, slamming the door on my way out.

I walked to the Metro station. Rage and regret ate into me as I waited on the train for Vincennes and Fort St Nogent. It was a long ride to Vincennes, and I blocked out the pain and my guilt at what I'd done. I swung in and out of my seat as the train clattered across points, lurching into bends on the track. I was a Broch Dweller longing for spring. I needed space and fresh air. I had to get back to the Legion. The world could go and fuck itself; bluster, all of it. I was heart sick at what I'd done to Cliesh.

I went to the bar near the Fort. I had a ham sandwich and a beer. Then, I drank Ricard and after a while it dulled the pain. I don't remember leaving the bar.

Hands ripped the covers off, tipping me out of bed onto the floor. "Get up, Ronsard, you lazy bastard!" I lay on the floor half drunk, eyes thick with sleep and mouth foul. Dieter stood over me.

"Go away, Westhaus. We're on leave for Christ's sake."

I rose, gagged and staggered from an attack of the dry heaves. Dieter caught my arm and bundled me into the shower.

"Get dressed. We're going out." In the bar near the Fort, Dieter poured coffee into me. I gagged on it and was sick again in the toilet. When I came back, he handed me a glass of raw eggs and Worcester sauce. "Drink it, Tim."

I managed not to vomit the lot up. The mixture worked, and I felt better. I looked round the bar. Some Legionnaires on leave sipped coffee and a hair of the dog as they nursed hangovers. The Pied Noir woman who ran the place kept a benevolent eye on us. Gradually I rejoined humanity. I was sick at heart at what I'd done, ashamed and disgusted. I bottled down the urge to vomit.

"You were lying there still drunk, wallet on the floor, cash, and Metro tickets spilled," Dieter said. "I saw the slip of paper with Cliesh's address, and reckoned you were in the shit."

"So what," I said.

"I went to see Cliesh. She told me what you did, Tim."

"Don't stick your nose in again, Dieter."

"Watch it, Tim." Dieter looked as if he might hit me.

"Sorry." I was so badly hungover that I couldn't see that Dieter was trying to help me.

"What the Hell is wrong with you, Ronsard, acting like that? She's a nice girl; too good for you."

"All I could think about was the way she left me." I stared at Dieter, and doubted my friend. Why had he gone to Cliesh's apartment? Was he after her; did he fancy Cliesh? Sometimes I got things terribly wrong.

It was close to Noon, and the bar had filled. An old couple sat quietly by a table in the corner. They talked in whispers and sipped coffee. Legionnaires from the Fort came in and stood at the bar drinking beer. I recognized the veteran Corporal who'd brought Cliesh's telephone message.

"Are you OK, Sergeant?"

"So-so, Corporal." He laughed and shook his head.

"OK, Tim. Are you calmer now? It's as well I did stick my nose in. You're too damned stupid to put things right yourself."

I had to agree.

"This girl Cliesh is special. Right?"

"Yes, she is."

"That's why I went to see her. She finds you again, and you behave like a clown; frighten her half to death. What a prick you are, Ronsard!"

"I know, I know."

The waiter brought coffee and cognac.

"Drink it."

Bile rose in my throat but I wasn't sick, and I felt better.

"She's everything you said. You're a lucky Ronsard. I fixed things for you. She'll see you tonight at seven."

"What did you say?"

"Never mind what I said. She's nervous about seeing you. She was in some state this morning. Just get it right, and don't upset her again or you're no friend of mine."

I'd really made a mess of things. Although she'd agreed to see me I'd probably lost Cliesh, and I'd disappointed Dieter, my best friend.

I shivered, and looked behind me. The old couple went out the door, the legionnaires were draining their glasses. My hangover slipped away and I felt the warmth of hope. I wanted it to be seven o' clock. And I worried about facing Cliesh.

I got off the Metro at the station not far from La Divine's cafe-bar. I didn't go in. I had time to find a flower shop. I rejected the roses; too obvious I was trying to impress. The florist waited as I moved among the flowers. I liked the delicate ivory, lilac and pink orchids.

"No, no, There's too many," the girl said. "Is it for someone special?"

"Yes. Someone very special."

"Then I suggest fewer blooms."

She placed the ivory orchids in transparent wrapping and tied it with curled white ribbons. It was a sunny evening, and I wore Ray Bans to hide my eyes, the black kepi low on my brow. I was smartly dressed, the competent NCO. But, I was ashamed and prayed that Cliesh wouldn't tell me to go to Hell.

I knocked Cliesh's door at seven, removed the Black Kepi, cradling it in my right arm. I kept the bouquet in my left hand hidden behind my back. I felt a damned fool after what I'd done to her. I stood easy and tried to appear calm as I heard her footsteps coming across the hall floor.

"Hello, Cliesh."

"Come in."

She wore a plain dark grey skirt of light wool, and a white blouse just opened at the neck, black court shoes. I missed the bright scarves she used to tie round her neck, sailor fashion. She'd pulled her hair back tightly, pinned up at the back; face white, eyes luminous, and heightened with kohl like Arab and Berber women. I handed her the orchids.

"Thank you."

I didn't know what to say.

"You look terrible. How are you feeling?"

"Not bad."

I managed a tight smile. Cliesh turned her head away. "Please sit down."

I sat upright on the settee at her mercy. "Cliesh, I ..."

She held up her right hand palm out. Her look was chilling. "Don't, Tim. If Dieter hadn't come here, I'd never have seen you again. You've a good friend in Dieter; better than you deserve. You terrified me; I thought you were going to hit me. That glass you broke was part of a set that La Divine gave me; and the china belonged to my grandmother. They meant a lot to me, and you destroyed them."

"I'd never hit you. I'm very sorry."

"Fine words, Sergeant Ronsard. Have you the slightest idea what you were like last night? You were a perfect fiend. I'm off my head seeing you at all. I'm afraid of you; you of all people. I'd never have believed it of you."

Silence. I looked at Cliesh. She was beautiful sitting at the edge of the chair; her slender legs pressed together, hands clasped on her lap. Eyes lowered. I would have died for her right then. I couldn't handle her silence.

I stood. "I'm sorry I spoiled everything for us. I'd better go."

"For Heavens sake sit down. Don't be a fool. I didn't agree to see you and send you away after five minutes."

We'd talk now about the way she left. It was something we needed to resolve. I told Cliesh about the row with my mother and the talk with my father in the pub. He was understanding, but I was to stop seeing her. I told her that I'd lied to him.

"Oh, I see. You were coming to break it off. Was that it?"

That hurt.

"What were you going to say to me?"

"I was hoping you'd find a way that I could still see you."

"What did you do when you read my letter?"

"I went to the small park near the Cross of Lorraine. I read your letter, over and over."

I carried her letter hidden in my wallet. I had her book, The First Forty-nine with my kit in Algeria. I got my wallet and removed her letter. The folds cut into the paper; the edges frayed from my handling. I opened it; her writing, the faded, ruby ink. Her words spilled out of me. "Tim, darling Tim, you sang of me in the days when I was fair."

I saw tears in Cliesh's eyes. "I sat there a long time, and I cried."

"Let me see." Quite forgetting we were at war, Cliesh sat beside me, and plucked the letter from my hand. "You kept it. Why?"

"It was the last thing I had from you; it belongs to me. I never had a photograph of you in Algeria.

"Oh Tim..." Cliesh put her hand over mine. "You remember the last day we spent together? I was ill at the thought of leaving you. I always liked you and then I fell in love with you. But I was twenty-four and you were sixteen. I was so miserable and upset on the train to Aberdeen."

I'd never forget that day I spent with Cliesh in her bed. I knew now that she had to leave to protect me and avoid a scandal. If only she'd been younger or I'd been older.

"I can see the two of us in my rooms sobbing and crying. I couldn't have left you. Tell me you understand."

"I understand. I'm so, so sorry for what I did yesterday."

"I'm sorry too. I never wanted to hurt you. Please promise you'll never do that to me again."

"I swear it."

Cliesh leant against me. "It's just wonderful; I called the Fort and found you again." She turned her head and smiled. "Are you feeling better; how about a Kir?"

"I could do with that."

We sipped the Kir. The dry white wine flavoured with a splash of cassis tasted good. I felt good again; and I was hungry. "How about a bite of supper?"

"That's a wonderful idea. Why don't we have supper here? I could make a Salad Nicoise. Would you like that?"

"Lets make it together. I can cook."

"Yes, so you can. Dieter told me. You learn everything in the Legion."

We laid the table and went to the small kitchen. Cliesh put on a bright floral apron. An old fashioned Peenie the women used to wear in Scotland. It covered her blouse and skirt. "I brought it from home."

Cliesh tossed me a white dish towel. I fastened it round my waist to protect my uniform. She prepared the leaves, tomatoes, and onions. I boiled a few potatoes and hard-boiled a couple of eggs, mashed tuna and put anchovies on a small plate. It was wonderful to see her warm smile and hear affection in her voice.

"Tell me about the Legion."

"There are good times in the Legion. Not all our days are hard."

"Do you mean parades with flags, and drums beating?"

"Not all the time."

"What happens at Christmas?"

"Legionnaires get a gift-wrapped present."

I always liked Christmas. Celebrations begin on Christmas Eve. The hardest of the Sergeants and Corporals rejoined humanity, buying cases of beer for the men.

"Really?"

"Yes; and it isn't rubbish. Good presents bought from the Regimental Fund; the profits from the foyer. The Company Commander arranges it."

"You're kidding me, Tim. Aren't you?"

"Not at all. I've known Legionnaires get radios, cameras, Cross pens, clothing. They're good presents."

"So, what kind of presents have you had?"

"Oh, a pullover and woollen scarf, a great knife, leather gloves; and this watch."

I held out my left wrist without thinking, exposing part of my tattoo that she disliked. Cliesh turned my hand, examining the watch.

"Nice watch. Stainless steel isn't it; can I take it off?"

"Sure, go ahead."

She turned the watch over and murmured, 'Legion Etrangere.' engraved on the back.

"Who is Aristiedes Spilyades?"

"Friend of mine."

"Why do you have his watch?"

"He's dead."

It'd been some time since I'd thought about Aristiedes. I regretted his death, and it showed on my face.

"Oh, I'm sorry, Tim. Was he a good friend?"

"Yes; like Dieter. Aristiedes was from Cyprus. We joined at the same time."

"Was he killed in an accident?"

"No, in a skirmish just after Christmas in 1958."

"Was he young?"

"About my age. Twenty when he was killed. He left Cyprus to get away from the war; he didn't want anyone to think he was a coward. We were going to Corporals' School together." I had to say more. "I wrapped him in his ground-sheet and placed his body in the helicopter. I'll never forget it. That's when I took his watch. It felt right; he was my friend."

"How awful for you. I'm so sorry."

I held her, like the first time; we kissed and smiled. I was glad she'd found me and forgiven me.

"Tell me more about Christmas."

We decorated the barracks, and dressed smartly. In the field, we managed to look smart and adorn our tents. Officers and NCOs served the excellent meal. The ritual mattered to men far from home. But, I didn't tell her that sometimes celebrations ended in drunken chaos. Then I kept my distance; next day we might be out on operations. Aristiedes died the day after Christmas.

"Did you get homesick?"

"No. I'd like to have seen my father, but he wrote to me."

"What about your mother?"

"She cut me off; never answered my letters, so I stopped writing. I suppose she's still at war with me. What about your Christmases in France?"

"I went home the first Christmas and the second I spent with La Divine and her family. She's been good to me."

"I often thought of you at Christmas, Cliesh." She pressed my hand.

The German Legionnaires singing Stille Nacht, Heilige Nacht brought tears to the eyes of the hardest cases, the friendly mood and goodwill. I always thought about Cliesh then. The concerts; the competition to create the most imaginative Nativity crib.

"It's true, each section has a crib. Someday, I'll take you to a Legion Christmas."

Cliesh smiled ruefully and I laid it on. "At Easter we exchange coloured eggs."

She bit me sweetly, painfully on the lobe of my right ear. "Right, Tim Ronsard; that's enough."

After the Salad Nicoise we washed and dried the dishes. We stood in the kitchen.

"I like Dieter," Cliesh said. "He's so polite."

"What happened?"

"I tried to shut him out, but I couldn't."

I pictured Dieter at Cliesh's door. A well-built impressive figure in Black Kepi, the eyes hidden behind the Ray Bans. The immaculate dress shirt-sleeves order set off by silver parachute wings on the right breast, the medal ribbons on the left, testimony to his service and bravery in Vietnam and Algeria. On operations, I'd seen him lean on door frames in Arab and Berber dwellings. He had a cool way when someone didn't respond, shrugging dismissively, arching his eyebrows, the lens of the Ray Bans glittering in the light; he'd pull down the corners of his mouth. Then people did what he wanted.

"He knew a lot about me," Cliesh said.

"Sometimes I missed you; I'd talk about you."

When my heart ached, Dieter listened; he was a good listener. Talking about Cliesh kept her alive. I wanted to keep her; didn't want to lose her. She was crying again. "Tim, I had to go away. How do you think I felt leaving you?"

"Oh, Cliesh, I know now; I understand." I held her. I promised myself I'd never leave her. "I love you Cliesh."

She kissed me. Her tongue opened my lips.

"Dieter told me you were so excited when you got ready to meet me."

"I never thought I'd see you again."

"Isn't it wonderful?"

"Yes; better than wonderful."

Cliesh loved that Dieter was so Scottish. He'd told her about his time as a POW. "He has an accent just like you, Tim. He liked Scotland and the people."

"I know."

She knew that I'd saved his life out in the Djebel. That he'd taught me to soldier. "He said you'd thought about deserting."

"Everybody does. But I stayed."

"I was glad when he told me that you're a good soldier. You're his best friend." Cliesh touched the scar on my face her fingers lingering lovingly. "Dieter told me how that happened; it was a good thing you did that night."

I shrugged. Cliesh moved away and reached for a handbag lying near the table.

"He gave me this." Cliesh handed me a coloured photograph. We all took black and white pictures with our cheap cameras, but this was a sharp photograph taken with Dieter's Leica Standard. He'd handed out copies. We'd just finished hammering a Fell band up in the Djebel. We hadn't taken any prisoners. It'd been hand to hand fighting, but we'd not lost any men, and just two wounded.

I was in the foreground at Dieter's side, the section spread out on either side of us. In the background two Shawnee helicopters, flying bananas, ready to lift us off. We wore camouflaged Tenue Leopard and green berets. Dieter had slung his mitraillette sub-machine gun, and a 7.5 MAS rifle hung from my right shoulder. Between Dieter's right arm and my left hung a Fell flag, a red crescent and star on a background of a broad green and white stripe. Dieter was solemn, but I grinned at the camera.

"Look at you; you're the boy I fell in love with."

"I was nineteen."

Then she cried, and she held me so close. "I thought about you a lot. I'd have worried myself sick if I'd known you were a soldier in Algeria."

"That war's over; it's finished." There would be other wars; but I didn't tell her that.

"I'm glad Dieter came. He asked me to let you apologise; to make it right between us. Oh Tim, he brought us back together."

She turned and looked at the kitchen clock. It was after ten. I touched her shoulder and drew her towards me; soon her head rested on my shoulder. Her perfume was delicate and fragrant. Eight years; I held her now. She put her hand behind and touched me.

"I know. I feel the same. How long before you go back?"

"A month."

"Will you stay, Tim?"

"Yes Cliesh, I'll stay"

I thought only of Cliesh; I loved and adored her; I was full of her, and out of the world. I carried her in my arms to her bedroom. I'd make up for the years that we'd been apart.

I helped her undress; I removed her shoes and caressed her slender legs. I knew Cliesh wanted me to; she was beautiful and shy. I turned and finished undressing and felt her hands on a rash of cicatrices on my back; grenade shrapnel. "Oh, God, oh God, my poor Tim. What have they done to you?" And I was beside her and we embraced. She smoothed her fingers across the pock marks and bumps, wanting them to vanish; then we made love.

I stood aft on the grubby little trooper watching the sunset far to the west. I gazed astern at the evening lights of Marseilles. Less than a day since we said goodbye; I missed Cliesh.

We'd clung to each other in Paris yesterday, just before Dieter and I boarded the train for Marseilles. I was miserable and close to cracking up. Tomorrow, Oran; then 2 REP. Memories of Cliesh were all I had.

I forgot about the movement of the ship and remembered the idyllic few days we had together in the Loire Valley: the fine weather, the breakfasts in the garden by the weir at the mill. The sounds of the little river calmed us and we forgot about my journey back to Algeria and the Legion. I thought we knew each other until we stayed at Moulin de la Planche when we found a deeper intensity in our love.

For five days, I shed my uniform for casual civilian clothes. It felt odd until I forgot that I was a soldier. I felt younger being with Cliesh. In the afternoons we walked, following the riverbank to the outskirts of the town, stopping at a small bar for a sandwich and a glass of wine. We paused in quiet places by the river, listening to the gurgling, swirling eddies. More than once, we lay on soft grass and made love, the sunlight shining through the trees, dappling our bodies.

We had dinner at Moulin de la Planche. We loved being alone, growing mellow and ever more loving as we sipped wine. On chilly evenings we dined indoors in a room with a smooth, stone floor. From the bright window we looked west across meadows to wooded hills. We lay under cool white sheets; I'd reach for Cliesh and find her. We'd never loved each other more than this.

A fine spray came aft, carried on the breeze bringing me back to the present. I was in shirtsleeves, the collar unfastened, tugged here and there by conflicting emotions. I thought I might leave the Legion, but I knew that I couldn't. There was too much of my life holding me to the Corps that had been my home for more than five years. I belonged there: LEGIO PATRIA NOSTRA said more about me than anything in Westburn. What was I going to do about Cliesh? I was wary about asking her to join me in Algeria. I made myself ill longing for her.

"You OK, Tim?" Dieter handed me a glass of Ricard. We sipped the pastis. I looked at its milky texture. The aniseed taste soothed and swallowed easily.

"What are you going to do about Isobel?"

"I don't know."

We moved with the rhythm of the ship burying her bows in the open sea, and corkscrewing in the swell.

"You know, what we do changes us. Oh, we're good at soldiering but we're not right for ordinary life. I think we're afraid of it. I'm nearly thirty-six. I've been in the Legion a long time. They're going to have to throw me out; or kill me. Every time I think about leaving, I remember, Kowalski."

Kowalski was a legend in the Regiment, a Pole who'd come in to the Legion in 1940 and fought in Norway with 13 DBLE. He'd come into 2 REP after Vietnam and the fighting at Dien Bien Phu. He was a wonderful soldier. One of the few men Dieter acknowledged as his superior in the arts of war.

He left the Legion after twenty-one years, the senior NCO in the Regiment and could have gone on for many more years. Everyone was surprised when he left to marry a Pied Noir woman and settle in Provence. A year later, he was dead. We never found out what killed him. Drink and despair; or out of his time and place; did he kill himself? He was forty-two.

Dieter handed me another Ricard. "To Kowalski."

I could leave the Legion in six months, for I'd signed a second contract for a year. Had I not met Cliesh again, there would have been no question of leaving the Legion. If I came out what was I going to do? I could live in France and become a French citizen, but I didn't want some miserable job skivvying after some bastard in a bar or an office; and I could not live off Cliesh. Leave the Legion and go to her, and I might destroy everything that mattered to me.

"Tim. You're in a difficult position. Isobel is lovely and I think the world of her. Be sure, about what you're doing. Don't leave the Legion and then take your regret out on her."

"She's waiting for me."

"Then go to her. Transfer out to a Regiment going to the mainland."

But I didn't want to leave the Second Parachute Regiment. It was where I belonged. We sipped our Ricards and stared at the wake of the ship. In Paris, I'd been alone with Cliesh most of the time. I'd moved out of the Fort and stayed with her. I met Dieter often when Cliesh was playing or teaching, but I felt awkward about leaving Dieter on his own.

"I'm fine. I've found the ladies. Anyway, I like what Isobel does to you. She makes you happy; be good to her."

Dieter was with me one afternoon as I waited for Cliesh in a café. "I wish that medic had done a better job on your face that night you stiffened Roche."

"It was a long time ago." I seldom thought about the scar it. But I knew the proud blue-black flesh shocked people when they met me for the first time. The scar had shaken Cliesh. These past weeks since I had been with Cliesh, I saw the scar as atonement for my past mistakes and the way I hurt her.

"You and Isobel look so well together. She's a nice girl. I should have paid more attention."

Cliesh waved and smiled, the satchel containing the sheet music, hanging from her right shoulder. I gazed possessively at her slender legs; I was glad of the sound of her elegant tan sandals. She was lovely wearing a lavender summer dress; her hair tied back with a fine piece of matching silk. I stood and kissed her. "Hello, Cliesh."

She smiled and whispered, "I love you, Sergeant Ronsard."

"Hello Dieter." Dieter shook Cliesh's hand and bowed from the shoulder.

"It's good to see you again, Isobel."

Cliesh held on to Dieter's hand, drawing him close, rising on tiptoes, she kissed him on both cheeks. Dieter flushed, pleased by Cliesh's affection.

"Well I'll be off."

"You'll do no such thing. We're all going out tonight. So just you stay here."

We dined at La Divine's. It was the first of several evenings we three spent together. Cliesh introduced Dieter. He took La Divine's hand bowing formally. La Divine welcomed him to her place. She was dining with us and glanced towards the kitchen then excused herself. I pulled Cliesh closer.

"What did you tell her?"

"I told her that if it hadn't been for Dieter we'd not be together."

I had Cliesh's hand in mine. "I am so, so sorry about what happened."

"I know, Tim. It's all right. I wanted La Divine to know that Dieter means a great deal to us."

Dieter enjoyed La Divine's place and got on well with her. But, he felt most at home in Cliesh's apartment. Near the end of our leave, just after we returned from Bourgueil, she invited him for dinner.

"Stay the night, Dieter. There's no point in trailing back to the Fort. I have a spare bedroom."

"I don't think so Isobel. You and Tim, you'll want the place to yourselves."

"Dieter! We want you to stay. Let's make it a good night. I'm not sending you out onto the Metro. You'll have plenty of time in Legion beds when you get back to Algeria."

"Cliesh's right, Dieter. We'd like you to stay."

Dieter brought wine; when we'd finished there were a few bottles left for Cliesh's wine rack. Cliesh made a wonderful meal. Mussels in white wine, followed by rabbit Provencal; desert was apple tart made with the most delicate short pastry. Afterwards, we sat quietly with strong coffee and Armagnac. Cliesh was so happy and content that she had a small glass of the digestif. It was late and we were all mellow, happy in our love and friendship.

Dieter rose and stretched his arms. "Time to turn in. You know, I can't remember the last time I was in someone's home; and I'm staying the night. I've forgotten what it's like." He grabbed both Cliesh's hands, and pulling her to her feet kissed her affectionately on both cheeks. "Thank you, Isobel; and you too, Tim."

Two days since that lovely evening. The ship surged through the heavier swell further out on the open sea and spray came aft dampening us. We steadied ourselves on the rails.

"Listen, Tim. I hear things. There could be opportunities for us in the Regiment. I have ambitions. Officers respect you. Hold on for a while; see what happens. Don't throw away your years of service."

I'd wait and see. I might find a way where I could follow my vocation and be with Cliesh.

Fights, drunkenness, and desertions had increased while we were on leave. The morale of the men had sunk. Dieter's prediction was right; treating the men as Pioneers, serving in a Labour Corps frustrated them. They loathed building work, the noise, the dirt of road making and building construction. They were elite Light Infantry. They had not come to the Legion, especially to the Parachute Regiment, to work on a building site.

"Some of the officers coming into the Legion now, Tim. It's a disgrace," Dieter said. "We used to get the best from St Cyr; now we get conscripts. Building and labouring work is destroying the Regiment. What a waste. We'll disband at this rate."

We were in the Sergeant's Mess. I ordered two more Kronenbourgs. It had been grim since we got back and we had been riding the men hard to get the camp finished. I wondered if the Regiment would be disbanded. We felt that we were hanging on by our finger tips. Another two beers appeared.

"I think this new CO is going to make a big difference," Dieter said.

I'd written to Cliesh; passionate love letters. Her letters, written with the ruby ink; her tender loving words. I read them often. But, I avoided saying anything about the future.

A few weeks later, I stood at attention in front of the Lieutenant. Dieter, as Senior NCO, stood to the right.

"CO wants to see you, Ronsard," the Lieutenant said. "It's important. Think carefully about what he says, and behave yourself."

"Yes Sir."

I knocked the door of the CO's office, waited and entered, marched, came to attention, and drew my right arm up in a perfect salute. I removed my beret.

"Sergeant Ronsard, Fourth Company, Lieutenant Ronet's Platoon. At your orders, Colonel."

"At ease, Sergeant."

I stood, legs spread, and feet planted firmly, hands behind my back, staring straight ahead, just above the Commanding Officer's head.

"I'm at ease as you order, Colonel."

"You had a good leave in Paris?"

"Excellent, Sir. Thank you."

"Everyone expected you to finish higher on the Corporal and the Sergeant's Courses."

"Yes Sir."

I'd worked hard on these courses, but finishing first, or second created high expectations among the senior NCOs and officers, and I did not want to wilt under their attention. It was difficult enough to establish my presence as a new NCO. I did not want to disappoint anyone; I wanted the freedom to get on with my work, so, I was content to finish in the top five. Since then I'd shown that I was more than a competent Corporal and Sergeant.

"Why, Sergeant? Come on man. Speak up!"

"I finished in the top five on each course, Sir."

"I know that; it's all in here." He patted my file on his desk. "You should have tried harder. Never hold back, Ronsard."

"Yes Sir."

The CO opened my file and studied it. "I see you were at Beni Sbihi back in 1957. It was a great victory for the Regiment. One hundred ninety-nine Fell, killed that day for our five dead and twenty-six wounded."

"Yes Sir. My first year in 2 REP"

"I know Lt Colonel Lefort. Good officer; he was in command?"

"Yes Sir"

"I've studied that engagement, Ronsard. Brilliant, the way he deployed and located the Fell." The CO grinned, sweeping his right hand back and forth, up and down, bringing back memories of the Regiment manoeuvering; I felt again the power of the helicopters disgorging legionnaires on to the hills of Beni Sbihi. "You were called on that day?"

"Yes Sir. One Corporal, killed and another wounded. Sergeant Westhaus was busy, Sir. The Lieutenant ordered Legionnaire Spilyades and me to stand in, Sir."

"You did well."

"Thank you, Sir."

"And you fought at Chelia; promoted to Corporal."

December 1960; Commandant Cabrio led the Regiment as it pulverized a Fell band in a fierce fight up and down tree-lined slopes. The Fell had fifty-four dead. We had ten men killed and nineteen wounded.

"You didn't hold back Sergeant. You were awarded the Medaille Militaire."

"Doing my job, Sir."

The CO stared hard at me then glanced again at my file. His attention to my details was impressive. "This last year was difficult."

"Yes Sir."

We hunted Fell bands while the French and the FLN negotiated. On contact, we wiped them out.

"It was hard work. You were out several times, Ronsard?"

"Yes Sir."

"Good job; we notice these things."

Sometimes we had curt acknowledgements from senior officers for work well done; this was the first time a Commanding Officer had spoken so openly.

"We used to get the top graduates from the Academy; now the Legion is open to all army officers; even conscripts. It's affecting the Regiment."

The CO was determined to arrest the decline, to stop the rot eating into the morale of the Regiment. "I aim to make the Second Parachute Regiment the elite in the Corps."

Many experienced Legionnaires were returning to civilian life. The cadre that had seen action had shrunk. Re-enlistments had declined, and the ranks filling up with new recruits.

"I need experienced men to stiffen these new officers and men; give them confidence. I want to promote from among the NCOs. Appoint one or two Acting Lieutenants."

The CO let his words take full effect. "Are you a career soldier, Ronsard?"

"Yes Sir"

"Being in command of men means personal sacrifice; the Legion is an officer's first duty. I know that you have worked hard as an NCO, that you lead your section very well indeed. Officers in the Second Regiment take on an enormous personal undertaking. There's going to be significant change in the Regiment. The officers will be working harder than they've ever done in their life."

"I can see that; I understand, Sir."

"I offered a promotion to Sergeant Westhaus and he declined. But he is staying. I need NCOs like him. I tell you this in confidence. I know that you're close friends."

"Thank you, Sir."

"You're twenty-four, Ronsard, but you have more experience than several older NCOs with longer service. I'm offering you an appointment as Acting Lieutenant. If you accept, you'll be deeply involved in re-training the Regiment. The work will be very hard. I have high expectations of all my officers. There is no guarantee of confirmation in the rank. I can return you to the rank of Sergeant at any time. Do you understand?"

This offer was a great honour. I'd reached a crossroads, but my future was brighter. "Yes Sir; thank you Sir. I understand."

I'd come to the Legion on impulse. I was eighteen; desperate to get away from Reid's foundry and the bitter atmosphere at home. I couldn't go on wallowing in misery, missing Cliesh. During the first year in basic training and the Second

Parachute Regiment I thought that I had made a serious mistake. Gradually, and no one was more surprised than me, I was a legionnaire.

Standing at ease in front of the CO, I remembered a Lieutenant, older than the other subalterns; a smart, tough officer, elegant in the tenue leopard and apple green beret. But, what had stuck with me, what I admired when we paraded, was his Medaille Militaire given for gallantry, but only to men who had served in the ranks; and it was from there that he'd been commissioned.

Back then, my ambition didn't stretch that far, but I thought how wonderful to attain that honour. I had the medal. But to be commissioned; it would be a dream realized. I belonged in the Legion. I had found my calling. I was proud of the Corps and my place in it; there was nothing I wanted outside the Legion.

The black hole in my life was that Cliesh was not with me. Meeting her in Paris had made me so happy. Seeing her again, loving her, knowing she loved me was another dream realized. But, it seemed I'd have to choose between my love and my calling. How could I remain in the Corps and have Cliesh with me?

I was afraid of outside. Leave the Legion and I'd be exchanging the security of the Corps and my rank for some dead end job. I'd never go back to engineering, but how would Cliesh feel about me working as a uniformed security guard, skivvying in a bar, or labouring on a building site? I refused to become another washed up ex legionnaire.

I was ashamed at what I'd done that first night in her apartment. But out of the Corps, black rage might come again; I'd ruin our love and lose everything.

"Well, Ronsard?"

Things were coming at me too quickly. That older Lieutenant I admired; with luck, I'd be like him and that pleased me. Why in Christ's name did I have to choose?

When we'd got back to Algeria I'd hoped the Regiment would move to France. I'd ask Cliesh to marry me. But how could Cliesh live here with me at Bou Sefr? Officers and NCOs had wives in Bou Sefr, but used to the ways of the Legion. Then I thought she might say no to my proposal. The thought of giving up Cliesh cut deeply.

"Yes, Sir, I accept. Thank you, Sir."

"Your contract has six months to run?"

"Yes, Sir."

When I had fallen in love with Cliesh, we were from different backgrounds, the music teacher and the Apprentice, and it hadn't mattered. I often wondered if we'd stayed together, would it have come between us. Now we had both changed. She was a quiet, free spirit, a musician, and teacher in Paris. I was a professional soldier stuck in North Africa.

If only the Regiment were withdrawing to France, we might have made it work. But I was sure we'd break up if I brought her to Algeria.

I knew the cease-fire and the tense relations with the FLN, about to form the new Government of Algeria. What could I tell Cliesh; would she understand? How could I tell her I was not coming back? I tried to convince myself that I was acting for the best.

"I'll sign a new contract for five years, Sir."

"Good. I'll have the papers prepared. You'll enjoy the course at the School of Infantry in Saint Maixent."

The CO rose smiling, leant across the desk and extended his hand. "Congratulations."

"Thank you again, Sir."

"You may leave now, Sergeant."

I put on my beret, came to attention, saluted, and marched out of his office.

I reported to the Lieutenant; he was delighted. "Congratulations, Tim. This is good news. I'm sorry to be losing a good NCO, but I'm glad I'll be working with you. I'll introduce you to the Officers Mess."

"Thank you, Sir."

"What's up, Tim? I thought you'd be really pleased."

"I am, Dieter. It's great news. I never expected it."

We drank our beers. I worried that my becoming an officer would make a difference to Dieter, and our friendship would wither. I'd be moving across an invisible, but palpable barrier that exists between officers and men.

"We're still friends?" I said. "How am I going to know what to do if I can't sound you out?"

Dieter looked at me across the rim of his glass, then drained it in one swallow. The glass clicked on the bar. "Of course we are. Is that what's bothering you? To Hell with this officer and men thing. You'll be moving to another company, but we can talk anytime."

I got two more beers.

"You'd be a fine officer, Dieter."

He grinned. "The Colonel and you can see more than I can see. I'm a better NCO, and I've been a Sergeant a long time, Tim. The CO wouldn't tell you, but I'm up for promotion to Adjutant. I'll have clout."

"Congratulations." I shook Dieter's hand. "You'll make Regimental Sergeant Major."

I could see Dieter at the heart of running the Regiment. Then, he'd have real clout.

I had to write to Cliesh and tell her what was happening and I was depressed.

"What about Isobel, Tim? Get her across from France; marry the girl when you get back from Saint Maixent."

"I think I'll tell her I'll be here for a while."

"You'd be mad to leave the Corps. I don't know how long the Regiment might be in Algeria. Maybe just a couple of years. Things could move quickly."

"Do you think Cliesh'll like Bou Sfer if I asked her to come?" I said.

"Well, it's neat. We built it," Dieter said. "And there's the married quarters, and families."

But would Cliesh adapt to married life with a legion officer in a French military enclave? One thing was certain; I was staying in the Regiment.

Bou Sfer; you'd hardly know it was once a vineyard. The entrance with the Regiment's title in metal letters over the gate, the barrier, and the guard. Beyond the entrance, a wide asphalt road running through the camp for about a mile and a quarter. It was a fine military base of one storey steel barracks mounted on concrete blocks. Here and there floral borders surrounding buildings. The place was painted white. It was a different world from Cliesh's feminine Paris apartment.

"I think she'll like it," I said. "Sure she can teach music and the piano."

But I worried what she'd think about armed guards, barbed wire fences and the tank traps.

Two cognacs appeared. "You need bracing," Dieter said. "Write the letter; have faith in Isobel."

Our parting in Paris had upset Cliesh. "You have to come back Tim. Promise you'll come back to me."

"I'll come back to you. I swear it." And I meant it, but that was before I had doubts about leaving the Corps. I was miserable leaving her. Somehow I meant for us to be together.

Bou Sfer was looking good. "I'm going to ask her to marry me; here in Bou Sfer."

"Right thing to do, Tim."

It wasn't hard to write the letter, not now that I knew what to do.

Dearest Cliesh,

All the time I think about the days we were together. I love you now more than ever.

There are significant changes in the Regiment. Shortly after I got back, my Commanding Officer offered me an appointment as Acting Lieutenant. There is every possibility that I'll obtain a permanent commission. It is a great honour, and I know you'll understand how important it is for me.

I can't get away, and I don't know when things will settle down. I've moved to a new Company and said farewell to Dieter. We're in Bou Sefr, and I'll be really busy as the Regiment re-trains once I get back from the course at the School of Infantry.

I don't know when I'll get permission to leave Algeria and return to France, perhaps as much as two years, possibly more, but I can't be certain.

My darling, we should be together, always. Please come and marry me.

The Regiment would welcome you. I'll arrange everything to bring you safely here.

Dearest Cliesh, write to me soon.

All My Love,

Tim

"Nothing yet, Tim?" Dieter said.

Two weeks had passed since I'd proposed to Cliesh; there was no word.

"Phone her. I'll fix it with the Signals Sergeant."

The Signals Sergeant left, and I sat alone listening to Cliesh's number ringing out. It rang out for a long time; finally she answered. The phone slipped in my hand.

"Cliesh, it's me, Tim. Did you get my letter?"

"Yes."

She was cool and distant, no warmth in her voice. "You were coming back to me. You had only six months till you finished with the Legion." Her voice was breaking. I heard her crying. "I want us to be together. Please come back, Tim. I love you so much. I'll marry you here. La Divine will give you a job; you could drive a taxi. We'd be together in Paris."

"I've signed a contract for another five years. It's chance of a commission. You know how important that is."

"More important than me?"

"Cliesh, be reasonable."

"You're the one who's being unreasonable."

Her anger and hurt were palpable, reminding me of her rage the day I made her jealous, back in Westburn and she cuffed me with the back of her hand. I was getting angry too. "But you'll be an officer's wife. They're decent people here, good families; schools, teachers. We can have a life."

"I'm not living on a Legion base in Algeria, or France." There was fear in her voice.

"Not good enough for you? I'm not leaving the Legion to skivvy for La Divine or anyone else."

"You don't need me. You're married to the Legion."

"The Legion's the best I could ever do for you."

She slammed the phone down. Cliesh it seemed, had no faith in me.

Dieter was waiting for me outside Signals. He knew I was upset and furious. "Isobel said no?"

"She said she'd marry me if I left the Corps and went to Paris. Otherwise, nothing doing."

"I'm sorry, Tim; for both of you."

Chapter 5

Blood Ties

It was the summer of nineteen-sixty-eight. The duty Sergeant at the gate of Camp Raffaeli said that a kid was looking for me.

"He speaks poor French. I think he's English. I'll send him on his way if you like, Sir."

I was curious. "I'll speak to him, Sergeant."

A stocky young man, fair complexion, and a head of red hair, a pack at his feet, looked around. I came forward, dressed in working uniform, apple green beret tilted towards the left brow. I looked him over, and his smile faded.

"I'm Ronsard. Who are you?"

"I'm Steve O'Hara, your cousin from Westburn."

Apart from a visit from my father, I'd had nothing to do with anyone from Westburn for many years. "We don't enlist here. Go to the recruiting offices on the mainland."

Steve O'Hara flushed, face a medley of embarrassment and anger. "I'm hitch-hiking in Corsica. When I go back, I have a place at the Royal Military Academy." That news impressed me.

His mother and my mother were sisters. When I left Scotland, he was a child I barely knew. But I liked the look of him. His appearance suggested he'd taken some trouble to get here. He was travel stained; dried salt maks on the side of his grey checked shirt, his khaki pants soiled. His hiking boots wanted a good polish. He was very tired. I felt sorry for young Steve O'Hara, and I wondered why he'd searched for me. He'd obviously not slept well for some days, and he'd feel shabby among the immaculate legionnaires of the Guard. Steve could do with a bath, sleep in a clean bed and a good feed.

"When did you last have a square meal?"

"I don't need anything."

I laughed, and he relaxed. "Behave yourself, Steve. I'm on duty right now and can't get away."

"All right, Lieutenant Ronsard."

He'd noted my rank; I liked that. I let go of his shoulder. "Have you got a room for the night?"

"No, I'm going to camp on a beach."

"Forget it. The police will pick you up. Go to the Café Bar Tizi. It's on a narrow side street near the Place Bel Ombra. Tell the owner who you are. Her name is Madame Ouzou. She'll let you have a room, and you can clean up and rest. She has good beds and hot showers."

"Is it expensive?"

"Don't worry about it. You're my guest. Legion hospitality."

"You're sure?"

"I'll meet you there at eight o'clock. There's a good friend of mine, Sergeant Major Dieter Westhaus. He was a POW in Scotland. When he was your age, he was a private in the German Airborne. If he's free, I'll ask him to come along. I think you'll like him. We'll have dinner, and you can tell me what's happening in Westburn."

"Thanks, Lieutenant."

"Look, Steve, we're cousins. I'm Tim. OK? I'll see you at eight."

Dieter found the Café-Bar Tizi, a discreet place not far from the Citadel. We liked Madame Ouzou, a Pied Noir woman who'd married an Algerian, a Harki: a soldier in the French service.

We'd never have beaten the Fell without the Harki. The French pulled out of Algeria, leaving the Harki to their fate. Madame Ouzou and her daughter had managed to get away when an FLN mob murdered her husband.

Madame Ouzou struggled to make the Tizi a quiet, tasteful Café-Bar. Dieter and I had a fair amount of cash saved living quietly in the Algerian enclave and at Camp Rafaelli, after the Regiment's move to Corsica.

We offered her money to carry out the improvements; not a loan and no formal agreements, but we suggested letting our interest grow with the business. It had worked well. With the surplus cash, we'd helped a former legionnaire operate a taxi from outside the Tizi. Wisely, Dieter had thought ahead.

"I'm not getting any younger. We could be injured and pensioned off. We might need something to fall back on. I like Madame Ouzou; we get on well."

"You fancy her?"

"Sure; I like her."

Steve O'Hara was resourceful, traveling light, but ready for anything. Madame Ouzou had lent him an iron and ironing board. At dinner we saw he was acting like a soldier: a crisp white shirt, mulberry silk tie, tan slacks held up by a smart brown leather belt, highly polished brown shoes gave the right finishing touch. He was more than a match for our smart turnout.

I was eager for news of home. "So, no trouble about you joining the Army?" I said.

"My parents accepted it. They insisted I go to University and think about the Army. I quit in second year; it was two wasted years. I'll be twenty when I go to the Academy. I just want to get started."

"Good decision," Dieter said. Dieter liked Steve. He jerked his thumb at me. "Four years service at twenty-two and made Sergeant at the start of his fifth year. Appointed Acting Lieutenant at twenty-four."

"Well, there was one helluva right row last April." Steve said. "My oldest sister had a baby girl, and my parents had a party after the Baptism. Your mum and dad were there. You know how close your mother is to my mother."

"What happened?" Dieter said.

Steve's father announced that Steve was quitting the university to take up a place at Sandhurst, the Royal Military Academy. Steve sipped the brandy, wrinkling his nose. He had a swallow of coffee. "My aunt and uncle-my father's sister and her husband-came, and he brought his cousin, an Irish priest who'd lived in Scotland for years. They got drunk."

Steve's uncle sounded off at the news. "How can you, good Catholics, let your son join the British Army? For God sake, think what they did in Ireland."

"Your father objected." 'Forget Ireland. The war's been over a long time. We're Scots now, and after Sandhurst Steve's joining a Scots Regiment.' "Then my uncle took on your father."

"I don't understand you, Ronsard. The British Army is no place for Catholics."

"Your father gave it to him straight," Steve said. 'That right enough? I was in the Royal Navy, and I understand you fine. You don't know where you belong. No wonder Protestants don't trust us.'

"My uncle lost the place." 'Shut up, Ronsard. That son of yours, a rascal, carrying on with that Protestant music teacher; a scandal. He's in the right place, among the riff raff of the Foreign Legion.'

"I thought your dad was going to kill him. He was round the table, grabbed his tie, hauled him out of the chair, and cuffed him hard." 'Tim's a Lieutenant. I'm proud of my son and his friends. You haven't a clue, Mister. You know nothing about Tim and the music teacher.'

It was a good feeling knowing the Old Man still cared about me; and about Cliesh.

"The priest was guttered, I mean really pished, shouting, 'Ronsard, you're a thug. How dare you. Your son, he's a disgrace.'

"Your Old Man was lethal. He picked up his whisky, turned on the Reverend, yanked him up and tossed the whisky in his face, then pulled him onto his tip toes. The whisky soaked his dog collar. I thought your dad was going to put the head on him. 'You're a damned fool of a priest, sit on your arse and shut up. Clowns like you waste the heads of Scots Catholics. Disappear, go back to Glockamorra.' "Then he shoved the old soak into his seat."

"I never met anyone like that when I was a POW in Scotland," Dieter said.

"That's the family," I said. "The Scots-Irish Catholics."

I was glad to be out of Scotland. I left the table and chatted to Madame Ouzou at the bar while I settled the bill. Back at table, we sat a minute or two finishing the last of the coffee and brandy.

"I'm on duty early," Dieter said. "Good to meet you, Steve." They shook hands.

Standing ouside the Tizi, I fancied a walk in the warm late evening. I wouldn't sleep for hours after the news from home. and I wanted more of Steve's company. "Let's walk by the port."

"Good idea."

We strolled in the quiet streets, and I thought about home. I'd imagined that out of sight, I'd be out of mind. But it turned out that my parents talked about me. My father mentioned it in his letter accepting my invitation to visit Corsica. However, my mother did not reply to my invitation. I was sad at her bitterness over Cliesh; and I was furious that she'd discussed Cliesh with her sister. I was glad and excited when my father came to Calvi.

I was at the port when the overnight ferry from Marseilles docked. My father came down the gangway carrying a case and a plastic bag of duty free. He'd changed; the aging of a decade. I was going on twenty-nine.

"Christ son it's great to see you." He shook my hand, hugged me, then pushed me to arms' length. His eyes glistened; my throat was tight. "You look great, Tim; never better." He touched the brim of my black kepi looked at my medal ribbons; touched the gleaming parachutist's wings, and shook his head. He dabbed at his eyes with his handkerchief. "It's the sun. Yer an officer son that's wonderful. Are ye happy, Tim?"

"Yes, dad. Very happy."

"What happened to your face, son?" His outstretched fingers fluttered above the scar running down my left cheek, from the eye to the edge of my mouth. "You should've told me."

"I didn't want to worry you; an accident that happened years ago. My eye's fine. How's Mum?"

"She's well enough."

"Then why didn't she come with you? I wrote to her."

"We both know the answer, son. She burned your letter"

Burning my letter; that cut; and yes, I knew. She nursed her hatred of Cliesh; blamed her for my leaving and joining the Legion.

"She doesn't answer my letters. I've given up writing."

My father gripped my shoulder and shook his head. My rift with my mother was hard on him. I'd come between them.

"Did she try to stop you from coming?"

"She said I could please myself. She's cutting herself to pieces, Tim."

He handed me the duty free. "Black Label. You and your friend Dieter'll enjoy it. There's a carton of Gitanes for him."

"You'll meet him while you're here."

"Good."

My dad was tired after the overnight crossing from the mainland. "Cabin?" He said. "Away wi' ye, I slept in a chair."

"Your staying with one of my men. He's a retired NCO, married to a Pied Noir. They let rooms. Bathroom's in the corridor outside the room."

"How much?"

"It's taken care of. Turn in for a few hours."

"Thanks, Tim. I'll see ye the night."

We sat in a cafe overlooking the harbour. My father looked well, shaved smoothly, white shirt sleeves and smart slacks. He enjoyed the warm evening, sipping whisky and beer chasers. I nursed a Ricard I leant on the table, hands bunched. My black kepi lay on an empty chair.

"The tattoo, son; why?"

"Saida; on my first pass from basic training, with my friend Aristedies. He was killed." My father nodded. "I wouldn't do it again." My father lifted my arm taking in the red and green square, the blue letters. "Legio Patria Nostra?"

"The Legion is my family, my country."

"You believe that, Tim?"

"I belong here. This is where I want to be."

"It's some haircut they give ye," he said, jerking his thumb at my cropped skull.

"Goes with the job. I like it that way."

"Anyway, ye look well, Tim."

A couple of local beauties in their summer dresses walked past.

"Bonny girls."

I guessed where this was heading. "It's all right dad, ask me."

"Have ye a girlfriend?"

"No." I swallowed Ricard.

"The music teacher, Isobel Clieshman wasn't it; did ye ever see her again?"

"I was on leave with Dieter; five years ago. I'd no idea she was in Paris. Cliesh, that's what I called her, saw us in the Marais and called Fort St Nogent. I went to see her."

"Ye never said."

"The Old Lady would've gone up the wall."

"She would've. What happened son?"

"I thought about leaving the Corps to be with her. I couldn't do it. I proposed; asked her to come to Bou Sefr. With the Commission, I thought she'd accept but she wanted me to leave. 'You're married to the Legion,' that's what she said. We fell out. Living on a Legion base in Algeria; maybe she was scared of that."

"Ah'm so sorry, Tim."

I had another swallow of Ricard." Me too."

On the Sunday morning I went to Mass with my father. He went to Communion. After Mass we stopped in a Cafe for coffee and croissants.

"Ah had a great time wi' Dieter and the Sergeants on Friday." My father said. I'd been a Sergeant, a good rank, the mingling in the bar; the conviviality. Standing at attention behind the chairs facing the set table, singing Le Boudin.

I wanted my father to experience it on his own without an officer present in the Sergeants' Mess.

"Good food. And the songs of the Legion. The wine flowed. A jeep took me back to my room."

"I heard. But you enjoyed it?"

"Ah did. Very hospitable."

"In a couple of days it's the twenty-ninth of September. That's a big day for the Regiment, the feast of Saint Michael The Archangel, Patron Saint of Paratroops, and our Patron Saint. Come to Camp Raffaeli. You'll enjoy the festivities"

The Legion Band was marching and playing throughout the day. Immaculate turnout in shirt sleeves order, white webbing belts and gaiters. The Chinese Pavilion percussion stick, an ornamental standard with a conical pavilion at the top, and hung with bells and jingles and horse hair plumes. The shrill piping fifes, the striking brass, and hypnotic beating of drums, carried bottom ring at the knee, the familiar melodies of Le Caid and Le Boudin. The speech by the Commanding Officer, the slow marching Companies parading.

What moved me was the veterans who turned up. Men who'd fought the Viets and beaten the Fell. Old gentlemen many of them, but gallant yet in navy blazers, grey slacks, and black shoes. The green ties and the green berets of the Regiment, slow marching onto the parade square, singing Le Boudin, our march since eighteen seventy. It would have brought tears to a glass eye. My life; I'd never give it up.

I was part of the parachuting display that day, landing first on a square of grass adjacent to the parade and followed by the legionnaires. Parachute stowed, and helmet removed I walked across to where my father was standing.

"Ah'm impressed Tim."

The CO came over; immaculate turnout, Parachutist's wings gleaming, a double row of medal ribbons for distinguished service. I came to attention. "Excellent display, Lieutenant Ronsard."

"Thank you Sir. May I present my father, James Ronsard, Sir. Dad, Colonel Lacaze, my Commanding Officer."

The CO saluted my father and shook hands. "You're being well looked after, Mr Ronsard?"

"Very well looked after Colonel, thank you."

"Visit the Regiment again, Mr Ronsard."

Senior NCOs and Officers mingled in the reception area of the garden. Orderlies serving wine, food and drinks. My men were packing up and one of them limped.

"I've got an injured man. Dieter will you look after my dad?"

We had a clear view from the battlements of the Citadel above the harbour. We looked down about a hundred feet to the shore. "I've climbed the walls," I said. My father shook his head. "Good God," he said.

The ferry for Marseilles was a blimp on the horizon. We walked to the port. "Don't worry, your case'll be there when we get down," I said.

The ferry berthed, passengers and cargo discharged, and she was ready to board. It was hard to say farewell to my dad. We embraced and shook hands.

"Next year, dad. We'll meet in Nimes. Visit Two REI. Dieter'll try to make it. Meet more of our friends."

My father nodded, unable to speak. He turned and mounted the gangway. He turned at the top waved once and vanished into the ship.

I'd never go back home, but I was chuffed that my father was proud of Dieter and me. I doubted that I'd ever see my mother again. But my father would come again to see me. Scotland, and its stupid parochial bigots, could sink in the North Atlantic for all I cared.

We sat in the port enjoying the late evening. "Tim, I'm sorry if I spoiled the evening by telling you what happened," Steve said.

"I'm glad you told me. Good to know my dad is looking out for me. What brought you here, Steve?"

"I admired what you did, joining the Legion. You're the Black Sheep, and you've done well."

"Oh away with you Steve. Now I've got a red face. I just try to do my job."

"I needed to talk to someone who'd understand why I wanted to join the Army. I hated studying law. And I can't stand the thought of spending my life in Westburn."

"Getting in to Sandhurst is wonderful. You made the right choice, Steve."

I could see that he wanted to ask me something.

"The music teacher; what was her name?"

"Isobel Clieshman."

"You must have liked her a lot."

"Yes I did. I called her Cliesh."

"That's a nice name. Have you heard from her at all?"

"No." I'd kept a note of her address. Probably she was still there, but it didn't feel right to get in touch. I'd not given Cliesh much thought during the intense training. "I'm the only one who called her Cliesh; I gave her the name. But it didn't work out. I haven't heard fom her since nineteen sixty-three; five bloody years."

"That's too bad."

It would soon be time to go back to Camp Raffaelli and get Steve to the Tizi for a night's sleep before his voyage to Marseilles the next morning. But we lingered, unwilling to end the evening.

"I like Dieter," Steve said. "He's a wonderful man."

"Yes, he is. He's a terrific soldier; taught me almost everything. Bags of authority. I'd just made legionnaire First-class when I saw him deal with an Army Captain, a parachutist who'd lost the place. There could've been serious trouble, but Dieter got a grip of the situation. He has a lot of presence."

"Tell me about it," Steve said.

"I like Army parachutists, volunteers, first-rate regulars. Up on the Djebel, we'd to execute a relief in place with a Parachute Regiment."

"Tricky," Steve said.

"Yes. But good preparations, advance parties in contact; a staggered relief from the rear to the front. One parachute section came down, and a Legion section went forward replacing them. The company was last to go, taking over from the Para company defending the line. Section by section the relief went smoothly."

There was a defile where only one section at a time could pass safely, and Paras late for some reason became entangled with the section. "A Para Corporal shoving legionnaires made things worse. He thumped a new man, an Italian, knocking him out."

"That's not too clever," Steve said.

"No, and the Fell might hear the scuffling."

Paras and Legionnaires locked: impasse. Dieter slammed the butt of his machine pistol into the jaw of the Para Corporal. Silence. He was out cold; a tooth was on the ground beside his face. "He'd need his jaw wired," I said.

Dieter's face was pale under the tan, and he closed up to the Sergeant in charge, and pushed him back. "Control your men," Dieter said, and looked him over. Legionnaires and Paras squared up. "Bad if fighting had broken out." I said. Dieter calmed the section with a wave of his hand. Then, a harassed Para Captain appeared. "What the Hell is going on?" He said.

Dieter, frosty, took charge "A bump. I'm helping the Sergeant; Sir."

Laughter in our ranks; Dieter turned, frowned; the laughter stopped. He slung the machine pistol behind his shoulder, bent over, picked up the Para Corporal and the Italian legionnaire. "Ronsard, Spilyades. Take care of him."

"We carried the Italian away, but I looked back. Dieter had his right hand on his machine pistol. He held the unconscious Corporal upright with his left hand and stared at the Captain." 'We need to be moving forward. Your men are late and they're in the way; Sir.'

"The Captain wilted, ordered NCOs to untangle the Paras and get them moving. Dieter pushed the unconscious Para Corporal to the Sergeant. He dragged him off the path. "Thank you; Sir. I'll get the section up to the line."

"Dieter can lead," I said.

"You saved his life out on the Djbell," Steve said. "He told me when you were settling the bill."

"Well, something like that."

"I hope I make friends like you and Dieter when I join my regiment after the Academy."

Steve wanted to know what had happened in the Regiment since the end of the Algerian War and the move to Corsica. I described the transformation from airborne light infantry to airborne commando.The hair raising escalades from the battlements of Fort Monte Christi overlooking the harbour of Oran. The low level jumps into the sea from a helicopter, off Mers el Kebir. The leap when Dieter hit the water first. "The water, hard as concrete," he'd said. Going on thirty-nine, there wasn't a harder or fitter man in the Regiment.

The Regiment got ready for its new mission. We parachuted of course; trained for amphibious operations; became expert in the use of plastic explosives and the demolition of pylons, buildings, and installations. We cinched anti tank operations. An even more potent esprit de corps took hold of the Regiment as the Algerian War slipped into our past.

Early next morning I went to the Tizi and picked him up in our taxi. and ran him to the ferry. The mood was good but we said little. I was tired from an unsettled night and little sleep and Steve, unused to modest quantities of wine and brandy, was feeling fragile.

We shook hands. "Time to get aboard, Steve."

"Is it OK if I write?"

"Write, and I'll reply."

I invited him to meet me. "When you get a leave, I'll meet you, here in Corsica if you like. We could do some serious stuff on the mountains. Next year then?"

"Definitely, Tim. I'd like that."

We wrote often, but it was three years before we met again.

Nineteen sixty-nine, and the Regiment was in Chad for several months dealing with Tubu insurgents. It was a grim place.

I was a Lieutenant commanding a platoon. We'd trained relentlessly, but this was my first engagement with an enemy since Algeria and several men were new. I was edgy, worried about my boys.

Well-armed insurgents operating out of Libyan bases waited in caves and dugouts ahead, protecting mortars. I was in charge of that battle area and in touch with the section NCOs by radio telephone, far enough back to control events, and let the NCOs and legionnaires respond as the battle unfolded.

Our job was to destroy two heavy mortars. Our mortar barrage lifted, and the rebels replied, with two mortar rounds that exploded in front of the skirmishers advancing up the slope on the Ennidi Massif. A cloud of dirty brown smoke rose into the bright sky. Two legionnaires went down. "Medic, medic," their voices penetrating the crack of MAS rifles and bursts of AK47s on automatic.

The medic left our lines, right hand laid on his pistol holster, sprinting and weaving towards the wounded, pouches bouncing off his back and thighs. He worked on both men, and I ordered covering fire. A Corporal went out dodging and weaving, a difficult target for the Tubu. He and the medic brought the wounded back. The medic did a great job, dressing torso, and shoulder injuries, giving the wounded men shots of morphine to reduce pain. I wanted the helicopter to come and evacuate my wounded men.

Two heads and shoulders appeared in a forward rebel position and threw grenades. An LMG gunner fired a short burst, dropping one; the other ducked below the rim of the dugout as dark blobs rose up, arcing towards the section.

"Grenades, grenades! Get down," I yelled. Metal fragments, and splinters hissed out of the explosions and swirling brown smoke, flying overhead. The CO requested air support, and the company pulled back two hundred yards to avoid casualties from the air strike. Four hundred yards now separated the section from the forward rebel positions. They yelled insults, thinking they had driven us off. One hundred and fifty yards to the front, the Air Officer and his two men observed the rebel positions from behind a low rocky out-crop, waiting to direct the air strike. Snipers searched for them and bullets ricocheted, sending rock splinters flying. Intermittent firing continued. From cover, I watched two Jaguar fighters booming overhead at low level. On the first pass, each fighter dropped a pair of bombs sending sand, brown earth, and rocks heaving up inside the rebel lines; on the second pass they fired salvoes of rockets that burst in and around the targets. I prayed they hit the mortars.

The fighters soared into a long swooping turn above the massif, flying in slow loops, waiting above the battle. Wounded rebels cried out and several men staggered out of caves. Bursts from the section's LMG gunners killed them. Two men flopped over the edge of a dugout; a legionnaire, lying prone in cover ahead of me, fired two shots from his MAS rifle, killing them. A few minutes later the CO came on the radio, advising another strike. The Jaguars came in low, passing four times, cannons strafing the rebel positions then climbing away, flying west into the sun.

My edginess vanished in a burst of adrenalin as the platoon advanced in open order. The platoon knitted smoothly, taking advantage of cover in shallow ground and behind boulders. The Company moved ahead and broke into the rebel positions. I advanced with the platoon, subduing pockets of resistance. Legionnaires fired machine guns into the mouth of caves. Others tossed grenades inside killing rebels. A handful of Tubu struggled on, but we killed them in bloody hand-to-hand fighting and occupied the position. My platoon had fought well. My hard work with the NCOs had paid off.

We enjoyed the quiet spells at the base. The villagers liked us; they figured we protected them. I admired the round houses with the thatched roofs twisted to a point at the top. The village kids were friendly and curious, peering from open doors of huts while the Company paraded for inspection on the village square. The small, black faces crowded the doorways when legionnaires wore the Kepi Blanc for a senior officer's inspection. They squealed with delight as boots stamped, raising puffs of dust, and the crisp slap of hands on rifles, when the men presented arms.

The weeks on long-range patrols: aircraft dropped supplies of food, water, and fuel at a rendezvous. Out in the emptiness the Company negotiated burnt out Savannah; moved through scrub and bush, and dragged vehicles free from muddy trails. Sometimes there was a firefight with the insurgents.

The company was in motorized column hunting rebels, and in a sandstorm, caught up with a band. The rebels launched the ambush from both sides of a broad track. A mortar round disabled the second vehicle in the column. Their machine guns lighted up the gloom giving away their positions. The Legion's mortars fired, blanketing the rebel positions and the heavy machine guns raked them. Heavy weapons ceased firing, and the infantry rose from cover advancing rapidly. I was sure of my platoon as I followed them into the smoke and low brush growing in the sand.

Ahead, the reports of AK47s and machine guns. Our grenades exploded, brown smoke drifting back as we made contact with the rebels. Several minutes of hand-to-hand fighting cleaned the rebels out.

The smoke cleared, the dead strewn about the battlefield, or slumped in foxholes. Detached arms and legs scattered here and there. The rebels had not dug in well. The column killed forty-five rebels, capturing three mortars, four machine guns, a few rifles, and small arms ammunition. We lost a Lieutenant, a Sergeant, and four legionnaires.

I laughed with the NCOs when they brought in stories of Legionnaires on operations mounted on horses and camels. We never saw them.

The platoon suffered the miserable heat and humidity; perfect conditions for spreading hepatitis and dysentery. Often, the men were near exhaustion and so was I. Four men in that column came down with amoebic dysentery and were lifted by helicopter down to Fort Lamy and evacuated to France. They suffered agonies, shitting blood. Two of them contracted bladder infections and were near crippled pissing. Three of the men were medically discharged from the Corps.

Serving in Chad taught me a good deal about command. It's easy to give orders; the men obey them, but earning their respect is much harder. The men give respect; you can't demand it. They let you know in quiet ways if they'd go through brick walls for you.

Near the finish of a long distance patrol, uneventful, apart from two skirmishes with small bands of insurgents. The section was tired and filthy and had no fresh meat since leaving the base. We survived on supplies dropped at rendezvous points. On the long leg back to the base, we navigated a large tract of wasted savannah. The sooty remnants of burnt grass and brush marked the vehicles. The legionnaires' combat fatigues were sweaty black and streaked with soot and dust. Underneath bush hats, soot marked faces hung from exhausted eyes. A couple of hours from the base, we stopped in a village and a man offered to sell a goat. There was an Italian Sergeant, from Sicily who'd farmed before coming into the Legion. *Edited to here.*

The goatherd offered a tough old she-goat. Her teats were dry; the animal a wriggle of bones. The Sergeant shrugging his shoulders, turning his back on the herder. He came after the Sergeant, plucking at his uniform. Reluctantly, the Sergeant stopped and faced the goatherd. After some histrionics, the Sicilian selected a fine young female from the herd.

The senior Sergeant, a German, came over. "We're going to roast the goat tonight, Sir, back at the base. Have a few beers. You'll be coming?"

"What's my share?"

"You're our guest, Sir."

"Thanks Sergeant. The beer is on me."

"That's good, Sir, thanks. I'll let the men know."

I knew then that I led them; that I had their loyalty and respect: they'd go through brick walls for me.

The goat lay trussed up in the back of a truck. At the base the men humped the animal off the truck and the beast bleated pitifully. The Sicilian Sergeant supervised hanging the goat by its hind legs, then, he cut its throat. The men stood around watching, as blood gushed into an improvised basin made from an old petrol tin. The flow of blood reduced to a minute or two of steady dripping as the goat quivered and ticked, its eyes glassy; then it died.

"The blood, Sir," the Sergeant said. "Good for sausages, but not in this heat."

Black Puddings, the Scottish Blood Sausage of Sunday breakfasts long ago. Suddenly, fried, black pudding appealed to me.

The Sicilian was a good butcher, skinning the beast, discarding its black and white hide, and removing the offal. He threw lungs and heart to the dogs. Slowly he browned the liver and kidneys in a pan.

The men drank beer steadily, slaking thirst and wetting throats dried out on the patrol. The Sergeants added to the dozen cases of beer I'd given. The Sicilian chopped the liver and kidneys. He raised the pan, handing it on to a man near him, "Pass it round." I enjoyed a chunk of kidney and a sliver of liver, washed down with mouthfuls of Kronenbourg, while the goat roasted on an improvised spit over an open fire; it smelt wonderful. The Sergeant dipped bread into the juices gathering in the tray fixed below the spitted goat. Eager hands plucked at it, the men chewing greedily and swallowing the juicy morsels. I devoured a satisfying crust.

I had chops washed down with beer. Aristiedes had relished chops from the goat. He'd have loved this session with the legionnaries. I wished that my friend had made it out of Algeria and like me gained a commission, serving still in 2 REP. I'd have missed him had he left the Corps, but I'd have been happy to hear that he was settled with a family in Cyprus.

Aristedies died for France; his bones resting in a neglected Legion cemetery in Algeria. It would have been good to have him around still, in 2REP, for us to have been NCOs or officers together.

Aristedies' sacrifice bound us: my shooting the man that killed him one bleak day on the Djbell. I remembered hitting the Fell twice in the chest, and he wasn't dead, raising his arms, surrendering, and how I shot him in the heart.

I belonged to the Legion and by the spilling of his blood Aristedies joined the immortals of the Corps. Together we'd been moulded by the Legion: enlisting as boys, we'd become men. Soldiering and honour strengthened our friendship. Years had passed, and still it grieved me that Aristedies died young.

I had the remaining chops served on a plate and took it to the Captain commanding the Company. He was always far too busy to feed himself. "Come on, Sir. You look all in. You'll enjoy the chops. I had some myself. They're very good. You could do with them."

He looked up, grinning when I uncovered the heap of small chops, garnished with tinned vegetables. "Thanks, Ronsard. I'm hungry."

"Right, Sir."

He waved me to a spare chair near his makeshift desk, opened a drawer, and pulled out a bottle of whisky. "You're from Scotland, Tim. Pour yourself a good one."

"Thank you, Sir."

The Captain devoured the meal. I sipped the whisky, the first in a long time. "Thanks again, Tim. I enjoyed that. Pour me a whisky and another one for yourself." It was good whisky, The Antiquary. Christ knows where he'd laid hands on it.

"The Colonel has mentioned us in despatches. It reflects well on the Company. You all did well out there. Honours given belong to the men too. Nothing is possible without good officers, and legionnaires."

'Yes Sir. Thank you, Sir."

Not long afterwards, my promotion to Captain came through.

When I met him at Calvi airport, Steve had changed. Active service in Oman marked him; hands fragile when I shook them, wrists, like bone china, sticking out below his shirt cuffs.

"How are you, Steve?"

"I'm so bloody tired, Tim. I got back from Oman to the UK two days ago, and I came straight here. I couldn't face going home. Congratulations on your promotion, Captain Ronsard."

"Thanks, Steve."

The last thing Steve should do was trek across the mountain route running the length of the island. Parts of it remained snow bound well into June. He needed rest and to put on weight.

"I've got you a room in the officers' quarters. Let's get you settled first."

That night I took him to the Tizi. Madam Ouzou was pleased to see Steve again; but his deep-set eyes and prominent cheekbones shocked her. We dined quietly; long silences punctuated our conversation. Steve needed to get Oman out of his system.

"Sleep well. Take it easy tomorrow. I've a couple of things to attend to before I start my leave."

The Commanding Officer invited him to the Mess. He wanted to meet the officer of a Scots Regiment. Life in the Officers Mess and resting in comfortable quarters for a day or two would do him good.

Dieter, now Regimental Sergeant Major, was keen to meet Steve again and had invited him to the Mess for dinner with some of the senior NCOs.

Staying quietly in Corsica was the right thing to do. If he had any lingering illness, he could draw on the regiment. But, I was careful not to suggest that he was not up for two hard weeks in the mountains.

"How do you think I'm looking, Steve?"

"Fit, but thinner than I remember."

"Chad took it out of me. I'd a touch of dysentery, but I'm over it."

"Well, Tim, I look bloody horrible. It's kind of you not to mention it. The last six months I got by on three or four hours' sleep, and that was broken many nights."

"I wouldn't mind laying low for a while, Steve. What about you?"

"That sounds good to me, Tim."

Steve and I spent our leave, staying in Piana, a village of five hundred souls. It was a lovely place, situated at altitude sixteen hundred and fifty feet, with beautiful views across the Golfe de Porto. We'd both scared up cash from our overseas postings and opted to stay in the fine old Hotel des Roches Rouges. We liked its spacious rooms and simple Thirties furnishings. The food in the restaurant was splendid.

There was a walk of three miles down the hill to the beach at Ficajola. Most days we walked there to swim. After some days, I could see Steve's strength returning and the gauntness retreating. We took a couple of easier hikes on trails at Les Clanache, a beautiful area of granite cliffs and outcrops, and the dark green foliage of chestnut forests.

Our friendship, begun at our first meeting and grown in our letters strengthened in Piana. Walking, swimming, the nourishing dinners, then deep, restful sleep, brought Steve back to health. I felt better myself.

Steve asked about Chad. I reckoned he wanted to talk about his year in the Arabian Peninsula. What he told me about Oman and the Dhofar made us brothers in arms.

The opportunity to serve with the Omani Army was a surprise, and Steve volunteered. "I was a Contract Officer. The year I spent there counted as service. The pay was good, but I wasn't a mercenary. If things went belly up, the Government might decide it didn't want to know. The job was turfing out Communist backed rebels in the Dhofar."

Service in Oman and the Dhofar was a sharp lesson in the realities of army life. It didn't take Steve long to figure out that Lieutenants are dispensable. "For six months, I was Acting Captain. There were British officers attached to the Sultan's forces. Christ, Tim, it was a strange place." Steve had much to say.

Steve's CO was a Scot, a Cameronian, Major Roderick Elphinstone. "Dressed in shabby khakis, scuffed desert boots and a soiled khaki puggarree wound round his head," Steve said. "His face hidden by a huge beard. I saluted, he returned it and shook my hand. 'Our job is to fight and don't you forget it.' he said."

"A nutter?"

"An eccentric, but he could soldier. I learnt a lot from him."

Steve saw Iranian Special Forces sent by the Shah, Baluchi mercenaries and grave, elegant Akari sentries, dressed in loose white robes and brilliant puggarree, guarding the airfield at Salalah. "One old India hand said it was like campaigning on the Northwest Frontier. Right out of Gunga Din but now troops moved by helicopter and plane."

I envied Steve's experience of soldiering in this corner of Arabia at the end of Empire. But had I joined the British Army it was unlikely given my background that I'd ever have been commissioned.

"The enemy was the Adoo," Steve said, "tribesmen from the Jebel, up north. I never completely trusted them. They changed sides."

Adoo became Firqat when they crossed over. Slight, dark men, Steve said, bearded and turbaned, a cotton dhoti covering their legs, armed with everything from AK47s to Lee-Enfields. "We trained them to use mortars and machine guns. Independent bastards and hard as nails."

"An adventure, was it?"

"It was tough. I was responsible for a part of the fort, sangars, packed with weapons: light and heavy machine guns, light two inch mortars, the heavier eighty-one MM mortar and a gun pit dug, for a twenty-five-pound field gun."

"Sangars?"

"Indian Army lingo; defences built of stones, sandbags, and empty fuel drums filled with concrete. We lived rough, just like the Legion."

"Impregnable?"

"I thought so until the Adoo attacked the fort." Waves of tribesmen flowed across the ground flooding the front of the walls. "They had all this Soviet kit. I wished I'd trained more."

"Soldiering is hard, Steve; train, and train again."

"It was a fucking inferno: rockets slamming into the fort, the air full of bullets. I was scared shitless."

I'd been sacred shitless and it was Legion NCOs and their training that helped me overcome it. I described the booby trapped well, sand bagging the broiled corpse. The ambush when Aristiedes died, killing Dalderuup. "You'd be off your head not to be scared. When you're not scared, you die. What'd you do?"

"The Adoo had bags of guts. They got through the perimeter wire, assaulted the front of the fort, and attacked the gun pit. Lose that twenty-five-pounder gun and we'd be overrun. I got a mixed bunch of six Omani regulars and Firqat in there with the gun crew."

"You were OK?"

"I got on with it. My Omanis and Firqat put up a wall of rifle and machine gunfire and let the crew work the gun. They levelled the gun, firing into the

Adoo at point blank range. The Adoo nearly overran the position, throwing grenades, but they bounced back from the lip of the gun pit, exploding, killing, and wounding them. My men fought well."

"That's because you led them, Steve."

"The Adoo got very close. I saw one man's rotting teeth and he stank. I shot him."

"Doing your job, Steve."

"I suppose so."

Steve's Omanis and Firqat killed about forty men. "The CO came down to the gun pit. He said I'd done well."

"He seems like a good man. Few of my COs ever said as much."

Steve had come through. It's a good feeling. I was proud of my young cousin.

The hotel was quiet in late spring. After dinner, a pullover kept out the evening chill, and we sat on the terrace, sipping local brandy, chasing it with tiny cups of strong coffee. I loved those evenings, catching up on Steve's life since he'd appeared at the gate of Camp Raffaelli.

One afternoon late, we walked back from the beach. A few hundred yards from the entrance to the village, a sudden downpour soaked us through. The rain stopped and the sun dried the black wet road. A rainbow bridged the gap in the two hills guarding the village entrance and we passed under it. My spirits soared and the feeling lasted until well after dinner.

"You're in good fettle, Tim."

"I can't explain it, but that downpour and the rainbow this afternoon, made me happy. Like something good was coming."

"What would be good, Tim?"

"When I made Captain. But meeting Cliesh, now that would be good." I thought about her and how we'd lost each other. No way round that. It would take more than a rainbow to make it right.

We sat quietly, enjoying the brandy and the coffee. "You have a girl, Steve?"

"No, not really. I met a Colonel's daughter at a Regimental ball. I took her out a couple of times. Then I went to Oman."

"What's her name?"

"Catherine. A nice girl; she wrote to me and I sent her two letters. Then I sent a post card and I didn't write to her after that. Oman was hard, Tim."

I knew how he felt. Chad had been hard. "You going to see her when you get home?"

"Maybe. I'm not sure. I'd like to."

"See her, Steve. Nice girls can slip away from you."

The waiter brought more brandies and coffees.

"Have you heard anything from the music teacher?"

"Cliesh? No, nothing."

"I wanted to ask you this before, but I didn't feel I knew you well enough. Why didn't you ask her to marry?"

"I did. I asked her to come to Algeria. She said she'd marry me if I left the Corps and came to Paris. But I couldn't; not with the Commission, and she knocked me back. You're married to the Legion. That's what she said."

"You really cared for her, didn't you?"

I gazed at the starry sky so clear after the rain. "She's the love of my life, Steve."

The next day at lunch, Steve wanted to know more about my time in the Legion and I obliged, going over the Algerian war and the operations in Chad.

"What happened to your face, Tim?"

I told him about fighting Roche. "He ended up in the Penal battalion. I got eight days in prison for fighting."

I showed him my tattoo; LEGIO PATRIA NOSTRA. Its colours faded. "I was going on nineteen; a daft boy. The Legion is my family, my home, my country."

"Do you believe that?"

In the early days at Fort St Nicolas in Marseilles, I'd struggled to make sense of the Corps. But I'd long accepted Legio Patria Nostra. "Sure I do. I've been here for fourteen years." I remembered my home town. "I'm from Westburn, and Reid's foundry. What'd I be if I'd stayed there? Another weekend drunk trying to forget the foundry. I'm proud of what I am."

"I've met officers and NCOs who feel that way about the Regiment. I'm glad you said it; I feel that way myself. Outsiders; either they think you're odd or don't believe you."

I'd served so long in the Legion, I ignored outsiders. They were simply not a part of my life. I was not like them and didn't care what they thought. In the Legion what mattered is what you can do. "No one cares a toss where you're from or gives a shit about your religion. The Corps takes care of its own."

Legio Patria Nostra meant a lot to me. James Malone used to discuss the Scots soldiers who hired out to foreign powers and fought all over Europe. "It's an old tradition I follow, Steve." The longer I served the closer the Corps drew me in. I was part of the rituals and customs that shaped our lives, always ready to deploy.

"Are you hiding in the Legion?"

I laughed hiding my surprise."Not at all. I made up my my mind, came from Barcelona to Marseilles and that was it. I signed my first contract. I was trying to find myself."

"I think you have."

I liked the harmony given to our lives: in the barracks, the camaraderie of the forced marches in Algeria, the comradeship formed in the hard circumstances of Chad. Watching men unswathe faces and shake out grit and sand from the long scarves, lifting goggles on to foreheads to reveal white circles round the eyes.

The immense, silent desert, lit by moonlight shining on the vast, starry sky. Now and then in damp weather, twinges in my joints brought back cold nights lying on hard sand. My nose wrinkled, at the memory of sharp smells from unwashed bodies.

But the dead and wounded stayed with me: the bloody casualties of relentless patrols pursuing the Fell in that final year of the Algerian war and the comrades lost in Chad. As I moved through the ranks, I absorbed the values and the ethos holding the Corps together. Someday, Steve might feel the same about his Regiment. "I like the life, Steve. I'm the dedicated unmarried professional soldier."

"There's a few officers like you in the battalion."

I laughed. "Maybe you'll be one of them."

I accompanied Steve to the airport for the return to the UK.

"I'm appointed Captain; going to the Regiment's barracks in Glasgow. I'm adjutant to the 3rd Battalion."

"That's great news. You did well in Oman."

"Look, Armistice Day is usually commemorated on the Sunday nearest 11th November. There's a reception in the Mess after the parade. Why don't you come? I'll speak to the Colonel once I'm settled in. He'll write to your Colonel."

I'd not been home in fourteen years. I never intended going back. My father had met me in Corsica and France, and would do so again. That was as close as I wanted to get to Scotland.

"Come on, Tim, come home for a week or two. Your Old Man will be dead chuffed."

I had plenty of leave due. I hadn't taken my full leave for several years, preferring to volunteer for additional tours overseas, and training elsewhere. Since I'd given up hope of ever seeing Cliesh again, I got down to the hard graft of perfecting my calling.

"I don't know. You've taken the feet away from me. Even if I wanted to come, I'd probably not get away. I've been on leave for the last couple of weeks."

"Think about it. I'd like if you came. Give you a taste of the battalion's hospitality. I'll make the arrangements."

"OK, Steve, I'll see what I can do."

Chapter 6

Falling In Love Over Again

"You're not looking forward to going home are you, Tim?"

"I'm not, Dieter. I haven't told my father I'm coming. I don't want any surprises, like being met at the airport. I don't know what to expect; it's been so long."

My mother had died during the deployment in Chad. I heard about it when the unit returned to Calvi.

Dieter drove me to Calvi airport and waited until departure. I checked in my bags. "You'll enjoy staying with Steve, and the Armistice Ceremony; that'll be good. Sure, the invitation came from his CO; and our CO is happy about it."

We shook hands. "Tell me all about Scotland when you get back."

"I'll do that. See you in a month."

There was time for a Ricard before the plane took off. I'd dressed in walking out uniform and the green beret, preferring it to the black officers' kepi. Corsicans often saw legionnaires so no one gave me a second glance. The plane to Orly was quiet, and I had a seat at the back well away from other passengers. I was in no mood for conversation.

I had a couple of hours to wait at Orly for the Glasgow flight, so I sat at a bar brooding over another couple of Ricards. Unlike me, the people there were happy to be travelling. It hadn't sunk in that soon I would be home for the first time since I'd left at eighteen. I'd sworn I would never set foot in Scotland again, but the invitation from my cousin's regiment, and I changed my mind. He was a Captain now and I felt I could not refuse.

I had another reason for taking leave. Steve had married Catherine, the Colonel's daughter. He'd asked me to be Best Man, but I couldn't get away for I was on attachment to 13 DBLE in Djibouti.

I had another Ricard. I'd sleep on the plane. Fortunately, the flight was quiet, I'd a seat to myself at the rear of the aircraft. The passengers clustered in the front, and I was soon asleep.

The call to fasten seat belts woke me and I looked out the window of the Air France Caravelle making its final approach from the north. There was no Glasgow Airport when I left. The hump of Ben Lomond filled the window, giving way to pale autumn sun shimmering on the river, lighting Dumbarton Rock and the castle walls. The plane bounced on the tarmac, tyres screeching briefly. I was home for the first time in fourteen years.

I saw the hat moving along in front of me. The walk and the rhythmic clicking of her heels hit me; sharp arrow heads. It was *her*. My hands shook. I had to speak to her; but I hung back at Passport Control to get a grip of myself. Cliesh veered left to the foreigners' gate. I was going there myself.

The Passport Officer gave me the once over and thumbed slowly, deliberately, through my passport. Cliesh had disappeared.

"What's the purpose of your visit, Sir?"

She was probably out of the airport by now. "I'm a guest of Captain O'Hara, Adjutant, at the barracks in Glasgow. I'm here for the Armistice Day ceremonies."

"Right, Sir. Enjoy your visit."

I hurried to the Baggage Hall and sighed with relief when I saw Cliesh waiting near the carousel. An announcement said the luggage would be a delayed a few minutes. Her stance was just as I remembered, weight on the right leg the left foot pointing out and turned at the ankle, the slender ankles and beautiful shapely legs. Her gloved hands, one crooked protectively around her leather handbag, the other roaming nervously. Eight years since I'd seen Cliesh and I was weak at the knees.

Cliesh turned, her eyes met mine and passed. She was so lost in herself that I was invisible. Her hat was wrong; not the discreet, feminine hats she wore when I was with her in Paris making her even more beautiful. The brim of the hat kept her face in shadow. Cliesh did not want to be seen.

The carousel started, and the small crowd moved forward. Her luggage would be too heavy for her to manage. I'd carried her hefty bag that long weekend we spent in the Loire Valley. She was on tiptoes looking for her bag. Sweet Jesus; my heart ached at the sight of her. I let her struggle with the bag. It slipped from her fingers, heading round the carousel.

My mouth was dry and I swallowed nervously. "Let me help you with that, Miss," I said. I heaved her bag on to my trolley.

"Why, thank you."

My uniform hadn't registered. "Hello, Cliesh."

Her head came up. Disbelief clouded her face. I was the only man alive who called her Cliesh. "It's you!" Then, she collected herself. "Hello, Tim."

"Let me get this." I hauled my two bags on to the trolley. I had her attention now, and she looked me over. I had the gaunt face of a fit professional soldier in an elite regiment, and underneath the beret, the cropped hair that she didn't like.

"So you're an officer in the Legion?"

"I'm a Captain; Second Parachute Regiment. My cousin invited me to the Armistice Day Ceremony at Glasgow Barracks. My first visit home."

"You've done well."

I blushed. "What brings you home?" I said. The crowd thinned.

"Oh, just family business. My second visit in two months. My father died. My mother died three years ago. I'm here to break up the family home. Sell the house." She shrugged, her shoulders slumped and she turned away.

I took her right hand, and I felt her fingers steal away. I held on and she looked up at me. Her eyes filled and tears spilled onto her cheeks. I laid a gentle hand on her shoulder and kissed her cheek. "Cliesh, I'm so sorry for your loss." She forced a thin smile. Her lips did not part.

I chanced my luck and dabbed away her tears with my handkerchief. "No one to help you; what about your brother?"

"No; we've never been close. He lives in Hong Kong now. He came the day before my Father's funeral and left the day after it."

"I see. Anyway, I'm glad to see you again, Cliesh. Look, where are you going; into Glasgow?"

"Yes, I must find a taxi."

"I'll give you a lift. It's no trouble."

I wheeled our luggage through Customs. I liked having her by my side.

"You're tanned and fit. Where have you been?"

I shrugged. Fitness went with the job; a tan was an occupational hazard. "I've been in Chad and Djibouti."

An immaculately turned out Sergeant waited at the rendezvous point. He came to attention and saluted. "Good afternoon, Ma'am, Captain Ronsard, Sir. Sergeant McNab"

I stood straight and returned the salute. "Good afternoon, Sergeant. Can we drop the lady at Falkland Crescent, in Dowan Hill?"

"Certainly Sir. It's not far from Captain O'Hara's address."

Sergeant McNab took charge of our luggage and marched us outside. In a few minutes, he had the car round, a gleaming, black, three-litre Rover. He loaded the luggage into the boot and opened the rear passenger door.

"Colonel Robertson's car, Sir. You'll be comfortable."

"You're famous, Tim?"

"Not really."

The coolest smile creased her face.

"Best route's the Clyde Tunnel, Sir. Shall I drop the lady first?"

"Right, Sergeant."

I handed her into the car. I wanted to make her happy. She pressed herself into the corner of the rear seat far away from me. We rode in silence. I thought back to the night we'd said farewell in Paris; the last time we were together. It was heart breaking. Dieter stood apart with our kit trying not to watch. We were catching the trooper for Oran the next evening in Marseilles.

"Cliesh, I love you. I'll miss you so much."

"Tim, you know how much I love you?"

I held her closer. I was biting my lip. "Yes, I know."

"You will come back; you have to come back, Tim. I'll be waiting for you."

I swore that I would be back; that I'd leave the Legion to be with her; and I meant it. That was before the doubts about civilian life set in and I accepted a commission.

"Tim, it's time," Dieter had said. "We have to go."

We walked to Dieter. He cupped Cliesh's hands in his hands and kissed her on the cheek. "I'm glad we met, Isobel. I hope we'll meet again."

"Take care of Tim for me, Dieter."

I was close to losing my composure. I didn't want Cliesh to see how bad I was feeling. The sharp blasts of whistles and the last calls for the train.

"Good bye, Isobel," Dieter said.

Cliesh waved half-heartedly to Dieter. I felt worse than when she left me and went to the North East coast. We clung to one another, and I couldn't let her go. "Oh, Cliesh ..."

"You'd better go, Tim."

We kissed one last time. I grabbed the last bag and ran for the moving train. Dieter caught my outstretched hand and swung me on-board. I watched Cliesh growing smaller waving to me. The train turned out of the station and she was gone. I just about cracked up.

"You need a drink, Tim. Let's have a Ricard."

Sergeant McNab braked hard throwing me against Cliesh. She pushed me off. "Do you mind?"

"Sorry."

"There are some head cases on the road, Sir."

I felt the weight of her silence. Twenty minutes later, we were in the affluent, leafy Victorian suburb of Dowan Hill. Falkland Crescent, a semi circle of large, well appointed honey coloured sand stone villas.

"Sergeant, I'll help Miss Clieshman with her luggage. Can you drop my bags at Captain O'Hara's place and tell him I'll be along soon?"

"Right, Sir. I'll drop off your kit. Captain O'Hara is at the Barracks. I'll let him know to expect you. Shall I come back for you?"

"No, I'll walk."

"Good bye, Sir; and to you Ma'am."

I followed her up the stairs to the main entrance. Cliesh unlocked the outer doors. She kicked at the mail heaped there. I arranged it in a neat pile on a small table. I left her bag on the hall floor.

Inside the house was damp and cold, the air fusty; no one lived here. I followed her to an oak panelled hall, deep cornice, high ceiling. A worn Baluchi rug lay on the centre of the hall floor. So reminiscent of her rooms where we were lovers long ago. She seemed to forget I was there, and I followed her into the kitchen. "You're going to live here for a couple of weeks?"

"Yes. I shut most of the house down last time I was here. I put dust covers on the furniture. My parents had some nice pieces. There's a beautiful piano, a small Pleyel grand. They both played quite well. I'd hate to sell it."

Cliesh leant against the dresser and removed her hat. She shivered in that chilly kitchen. Her face confirmed that she was worn out. "You think you'll be OK here?"

"I'll eat in the kitchen, and sleep in my old bedroom. I must air the bed. I left the study furnished, and the phone's connected."

I shivered. "I'll put the heating on," Cliesh said.

Cliesh stamped her foot. Something was wrong with the heating. "The pump is down," I said.

"Damn!"

Back in the kitchen, she switched on a small electric fire. The cold and damp won. Staying in this freezing house would make her ill. A neighbour had left a basket of food. Cliesh made coffee. We sipped the coffee and nibbled biscuits. She let the phone ring. I looked at her.

"Tim, would you mind answering that? Please."

It was my cousin. I told Steve about meeting Cliesh at the airport; that she looked ill. "My cousin Steve O'Hara. Sergeant McNab mentioned your name, and Steve looked up your number."

"Thank you for the lift. Perhaps I'll run into you."

"My cousin's invited you to dinner and to stay the night. So pack a small bag and let's get out of here. You're perishing in front of me. Look at you."

"I can't do that. I've never met your cousin."

"Cliesh; for heaven's sake, you can't stay here. The house is freezing. The bed is bound to be damp. What you need is company and a dram to warm you up."

Such a determined look on her face, I thought she was going to refuse, or tell me to go to Hell.

"All right, I'll come. Thank you."

I carried the small bag containing her overnight things. The West End is handsome. It reminded me of where she lived when I first met her. We passed through squares with private gardens. Residents sat there in fine weather. The empty flower beds; here and there a late autumn rose hung on. She rebuffed all my efforts at conversation with a curt yes or no. At a road junction I took her arm, to hand her across, but she shook her arm free.

"Here we are."

Silence. Steve rented the main door flat of a handsome Victorian house. He answered the door in his working uniform. We shook hands warmly. I introduced them.

"Come in, Isobel. I'm glad to meet you. I've heard such a lot about you."

"Hello, Captain O'Hara. How do you do? Thank you for inviting me." I hoped Steve wasn't surprised by Cliesh's coolness.

Cliesh let me help remove her coat.

"When you've settled in, Isobel. Come through to the Good Room. There's a fire on and I'll get you something to warm you up. You look chilled."

She turned to Steve. "Thank you."

I carried her bag to the door of her room. I sat by the fire sunk in reverie while Steve poured drinks. During the time we had been together in Paris and the Loire Valley, Cliesh was radiant. We'd never been happier, making love when we wakened. I loved the breakfasts we had at the little guesthouse in Bourgueil. The owners of Moulin de la Planche served us on the terrace by the weir. Cliesh would linger over the last cup of coffee; listening to soothing murmurs of running water, stretching her slender legs and smiling contentedly.

"Glad you came, Tim?"

"What do you think?"

"I think you love me, Tim Ronsard."

"How can you tell?"

Cliesh would just smile.

Sometimes our playfulness turned serious, and Cliesh rested her head on my shoulder. I was leaving for Oran soon after we got back from Bourgueil. We couldn't talk about it.

I was regretting bringing Cliesh to Steve's house. The coolness was so unlike her. We waited for her in the Good Room. I'd shed my uniform jacket, a little happiness kindling in me as we sipped our drams and I chased the whisky with a swallow of beer.

"Well, Tim, I see old habits thrive, drinking whisky and beer together. You can take the boy out of the foundry, but you can't take the foundry out of the man."

"Really?"

"Sorry, Tim. Are you worried about her?"

"Yes, I am."

"How was she on the road in?"

"Quiet, and then pretty brusque. I thought we'd at least be friends."

I heard her footsteps coming towards us. She looked a little better when she entered the Good Room. Hair tidied, makeup freshened. She carried herself haughtily. But she couldn't hide her beauty no matter how miserable she was. I wondered what she felt. Perhaps she'd rather have spent the night rattling about an empty house and sleeping in a damp bed. I wanted to hug her and tell I'd help; make a start to wiping out the last eight years.

"You better now, Cliesh?"

"Yes. You don't have to keep asking."

I was about to say something sharp, but that would have sent her flouncing out of Steve's flat back to that freezing house. Steve gave her a small glass of sherry and sat her by the fire. The heat softened her features and she sat back in the chair showing off her slender legs. Did she remember how much I liked it when she sat that way?

"How's the sherry?" Steve said.

"Fine."

"Are you warm enough?" I said.

"Yes."

She grew pale and moved restlessly in the chair, crossing and uncrossing her ankles; sitting back for a moment, then coming to the edge of the seat. I saw the film of sweat glisten on her brow. Her face turned from white to grey. I wanted to go to her but feared a rebuff. Steve and I exchanged glances. She stood and her glass fell, spilling the dregs of the sherry on the carpet.

"Please, excuse me."

We both stood but she waved us back. Her right hand covered her mouth, left hand extended for balance. Her narrow skirt hobbled her step and her feet skittered across the floor as she rushed for the bathroom. She was retching now and flecks of vomit escaped her hand. She was so vulnerable. We stood outside the bathroom and heard her vomitting; her retching was heart rending. She flushed the toilet and we heard her footsteps on the tiled floor.

'I'm sorry, Steve. I'd better go. I shouldn't have come. Tim, please call me a taxi."

She looked terrible. Eyes watering, brow covered in a film of greasy sweat. Poor Cliesh. She steadied herself on the doorframe, a fountain of bile shot from her mouth and cascaded over the hall floor. The force of the purge dragged her head down and she gasped and retched, finally cleansing her system. Bile spattered her shoes. She swayed and started crying, her nose running. I gave her my handkerchief. My poor Cliesh.

"I'm so sorry for this. Please let me clean it up."

I put my arm round her shoulder, and she leant into me. Her breath was foul, but I didn't care. I was glad to hold her. Steve pointed to her bedroom door.

"My ears hurt," Cliesh said.

"Tim. Take care of her. I'll fix this lot up."

"You're sure? I mean is it all right, Steve? Oh God! I'm so sorry."

"Come on, Cliesh. Bed. You need rest. You're not going anywhere," I said.

The bedroom had soft lights, and it was warm. I switched on the electric blanket and sat her on the bed.

"Take off your shoes."

"I can't. I'll be sick again. Help me with my shoes."

Did she remember the day we became lovers, she asked me to help with her shoes. I'd have made love to her at that moment. Poor Cliesh. She was just so ill. I removed her shoes.

"Can you stand?"

"I think so."

She stood flatfooted, helpless. She swayed with tiredness. I unfastened the zip on her dress and drew it down. "Can you manage now?"

"Yes. Don't go. Hand me my nightdress. It's on the pillow."

I turned away. Listening to the rustle of her dress and underwear as she undressed. When I turned to look she was swaying again. "I feel terrible. I don't know what's wrong with me."

She was crying as I turned the bed down and sat her on the edge. Her eyes closed. I turned the corner of the covers and lifted her legs into bed. She lay down and I tucked her in. Her head peeped above the sheet edge. She looked so alone lying there, her white face framed by her chestnut hair spread on the pillow. Her hand came up and touched her right ear.

"Sleep now, Cliesh. I'll help you with the house. I'm here for a month. Don't worry about anything. We'll talk in the morning."

Cliesh was asleep by the time I reached the bedroom door.

Catherine came in and greeted me like family, kissing me on the cheek.

"Tim! I am glad to meet you at last, after Steve has told me so much about you."

We had drinks and chatted by the fire. "Where's Isobel?" Catherine said.

"In bed," I said. "She's unwell."

"Let me get dinner ready," Catherine said.

Cliesh called from the bedroom, her voice faint."I'm burning and I have a dreadful earache." There was no dinner that night. Much later we made do with ham sandwiches and coffee.

I dried Cliesh's soaking brow and called Steve and Catherine. Cliesh was shivering uncontrollably under the blankets. "I'm so cold."

I turned back the covers, damp sheets, wet night dress. Catherine fetched a fresh night dress and sheets. I helped Cliesh up; Catherine helped her change and got her into her robe. Cliesh touched her right ear. "It's so painful."

I'd seen fever more than once; had it myself in Chad. I felt Cliesh's pulse and it was a drum roll. She was really sick. I got her back into bed. Steve phoned the doctor attached to the battalion. "He'll be here soon. He's at the barracks. It's not far."

Cliesh's ear infection caused the fever. The doctor put drops in her ear and dosed her with penicillin and left codiene tablets for the earache. "She'll be OK, but keep your eye on her tonight. Call me if she gets worse."

I changed into pyjamas and robe. I dozed in the chair and kept Cliesh company. I gave her plenty to drink. Put drops in her ear and fed her codiene tablets. She slept most of the night and by sun up the fever was gone.

"Tim, was I horrible yesterday?"

"Yes, just a little bit horrible. You were sick."

"You've all been so kind taking care of me. Everything has been so wretched these last few months and more. I felt I was going mad."

I showered and shaved and put on a working uniform. I just couldn't accept wearing civilian clothes. I walked over the hill to Byres Road to the bakers and purchased a dozen morning rolls. I'd never missed them before. Now I wanted to eat maybe four, spread with salted butter along with eggs, bacon, and coffee. When I got back, Steve was departing for the Barracks and Catherine was on her way to work.

"It'll take a couple of days for Isobel to recover," Steve said. "We'd like her to stay."

"Yes," Catherine said.

"I'll take care of her," I said.

We'd been back in Scotland for almost two weeks. One morning we lingered in the kitchen after washing the breakfast dishes.

"Tim, why are you doing all this for me?" Cliesh said. "I mean I'm grateful. I don't know how I'd have got on without you."

"I wanted to help." We'd worked at her house. Steve organized a plumber from the battalion and he fixed the pump on the central heating. Sergeant Mc-Nab and a couple of Jocks had come down and got rid of rubbish. They moved things to the auctioneers. The house was empty. The lawyer was ready to sell it.

Her family ghosts were gone. Our footsteps rang on bare wooden floors. Only the Pleyel and the Baluchi rug remained. Cliesh couldn't make up her mind what to do about them.

Since her illness, Cliesh was warm and friendly and free of any embarrassment after being sick. Catherine and Steve liked her and would not hear of her moving out. Dinners were happy, and full of laughter. She washed up and helped Catherine cook dinner. Cliesh cooked well.

In the morning there was just the two of us in the house. I tried to get closer to her. She enjoyed the breakfasts I made: poached, or lightly boiled eggs; grilled bacon. I went out for fresh rolls. I made brown toast for the honey and marmalade. I bought fancy teas: Earl Grey, Lapsang Suchon. Strong, Nilgris leaf. I remembered how she tasted the brews with genteel relish when I first knew her.

"I'd forgotten you cooked," she said.

"We do everything in the Legion."

"Why did you want to help?"

"You'd not have managed it on your own."

I did everything to be near her. I loved to look at her. She was nearly forty and so beautiful. Catherine and Steve said she looked about thirty. That made me happy.

Things needed saying and I wondered what the men in the company would think of the Captain a nervous wreck. I couldn't bear the thought of losing her again. Sometimes sleep came hard. She was just through the wall and I longed for her. One morning Steve nailed me.

"What the Hell is wrong with you? You told me how you feel about Isobel. Go to her."

"I can't. Don't ask me to explain it. I just don't know. She's so distant. I think I'll go back. I hate leave."

"Distant? I don't think so. For heaven's sake, behave yourself. My CO pushed the boat out. He's told me off to introduce you as soon as you come to the Armistice Ceremony. Robertson soldiered with I REP at Suez. He has the highest regard for the Legion. If you go back early to Calvi you'll make an arse of yourself and your regiment. You'll make me look a bloody fool."

"OK, OK! I'll stay. But it's all up with Cliesh."

"She fancies you and then some. I've seen the way she looks at you. Catherine's seen it. The only idiot who hasn't is you. What ever it is that's not right, put it right. We think she's wonderful. Get a grip, Tim."

The weather was unseasonably cheerful. Cold, sunny, autumn days that kept south facing rooms bright and warm. "Let's go for a walk Tim." Cliesh said. "We'll cross Byres Road and University Avenue. I haven't been over there in years. Then we could walk in the park."

Piles of leaves lay on the turf. We sat on a bench; Cliesh wore a tan wool coat against the cold. One of her discreet feminine hats pulled into shape showing her face to advantage. She looked just great; kind of prim sitting there with her legs pressed together and to the side.

When I returned to Algeria, Cliesh believed I'd come back to her. Then, she received my letter. "Your letter shattered me," Cliesh said. "I wasn't myself for a very long time."

"How do you think I felt?" I said. "I'd asked you to marry, and you knocked me back. Anyway, you're a dab hand at letters."

"For God's sake," Cliesh said. "Not that again."

"In Paris I'd have ended up living off you. You could've been an officer's wife."

"I was afraid to go to Algeria. I was terrified I'd make a fool of myself. Why couldn't you come to Paris and marry?"

"I couldn't see what I'd do on the outside." What I then said was painful to me, but I owed it to Cliesh. If I didn't tell her now I never would. "Look Cliesh, the outside scared me. Friends of mine fell apart when they left the Corps. One senior NCO died. Drink and a bad marriage; another one finished up in prison for petty theft. I'd hate that."

"Damn you Tim Ronsard; excuses, excuses. You promised. Shame on you; you don't bloody well deserve me."

"I wasn't ready for life on the outside. And I'd not have promised if I'd known I was to be offered a commission."

Cliesh pressed her lips together. "Even without the commission, you'd not have left the Legion, would you?"

"You're right, that's the truth. The Corps; that's what I do. Out of the Legion, I'd be nothing."

"I wish I'd known. It might have made a difference."

I was glad she said that. I needed Cliesh, but still I couldn't see us together; not after what I'd told her.

We walked back. I was lost in reverie of my beloved. I remembered everything about her; how I'd clung to the details of her appearance, in the long periods of waiting in barracks at Calvi and the lulls between operations in Africa.

I knew what she wore at different times and places where we had been together. There was desperation in the way I hung on to memories of Cliesh's
personal things. To let go would have diminished me. A cooler man, not connected by a deep and enduring love, might have dismissed me as eccentric.
Lunatic even; I was obsessed by Cliesh. These traces of her were all I had. The
textures of her clothes, the times I removed her shoes and the kisses I laid on
the small birthmark on her right shoulder; bittersweet consolations.

"I'm sorry about the way I went on when you took me to Steve's," Cliesh
said. "I was ill. I'd had a hellish few months, and it just boiled over. I'm glad
you looked after me. It would have been awful for me if we hadn't met in the
airport."

"You're distant." But she wasn't distant. I'd just made another excuse. She
was near; I saw how she looked at me, and she knew my hot eyes. I wanted to
go to her. I wanted to be with her for the rest of my life, but I was scared that
she'd knock me back again.

"In the name of God, Tim! What are you afraid of? I asked Steve and Catherine what was up. I heard you when you said you were going back early. Were
you really going to go?"

"I'm not afraid," I lied, and Cliesh knew. "I thought about it. But, I wonder
now why I came at all. I was a damned sight happier soldiering. Leave just gets
in the road."

"Don't be ridiculous. You know that's rubbish. What did you say to Steve
about me?"

"I told him your name. I said I liked you."

Cliesh insisted on telling me about the Spaniard she'd lived with for almost
six years. After we parted she was low and not making much of a living playing
and giving piano lessons. This man owned a music shop she frequented. She
bought sheet music and the odd record from him. They got on well. He offered
her a job, to tide her over. Then she moved in.

"I didn't give up my apartment, and I didn't stay with him all the time. But,
I was with him often."

"Was he good to you?"

"Yes. He was a decent man."

"I'm glad."

I wasn't glad; I was so jealous; I could barely contain it. Her words hurt more
than the knife wound on my face. "Did you love him?"

"I was content with him."

I didn't want to hear any of this.

"He was fifteen years older. He died two years ago and left me the music shop. It was hard at first. I missed him. There was debt to pay off. That was hard too. I've just finished paying. I make a modest living running the shop, doing some teaching and the odd bit of playing. I like the music shop. Good people come into it. Is there anyone in your life?"

There was no one in my life. I went to the Legion brothels, and I picked up pretty German tourists when they were around. I said nothing about that. "No, there isn't anyone."

Spitefully I almost told her about the beautiful Somali prostitute. I'd met her in Djibouti and went to her often, for she was unlike the tarts in Algeria. With her fine features and gorgeous smile, it was easy to imagine her tender and sweet. When I lay with her, she seemed interested in me and her talk was warm. I cursed whomever or whatever gave her to whoring.

"Tell me about the way you live," Cliesh said.

"I live quietly. I have a simple room."

"Simple?"

"Well, a thin beige carpet covers the floor; plain walls covered in a lighter beige emulsion, the door, and window, painted light grey. There's a wardrobe and a chest of drawers for my kit, a straight back wooden chair at a good-sized desk where I work. Further back, an oak bookcase and a comfortable easy chair where I read and listen to music. I have a decent radio and a gramophone. And there's a bed, narrow and hard. I like it that way."

"What do you listen to; something I know?"

"You know the music I like."

"Yes: Spanish composers, Albeniz, Granados, the French Impressionists. I remember you liked Poulenc and Movements Perpetuel?"

I was happy she remembered so much about me.

"What else do you do?"

"I'm an officer and I'm responsible for my men."

"You told me about Algeria years ago. What's it been like since then?"

So I told her about life in Bou Sfer; the training and transformation of the regiment; the move to Corsica and the sketchiest outline of Chad and Djibouti.

"We could've been together," I said. "There was nothing wrong at Bou Sfer."
I waited but Cliesh said nothing. "I'm in for as long as the Legion'll have me:
Legio Patria Nostra. The Legion is my family, my home, my country."

"You believe that, don't you?"

"Yes. It's not an easy life, and it is not for most men, but it's better than living
in Westburn and working at Reid's foundry. I know what outsiders say about
the Corps and frankly, I don't care. I'm proud of what I am."

"I can see that."

"I'm not a mercenary. No one's in the Legion for the money. I'm a soldier
and it's an old tradition I follow."

"The wandering Scots knight?"

I laughed.

We'd walked halfway up University Avenue past the main building of the
University. The street was quiet, and I stopped at the main gate. A few benches
lay against the ornate cast iron railings. "Let's sit down," I said.

We sat close together. I leant forward, my elbows resting on my thighs,
hands joined loosely. "I do things I never dreamt of when I was an apprentice.
Sometimes it's hard, very hard, delivering my responsibilities, but I've managed
pretty well. I worry about my boys; about getting them back safely. If I'd stayed
in Reid's foundry, whatever I amounted to would have been much less."

I grinned and pressed her gloved hand. "Anyway, Cliesh, if I hadn't signed
that first contract, we'd probably never have met again."

I felt her warmth through the fine leather of her glove. Cliesh smiled a beautiful meld of regret and gladness. "I know. I've thought a lot about that these
past days."

"You should see me handing out the Christmas presents to my men."

"Tim, Tim. Why did you have to choose such a hard life?"

"Perhaps it chose me."

We walked on. A force drew us to Cliesh's house. It was empty now and
would be up for sale soon. All that remained was the Pleyel piano shrouded
in a dust sheet, the stool in front of the keyboard. The old Baluchi rug on the
floor beside the piano.

She tugged the dust cover from the piano. I helped her fold it. We propped the
lid open. She removed her hat and gloves and sat at the keyboard. I stood behind
her. Cliesh played the Evocacion and Triana from Iberia. Then, she played from

Movements Perpetual. It was so beautiful, just like the innocent days when we fell in love. I kissed her chestnut hair. She stood and came to me, and I held her.

"Sit on the piano stool, Tim."

Eight years of waiting. Sweetly, tenderly, we joined .

"Have you always loved me?" Cliesh said.

"Yes; always."

"What did you say about me in Calvi? Please, Tim."

"That I'd give anything to see you again. You're the love of my life. You knew, didn't you?"

"Yes. But, just to hear you say it. Oh, Tim, darling Tim, I'm so sorry."

"So am I."

"I missed you all these years. No one ever felt about me the way you do. No one ever loved me like you do."

Afterwards, we held each other, not ready to let go. We dressed and Cliesh was lovely, her face serene under the brim of her hat.

We locked the doors on the house. This time Cliesh hung on to me as we walked to Steve and Catherine's house along the tree-lined streets, beautiful in the brief twilight. The leaves from plane trees, chestnut, and oak drifted to the pavement. The air resonated with the calls of starlings swirling and turning above us.

When we got back to the house, Steve and Catherine had gone out. Catherine had left a note telling us to help ourselves and make an evening meal. They would be back late.

We sat together on the settee by the light of the fire in the Good Room. Cliesh had her legs tucked under her, shoes standing on the carpet. We sipped dry sherry. I held her and she cupped my hand on her breast, turning her head, kissing me.

"I love you, Tim."

She wriggled free, her feet searching for her shoes. "I'm going to make us supper. Something light."

"I'll help."

Cliesh touched my lips She let her fingers stay a moment. "I'll do it. We'll have it by the fire. I'll get you another sherry."

I liked this room: well proportioned, a deep cornice of ornate plaster, old comfortable furniture, and the soft wool carpet bordered by the polished wood

floor. I admired the well maintained Zimmerman upright piano. The fire flickered, lighting plaster roses and fruits. I placed more coal on the fire. It soon
caught, sending the light from soft yellow flames into the corners of the room,
brightening the walls. I noticed the small vase of late Icelandic poppies by the
window. I was happy; Cliesh was near. I heard her in the kitchen and wondered
what she would make. She came in with the tea things and laid them on the
low table near the settee.

"It's an Earl Grey."

She returned with two trays balanced on either hand and placed them beside
the tea tray. Steve and Catherine kept a full larder. On one tray lay a variety of
small sandwiches, with trimmed crusts and, there were sardines on toast. On
the other tray lay slices of Dundee cake and an assortment of shortbread.

The sherry, the tea, and the food took us back sixteen years to the Sunday
afternoons in Cliesh's rooms. She was beautiful, sitting in the firelight. We ate
quietly, happy to be together. I stood.

"I, ah ... Cliesh, I want to ask you something."

"Yes?"

I coughed behind my hand.

"Is there something wrong, Tim?"

"Well, ... before, when I was a Sergeant, in Paris, I had to go back to Algeria.
It was an odd life ... I mean, you know." I knew that we loved each other, but
I worried that she was still afraid of the Legion.

"Know what, Tim; what is it you want?"

Cliesh came forward to the edge of her seat, clasped her knees, pressing the
points of her shoes into the carpet. I had an attack of the jitters. I tried again.

"Well, now I'm a Captain. It's different, we could do something. I'd be away
now and then .... Maybe you'd not like Calvi or some of the places we go to."

"Different; do something; not like Calvi? What do you mean?"

"Sure, you know what I mean, Cliesh."

I looked at the fire searching the hot coals.

"Whatever it is, why don't you just tell me."

I coughed again.

"I can see it in your face, Tim Ronsard. You're going to tell me it's over that
you're going back. That's it isn't? After all, I'm almost forty. This afternoon
was all a sham."

She held my gaze. She was so fragile sitting, waiting for bad news. Cliesh thought I'd betray her again. I took her hands and drew her to her feet. She teetered, off balance, and I steadied her.

"It's all right Cliesh. Everything is all right."

"Is it, Tim?"

I held her, and she was stiff and withholding, turning her head away from me, shoulders rigid. Her eyes hurried round the room. Cliesh looked older, expecting I would strike her even lower than she had been when we met at the airport. Cliesh smiled ruefully, mirroring my sorrow for our wasted years. I loved her so much. I took hold of her by the shoulders. I wanted her to see my eyes.

"I couldn't leave the Legion and come to Paris. Please try to understand."

"I do understand; I'm not afraid now, Tim."

"I've been trying to ask; now, will you marry me?"

Cliesh's eyes filled with happiness and excitement. Her shoulders slackened, and she let her weight fall on her heels.

"Yes, Tim, I'll marry you."

Getting that question out drained me. We held each other for a long time. In the soft firelight Cliesh was young again.

"Oh Tim, I thought I'd lost you. This afternoon you made me so happy. I never expected to feel that way again. But I'm even happier now."

"I love this room. It's so like your rooms in Westburn."

"I'm glad you brought me here."

"Coming to your rooms meant everything to me. I lived from one Sunday to the next."

"I know. Sunday afternoons were wonderful. I loved when you came."

We touched each other giving in to love and pleasure.

"I'd like to marry soon, Tim. I don't want to wait until we go back to France."

"I wish we could get married tomorrow. I want to tell Dieter; I should let my Commanding Officer know."

We had much to discuss for I was halfway through my leave.

"Oh, not tonight. I know there's a lot to do but let's start tomorrow."

It was early; had not gone nine o'clock.

"Let's sit here by the fire. You've made me so happy. Lift me up again; take me higher?"

"Yes."

She blushed and laughed. "Help me with my shoes?"

Now that we had decided to get married, I wanted to see my father and tell him. And I wanted to see how he was coping after my mother's death.

I'd not thought about my parents in the excitement of meeting Cliesh again. Had my mother been alive, announcing our marriage would have been difficult. Of course we had our long running war over my hated apprenticeship in Reid's foundry. But most painful for me, was her rejection of Cliesh. It stung, when I remembered the venom in her voice: "That bloody music teacher."

My mother had never accepted how I felt about Cliesh. Our love was too powerful for her, and out of her reach; well beyond her powers of control. She felt Cliesh came between her and her son.

I went out with girls when I worked at Reid's foundry. A few kisses and an unconsummated fumble in some darkened tenement close. None of my dates blossomed into relationships. My mother would have been delighted had I fallen for a freckled, plump Catholic beauty; then she'd control us.

I was often miserable from missing Cliesh and my mother knew; she would erupt in fury. I knew she wanted me to admit that I longed for Cliesh, then she'd get the hook in and tug mercilessly. I remained silent. I would never admit to her that I loved Cliesh, but she knew, and she resented it. My father was glad to be away on the Irish boats; then, he had a day or two of peace. He gave up trying to stop the domestic guerrilla war.

My mother never accepted my joining the Legion, refusing my invitation to Calvi and and my father came alone.

"Good God, Tim, that's awful," Cliesh said. "No wonder you went away. I never realized how much she disliked me. There's nothing we can do now."

Cliesh frowned. "What's up?" I said.

"I'm so worried about meeting your father. Do you think he'll like me?"

"Don't worry. It'll be fine." I hoped I was right.

In spite of parting on bad terms, I was trying to make it up. The failure, and yes, the loss, was something I had to live with. I often remembered when she was Mum, and I'd welcomed all her love and given her all the unquestioning love of a young son.

I had always known that my father was disappointed that I was unhappy in engineering. But in that long war with my mother, he let me know in quiet ways that he knew and understood how I felt about Cliesh. He hated forcing me to give her up. He had no option. When my mother went too far, taunting me, he would stop her.

"Has your father been in France? Did he come to see you?"

I told Cliesh about my father's visit to Calvi.

"Did your father and Dieter get along?"

"Oh yes. They hit it off at once. Dieter invited him to the Sergeants' Mess and he had a great time. I left them to it. My CO made a point of welcoming him."

"Being Dieter's friend made him very happy."

"That meant a lot to you, didn't it?"

"Yes; an awful lot."

I called my father from Steve's and arranged to go down to the old town by the river the next day. We were due at the house late afternoon.

"I want to bring a friend from France with me. Is that OK, dad?"

"That's fine, son. Ye'll huv yer meal here and stay the night. I huv nae seen ye fur a good while."

We walked to the close and up the stairs, where I'd lived. What is it you notice about a place you once knew well? It wasn't the appearance of the tenement that brought everything back, though it helped; it was the smells. Homey, family smells of lives lived here. My nose wrinkled at the aromas of home.

Cliesh was worried. I had been vague about who I was bringing. I put the knuckles of my right hand to the door and rattled out the old familiar knock.

"Son. Ah'm gled tae see ye." He just about shook the hand off me.

"Hello, Dad."

The Old Man looked fit and well, but older in the year since I'd seen him. His aging vexed me; I wanted him to remain the same. "This is my friend from Paris, Isobel Clieshman."

They shook hands and my father took Cliesh all in. A flash of recognition lit his face. "Ah'm pleased tae meet ye, Miss."

"How do you do, Mr Ronsard? It's so good to meet you."

Cliesh's name had registered, but he never let on.

My father ushered us into my old room. The wallpaper was different and the paint smelt fresh. Two single beds had replaced my old double bed. The wardrobe and dressing table were unchanged. My small bookcase was still there and my books. Old friends. The chair where I'd sat to read was there too. So my mother had not eliminated my presence.

"Put yer things out and come on through to the living room." My father left us.

"Do you think everything is all right, Tim?" Cliesh said.

My father knew it was the music teacher from years ago and what she meant to me. I was worried; this might just be a tough meeting. But I wanted Cliesh to feel good. "Yes, it's fine. He likes you. I can tell." But I was far from sure.

The coal fire had gone from the living room, replaced by a new gas fire. The furniture had lasted well. I drew my hand across the top of an easy chair, enjoying the soft familiar texture. Everything was comfortable and clean, but the room lacked a woman's touch.

Over by the windows he had set the gate-leg oak table. It was covered by a white table cloth. Three places set, white napkins, folded as jockey boots; a nice touch. My mother had loved that table.

"Ah learned a few tricks on the Irish boats. Ah wish Ah could tell ye that Ah cooked it a' masel'. It's broth tae start an' Ah made that. Then, there's Game Pie. The cook on the boat made it, so it should be a'right. An' he made the dessert; it's apple tart. Ah hope ye enjoy it. Oh, aye, before I forget, there's wine. I asked the Chief Steward about it. Seein' yer livin' in France, Ah thought ye'd like some."

"Its lovely, Mr. Ronsard." Cliesh said. "You've gone to far too much trouble."

"Ach its no trouble, Miss. No trouble at all. Look Miss, ma name's, Jimmy. Ah'd like it fine if ye called me, Jimmy."

"Then you must call me, Isobel, Jimmy."

My father was as nervous as we were. I had an inkling that everything would be all right. He went to the sideboard and brought out a bottle of good burgundy and uncorked it. He put it on the table.

We sat by the fire. My father had poured drinks. Cliesh sipped a dry sherry. We took sips of Tulamore Dew chasing it with good swallows of pale ale. We made polite conversation. Cliesh sat demurely on the edge of her chair. My father glanced at her. Was he finding it hard to believe his soldier son was with this beautiful woman?

"Isobel, you're the music teacher; Tim used tae go tae yer rooms on a Sunday?"

"Yes, Jimmy."

"Will ye tell me how ye met again?"

We told him our story.

"An' ye met again at Glasgow Airport?"

"Yes we did," I said. "Are you not pleased about it?"

"Look, Isobel, Tim. Ah know how hard it was for ye both. Son, ye were sixteen. Isobel, whit age wur ye then?"

"I was twenty-four, Jimmy."

"Tim, Ye wir jist sixteen. Ye jist could nae be the gither."

I sighed in relief. "Dad, it's all right."

"Its no' a' right; the day Ah had tae tell ye no' tae see Isobel again; Ah hated it. It was wan o' the worst days o' ma life. Ah knew how ye felt. Ah had nae choice, surely ye know that. If there had been some other way, … if only ye'd been older, Tim. He wis jist too young, Isobel."

What my father said moved me. Cliesh was dewy eyed. She went over to my father.

"Mr. Ronsard, Jimmy. It was so kind of you to say that. It means so much to Tim, and a very great deal to me."

"That's a' right, Isobel. It's nae mair than the truth. It needed sayin'."

Cliesh took his hand and kissed him on the cheek. "Thank you, Jimmy."

My father turned a delicate shade of pink. He moved to the table and drew out a chair. "Isobel, you sit here. Tim, you sit facin' Isobel. Ah'll sit here."

My father served the meal himself, dismissing our offers of help. The food was exceptional and the Burgundy was soothing. I felt we belonged. Cliesh smiled.

"We've something to tell you, dad."

"Aye, Tim?"

"We're getting married next week."

"That's great news. This is a great day. Ah'm pleased right enough."

"So you'll come to the wedding, Jimmy?"

"Ah certainly will."

Then, Cliesh did something spontaneous and inspired. "I'd like to ask you a favour, Jimmy. It's about the wedding."

"Ask away, Isobel."

"My parents are dead. Steve O'Hara is Best Man and his wife, Catherine is the Matron of Honour." Cliesh rubbed her hands. "Well, you see, I wondered if you'd give me away. You wouldn't mind, would you?"

My father struggled to master his composure. "There's nuthin' that wid gie me mair pleasure, Isobel. This has tae be wan o' the best days o' ma life."

My father got up from the table and brought over three glasses and the bottle of Tullamore Dew. We all needed a bracing drink. Later, my father got up to clear the table.

"Come on, dad, sit down, and chat to Isobel. I'm good at doing the dishes. I learned some useful things in the Legion."

They moved on to the settee. My father liked Cliesh. Warmth spread out from the gas fire. I cleared the table.

"Isobel, Ah'll show ye some pictures o' his nibs."

I left them looking through the unsorted pictures kept in an old leather satchel. My father knew each one intimately; so did I. They were laughing, as I ran hot water into the sink. He'd show Cliesh the picture of me in the Apprentice School, just before I met her again. Then, the pictures when he was in the Royal Navy. The studio photograph, taken at the start of the War. My dad in the Petty Officer's uniform, his jaunty cap.

"Dover Patrol; mine sweeping through the Heligoland Bight", my father said. The places that mattered in nineteen forty.

One picture I loved. My father was about twenty-two, standing on the stern of the steamship, Athol Duke, a short oilskin covering his white engine room overalls, hair streaming in front of his face,looking at the camera. The mountainous sea behind the ship, whipped to a creamy fury by the gale, as she slid down the wall of water, into the trough between the waves.

I washed the dishes. This leave was to be a pleasant interlude. I was settling in for the last part of the long haul: another fourteen or fifteen years in the Legion. I hoped I might remain another twenty years in the hermetic world of the Second Regiment. I wasn't counting on another promotion. Regular officers, the graduates of St Cyr, were destined for the higher ranks.

There was plenty of interesting work for a Captain. In Kourou, French Guyana, The 3e Régiment Etranger D'Infanterie guarded the Space Centre and ran a school of jungle warfare. It was likely that Companies from 2 REP would train there. But what a difference a few days had made to my life. How wonderful it was to find Cliesh again; knowing that she loved me as much as I loved her. Cliesh enveloped me: her smell and taste; our touching; and the sheer joy of being with her.

I'd put in plenty of straight duty in Africa. Now, I thought about an appointment, where I'd seldom be away and we'd be together.

"Tim! Come an' see this picture," my father said.

I wiped down the sink and dresser. Cliesh passed me the picture. It was the official photograph of the choir at St Mary's, at the prize giving long ago. The boys dressed in white shirts with tightly knotted school ties and dark grey trousers. I was grinning at the camera. Cliesh was on the left of the choir wearing a white blouse, a long dark skirt of grey wool and black court shoes, her hair caught up by a wisp of pale red silk. A smile played on her lips. She was so young and beautiful.

"You remember that night," Cliesh said.

"How could I forget it?" I said.

My father reached into the leather satchel.

"There's another picture. Ye used tae keep it yer room. Ye left it here when ye joined the Foreign Legion. It belongs tae both o' ye now."

I went on holiday to Barcelona intent on pleasure. Had I known I wouldn't return home, I'd never have left that picture behind. The photographer had warmed up taking pictures before the official photograph of the choir. We'd finished singing I Met Her In The Garden Where The Praties Grow. The choir moving about the stage excited by the applause. A raw, fuzzy picture.

Cliesh stood by the piano and I'd moved closer to her. Long before we could have acknowledged it, the photographer caught how we felt. There was longing in her gaze and desire in her stance. Anyone could see that I worshipped Cliesh. Cliesh gave me the picture just before she left for the north east coast.

I heard my father in the kitchen. He went to the bedroom. I put my arm round Cliesh's shoulders.

"I never realized it was so obvious how we felt. Did you?" I said.

"No. I tried to hide it, and I pretended it was no more than fondness."

"My mother must have hated that picture."

"Perhaps your father wouldn't let her destroy it."

"I think you're right."

"I like your father."

"He's OK isn't he?"

"He's a lovely man. I'm going to make sure he comes often to Corsica."

My father came back to the living room. "A cup o' tea before we turn in?"

"We're fine, dad. Why don't I make up the bed settee? Cliesh can sleep in my old room."

"Ye'll dae no such thing. Dae ye think yer old dad is daft, eh? Ye've been kept apart long enough. Away yez go tae the bedroom. I put on the fire and heated the beds. Ye'll be fine in there."

For the second time that day, Cliesh kissed my father. "Thank you, Jimmy."

"Away wi ye, Isobel. Yer spoilin' me."

The lamps lit the bedroom with a soft glow. The single beds pushed together. Bumps where my father had placed two hot water bottles.

We settled down for the night. I felt strange lying beside Cliesh and my father through the wall, sleeping in his bedroom. Not that we lay in my old double bed; that might have been too much.

Cliesh fell in and out of sleep, as the house cooled down and the floorboards creaked, hinges protesting as a draught moved a door. The bed was warm, but the room was cold.

"Are you cold? " I said. Cliesh curled into me, and I put my right arm around her.

"Are you all right, Tim?"

"No, not really. I feel embarrassed. It's ridiculous." I thought about my tumescent youth when I slept in this place; and dreamt of Cliesh.

"Something strange is happening. I feel it, here in the room. What is it?"

"Its all right, Cliesh. It's nothing." But there was something. Cliesh fell into a deep sleep. I joined her in a tight, defensive curl. Cliesh shielded her small, beautiful breasts with my right hand.

"Between Heaven and Hell the ghosts wait, and they tell you what they want," Dieter, half cut had said, one night years ago in Algeria. The Church denied it; I believed it.

There was someone in the room with us, and I was afraid. I saw a faint, grey, wispy shape clad in white floating near the window. Then, it drifted to the foot of the bed. I wished for salt, to scatter before this shimmering wraith. Salt, that restless souls can't pass over.

But, this was no poltergeist bent on mayhem. The apparition looked down on me; I shook and Cliesh moaned, then her breath steadied, and she pressed closer.

The wraith was still and clear. I saw my mother wan, melancholy, a far remove from the warm and pretty mum of my childhood. My mother must have haunted my old bedroom waiting. God let her to reach out to me in supplication. She joined her hands asking for my prayers to end her suffering, and I knew she sought forgiveness for her hatred of Cliesh, and cutting me off during our long war. She had made all of us, my father, Cliesh, myself and herself unhappy for many years. Then, I knew that she was Mum and I loved her.

My mother's soul had left her body after death, but her spirit had yet to leave the Earth. I raised my hand to her. "It's all right, Mum. I'll pray for you." And I began reciting the rosary, the Joyful Mysteries praying for the repose of her troubled soul.

Anguished murmurs came from Cliesh, and breath rushed from her nose. She whimpered and pressed further into me.

My mother came to me resting above my head. I loved her now as I had loved her as a young son, and my prayers to the Virgin intensified, asking Her to heal my mother's soul, and to accept my love for Cliesh. The darkness brightened, tranquillity came, and my mother stayed with me a while. Then, left us in peace and understanding.

Pale, fingers of light crept into the room. Cliesh relaxed against me, her breathing deep and restful. I slid away quietly, and tucked the bedclothes round her. I pulled on my robe, and went to the living room, to stand by the window and watch the new day. I listened to the birds singing.

I was back in the bedroom. Cliesh stirred. "Where have you been? I missed you."

"I watched the sunrise."

"Tim, I slept well, but I feel drained. Was I dreaming?"

"Yes. You were dreaming. Everything's fine."

My father wouldn't rise so early this morning. We had time.

"Come back to bed." Cliesh raised the covers as I dropped my robe. The cool morning air chilled me. I crept in beside her and she warmed me for a while. Then we celebrated life and made love.

Chapter 7

Shining Hours

Cliesh, obsessed with fate wrecking our marriage, wanted Steve, my father and me out of the house on the eve of our wedding. "It's bad luck if we meet. Please Tim."

Catherine called me into her kitchen. "Does Isobel have any friends here; someone close?"

"No one; she's been away a long time. Why do you ask?"

"It's flattering of Isobel to invite me to be Matron of Honour, but we've just met. She's lonely, Tim, and she's anxious about the wedding. Isobel needs someone."

"La Divine would be perfect. She must have slipped Isobel's mind."

"Let's surprise Isobel. Why don't you invite her? La Divine can stay here. She can have your room." Catherine smothered a grin; now, I spent every night with Cliesh. "I shouldn't laugh; we're so glad you're together."

"La Divine's a great lady; she'll come."

I called La Divine that afternoon.

"La Divine Speaking; who is calling?"

"I'm Tim Ronsard, friend of Isobel Clieshman; you remember me?"

"What do you want? Isobel is not here. She's in Scotland."

"I know. Isobel's with me."

"What's wrong; is she all right?"

"She's fine. We're getting married. Will you come to Scotland? You can stay at my cousin's house."

"I'll be on the late morning flight tomorrow. Will you meet me? I've never been to Scotland, and I speak little English."

"Yes, of course. I'd like to pay for your ticket."

"I'll pay for my own ticket. Are you still in the Foreign Legion? Wear your uniform. It's been a long time since we met."

La Divine emerged with the stragglers from Customs and the baggage hall; eight years since our last meeting. Her walk, slower, but the stride confident. La Divine carried her years well. She put down her case.

"Well, Captain Ronsard, we meet again."

She extended both hands and I squeezed slender fingers through her gloves. "I'm so glad you've come."

A smile played at the corners of her mouth, as she appraised me. "You look well, Tim. Thanks for inviting me." She drew me on tilting her head, offering her right cheek. I kissed her and catching her fragrance, kissed her again on the left cheek.

I picked up her case, and she took my right arm, as we walked to the café. People stared, an officer of the Foreign Legion, and a beautiful older women. La Divine liked the attention. We had coffee; thin stuff. La Divine wrinkled her nose. "How is Isobel?"

"Very well. She'll be so happy to see you."

La Divine grabbed my hand. "How did you meet again?" I told her what happened at the airport.

"I'm glad. Your letter made Isobel so unhappy for such a long time. Why did you write it? She waited for you in Paris."

"I'm a soldier; my CO offered a commission. We could've had a life."

"I know. But she was afraid. It almost destroyed her when you didn't come. Going to a Legion base frightened her. Often she'd wished she'd gone to Algeria."

"How do you think I felt?"

"You're right for Isobel and God knows she's so right for you. I prayed you'd be together. I always liked you, Tim."

When La Divine and Cliesh became friends there was no man in her life. "I thought perhaps she was Sapphic; you understand?"

"Yes."

"She told me that there was someone younger in Scotland she'd cared for. It broke her heart to to leave him, knowing that she might never see him again; it upset her to talk about it."

"It was me, and I missed her. I was sixteen when she went away."

La Divine caressed my hand and shook her head. Her eyes shone. "Isobel loves you. When you turned up with Dieter, she told me all about you when she came in to arrange dinner. Oh Tim, you made Isobel a young girl again. I'd never seen her so happy."

"Thanks for telling me that."

"I thought you'd want to know."

"How have you been, La Divine? You look well."

"Up and down, Tim. Three years ago I was quite ill. When my husband died I sank low."

La Divine couldn't cope with widowhood. "I didn't look after myself." She looked into her empty coffee cup. "I drank far too much, and I ate cigarettes. I hardly touched food. I refused to listen to anyone. It went on for more than a year, and I neglected my business."

Many customers remained loyal and Cliesh was there, a witness. The troubles broke when La Divine collapsed behind the bar of Le Coq d'Or. "My heart beat was irregular; my fingers turned blue. My lungs filled up; I was drowning, and felt like death. I had bronchitis, and it was hellish; disgusting, the filth I coughed up. I wasn't myself for three months. I had plenty of time for remorse."

La Divine spent ten days in hospital. A course of antibiotics set her on her feet to convalesce. "My daughter moved to Strasbourg with her husband's work and with three children, said that she couldn't come to Paris to look after me.

"Isobel got me through it. She stopped me from selling my business. Somehow, she kept my café-bar going. She lost a few pupils and some engagements taking care of me. Isobel's more than family to me. Without her, I'd have lost everything, given up and died."

It was a gift to hear that the woman you love is greater than you could ever imagine. I wanted to bring La Divine to her. "Come on, La Divine, let's go."

"Yes, let's do that, I'm dying to see Isobel."

Cliesh opened the door, blinked eyes wide. "La Divine! I meant to phone. I'm so sorry, but its been so confusing and exciting since I arrived." They embraced. "Its all right Isobel, I understand. Tim made sure I'd be here. I'm so happy for both of you."

Catherine took La Divine through to the Good Room. Cliesh held me back.

"Oh, Tim, such a lovely thing bringing La Divine over for our wedding. Thank you." Her eyes glistened.

"You're crying."

"No I'm not. I'm just so happy." I gave her a hug. "Your father's here with a wedding present," she said. "Let's go in."

We went to the table where my father stood. "It's lovely present," Cliesh said, and we admired a gorgeous boxed set of stainless steel cutlery.

"La Divine, my father, James Ronsard. Dad, La Divine, a good friend from Paris."

"How d'ye do?" My father said, shaking hands.

La Divine's eyes lingered on my father, smart in wool jacket, and slacks, beige and brown checked shirt, solid maroon wool tie. "I'm well, Mr Ronsard. Such a pleasure to meet you." Her English surprised me.

"May I?" He said, and helped La Divine remove her raincoat. My Old Man dragged his eyes from La Divine's pale complexion and prominent cheekbones, the close cut black hair peppered with grey, the red, blue, and green paisley patterned silk scarf brightening her throat, to the cream blouse, and tan skirt that drew attention to her willowy figure; a frank gaze to her shapely legs.

I helped Cliesh with the tea things in the kitchen. "My Dad has clicked with La Divine."

"Definitely." Cliesh smiled mischievously.

Later, my father put down his cup and saucer. "I'm off." La Divine got up and came with us to see my father out. "Your gloves, Mr Ronsard," La Divine said, picking them up from the hall table, laid there while he put on his coat. She gazed at him, smiled and pressed the gloves into his hand.

"I'll see you all soon," he said, "the night before the wedding."

"Your father, Tim; such nice man," La Divine said, her face a delightful pink.

After dinner, we sat round the fire in the Good Room. "Everything ready for the wedding?" I said. "Almost," Cliesh said. "That's right," Catherine said. Steve and I exchanged a glance. La Divine, clearly far away stared into the fire.

"La Divine, I'd like you to be a Matron of Honour," Cliesh said.

"Pardon, Isobel, what did you say?" La Divine came back from reverie. Perhaps she was thinking of my father.

"I'd like you to be Matron of Honour; along with Catherine"

"Yes; it would be good," Catherine said.

Steve and I exchanged an approving nod.

La Divine smiled. "But surely I am much too old?"

"Oh please say yes," Cliesh said.

"All right, yes. I'm touched and so happy that you asked."

We stood in front of the small oak table, a plain white linen runner down the centre, a small lectern to one side, holding an open King James Bible. I fingered the snake clasp of my ornate black belt and brushed imaginary dust from my shoulder boards. Steve tugged at the hem of his bum freezer, lowering his eyes to inspect his gleaming Sam Browne belt. I glanced at the musicians on my left. The pianist a music student and member of the Regimental band, the violinist, a young woman, a student, at the same institute. Steve had found them.

Our wedding was a small affair, but the day itself had a delightful epiphany, the work of Cliesh, and my father.

"Jake, Fergie," I said. "It's great that you're here."

We shook hands, and I introduced Steve. "Tim, away you and Steve tae the front and wait on yer bride. We'll see ye soon," Jake said.

Any wedding ceremony would have suited me for I had no church now, though I paid lip service to the words of Legion Chaplains. Cliesh could not stand the thought of a cold bureaucratic civil wedding, and wanted a religious ceremony, a sacred wedding with God's blessing. But, she'd been away for so long, and was reluctant to approach her family's parish church.

Steve rescued us, introducing us to the Battalion Chaplain, Matthew Thompson, a tolerant Presbyterian, and soldier, who understood how I had lived in the years apart from Cliesh. He agreed to marry us in Steve and Catherine's house.

For the wedding Cliesh chose from Granados' Sentimental Waltzes. When we signed the marriage documents, the musicians played a selection from Granados' Love Letters.

I loved the music when Cliesh played it on Steve and Catherine's piano. Perfect: Granados, gentle, loving man, the Spanish Chopin. Love Letters was an engagement present for his wife, Amparo. They had six children.

Sentimental Waltz, Number Six and I turned to see my father and Cliesh coming towards the front, her left hand resting on my father's right arm. He was smart in a dark gray suit and white shirt, a small pink rose in his lapel; the bright, carefully knotted tie of gay red and green stripes - Legion Colours - complimented Cliesh.

She was lovely in a champagne dress with short sleeves, her hair garlanded with Lily of the Valley. A fine veil shielded her face. She carried a small posy of ivory orchids, and so did Catherine and La Divine. They walked behind Cliesh, garlanded, Catherine in an ice blue dress with short sleeves, and La Divine wearing a dress of Wedgewood Blue with tight bracelet sleeves.

The Chaplain, turned out in regulation khaki jacket, parachutist's wings on the right sleeve, three finger widths below the shoulder seam, Sam Browne and McKenzie tartan trews, stepped forward to meet them and brought Cliesh to my left side. Steve joined Catherine to our rear.

"We're all relatives or friends of Isobel and Tim, and have an inkling of their story; prejudice and circumstances kept them apart for many years. That is a matter of regret, and we should rejoice now that they are together. They desire to affirm their love in front of God and you, their witnesses." He glanced at the King James. "And I will betroth thee unto me for ever; yea I will betroth thee unto me in righteousness and lovingkindness, and in mercies."

Cliesh chose our words. She turned to me, eyes shining. "My beloved is mine, and I am his. I found him whom my soul loveth: I held him, and would not let him go"

I saw only Cliesh. "You are all fair, my love. You have enchanted my heart with your eyes. Your love is sweeter than wine."

We wanted no words of obedience in our vows: giving ourselves to each other, in honour, in cherishing, and loving faithfully; gracious words for a good marriage, Matthew Thompson said.

Steve had the Battalion Chef make a cold buffet; the centerpiece, a splendid poached salmon. The Chef served us. We sat around a well laid dining table, and drank wine, the musicians played Gershwin, the first time I heard his music played by a duo. A delightful Rhapsody in Blue, and we yielded to the tender Embraceable You. I sought Cliesh's hand under the tablecloth and found her slender, stockinged leg. She took my hand, and continuing her conversation across the table with La Divine, squeezed my fingers.

I was happy when we caught up on Jake and Fergie's lives. "Nice service," Fergie said. He puckered his lips at the dry sparkling wine.

"Lovely," Ute said.

"Right enough, Missus Ronsard, it wis good words. An' the tunes, we liked them fine," Jake said.

"Very nice," Edie, Jake's wife said.

A sly grin tugged at Jake's lips. "The Reverend's got the right behind fur that bum freezer jaiket." We laughed.

Jake and Fergie looked well: hard work and active middle years kept them fit. Patches of gray at Jake's temples and Fergie's retreating hairline measured time passing.

Fergie wore the black eye patch. Our wedding was the occasion when he might have put up with a glass eye in the painful, empty socket. "Ah tried wan o' they new movin' gless eyes. Nae use; it hurt too much."

Reid's foundry lurched from one crisis to the next, struggling to manage the order book, dying a slow death from scant investment, and the onslaught of competition in the Far East. It was an open question how long the place would remain open. I cared nothing for the remaining hard-core of old hands, or the successors. I regretted that many of Reid's workers would finish up without work and with little chance of decent new jobs. But I had no sorrow for Reid's; it was a grim place.

"Ah got oot a few years ago," Jake said. "Ah wis offered the Foreman Engineer's job at the Dry Dock; ye know Tim, Siberia."

"I remember."

"Me as well, Tim," Fergie said. "Jake offered me the Charge Hand's job at Siberia, an' Ah' took it. It's no' a bad livin'."

The dry dock had a bright future in ship and engine repairs. I was glad Jake and Fergie had found a secure niche.

"Are you glad they came?" Cliesh said.

"Yes. How did you find them?"

"Your father told me about them the night we stayed with him."

"They helped me see through Reid's and scare up the courage to get out of the place."

The company withdrew from the table to the Good Room. We drank more wine. The musicians played love songs.

La Divine, striking in her blue dress the tight sleeves flattering her slender hands, and the hem showing off her rather good legs, chatted up my father. I joined them. "Good day, then?" I said to my father, saying it again in French, to La Divine. La Divine, smiling prettily, impressing my father, turned, "Look, Isobel's waving to you."

I turned and saw Cliesh talking to Jake and Fergie. She had little need of me. I looked round; La Divine and my father had moved closer together. La Divine grinned slyly, pleased that I was out of the way.

We came to the Old Hotel in Westburn for our wedding night. Driving from Westburn to Glasgow and would go back the next day. There was no time for a proper Honeymoon, with the Armistice Day Ceremony and our imminent return to France and Corsica.

There had never been anything conventional about our love. I'd have been happy to remain at Steve and Catherine's, for the wedding party ran full tilt.

Cliesh wanted to go away, even if only for one night. Everyone thought it a wonderful idea. We chose to return to Westburn. Sure, it was, in many ways, a grim town and a source of unhappiness for Cliesh and me. But, it was where I grew up; and it was where we met and fell in love.

We arrived at the Old Hotel in time for a supper of plain omelette and salad. We liked the intimate mood of the oak panelled dining room. I'd often passed the Old Hotel on my way to Cliesh's rooms.

"This is the first time I've been here, Tim. I used to walk past it every day."

"Of course you would, Cliesh. Have you had enough to eat?"

"Oh, yes. I'm tired after the excitement today."

She clasped my hand. "Let's go up to our room."

The room was well maintained, retaining its early Victorian features: panelled doors, an ornate cornice adorned with duck eggs. A partnership of architects and builders had worked in Westburn; Cliesh's rooms had similar features.

"I like this room; it reminds me of your rooms. I loved coming to see you; the rugs, the furniture, the Petrof, the vases of poppies."

We sat on the sofa set in the bay window. Cliesh perched awkwardly, on the edge of her seat. She had removed the navy bolero jacket. She was lovely in the white blouse, straight navy skirt, and matching shoes.

"Are you all right?"

Cliesh and I had been lovers again since we had made it up. There were few intimacies we had not shared. We had indulged each other, given in to our carnal fantasies and desires.

"Yes, but suddenly, I'm a married woman."

I held her. "Tell me, what's wrong?"

"There are so many memories. I keep seeing you coming to my rooms on Sunday afternoons. The first Sunday when you came in your best suit, the sober tie, clutching the little parcel of Terry's chocolates."

"Was I awkward?"

"Oh, just a little. You were such a sweet boy. I always liked you; and then we fell in love."

"You made me so happy."

"I never thought that we'd be here now, like this."

"We belong to each other."

Tomorrow, we'd walk to Cliesh's old rooms. We'd look at St. Mary's School. I'd take her to the garden beside the Cross of Lorraine, the memorial to the sailors of the Free French Navy, the place where I'd read her letter of farewell. We'd look across the river to the mountains. But for now I held Cliesh closer, her head on my shoulder.

Late afternoon the next day we got back to Steve and Catherine's flat. Cliesh brought in a note Catherine had left in the kitchen "Your father and La Divine went to Edinburgh. They're coming back late tomorrow morning."

That evening, I sat with Cliesh in our bedroom. "Catherine told me more about it," Cliesh said.

"Steve mentioned it. Was she annoyed?"

"No, not at all. She said they hit it off rather well."

"Steve was matter of fact. He isn't angry. He laughed and said, La Divine had the hots for my Old Man and got off with him."

For Steve, it was a horny encounter between two older players. Catherine saw the nascent tenderness. "It was so sweet. La Divine's striking and a bit of a handful; your father quiet and correct. The eyes, the way they sat together, so full of yearning."

I'd worried about my dad facing old age. His widowhood must have been hard to bear, for in spite of the difficulties with my mother over me, he was true to her. He never complained: not in his letters or when he met Dieter and me, but there was no joy in his life.

His suddenly finding love with a radiant La Divine was unexpected. My father and La Divine deserved some loving.

"What makes us love, Tim?" Cliesh said.

"The first time I saw you. I got carried away."

"Oh, stop it, Tim! This is serious."

"I'm serious. I'm trying to understand what happened between my father and La Divine."

"Her name is Hugette. That's what she'd ask your father to call her."

"Is that what you called her?"

"No. I always call her La Divine. Anyway, I'm not her lover."

"How do you feel about it?"

"I'm surprised, but I'm pleased too."

Cliesh laughed slyly. "Your father's a fine man and La Divine's good looking, and she's sexy; but, she's been so ill and she was lonely."

But now my dad would look well, having fallen in love with a blooming, loving La Divine. I was glad for them.

"Are you unhappy about it?" Cliesh said.

"No, I'm not. What made you ask that?"

"You're frowning and I hate it when you frown. You look so grim."

"I'm trying to understand it, that's all. Cliesh, I'm pleased about it. What did my father say to La Divine; what did she say to him?"

"Well, she has a little English; more than she lets on."

I remembered Marcel, a Free French sailor my father brought to the house. "My father has some French, picked up at sea. He doesn't say much about it."

"Your father was awkward at breakfast. La Divine was breezy and contented. She fussed over him, pressing his hand and calling him James, pronouncing James with a soft J. Your father called La Divine, Hugette, stressing the G. That's what Catherine said."

I tried not to, but I burst out laughing. So did Cliesh. "What did he say?"

"He thanked Steve and Catherine for putting him up. They didn't know he was in the house with La Divine until he appeared at breakfast, face crimson."

I couldn't stop laughing.

"Behave yourself, Tim. They'll be here tomorrow."

My father was awkward when he came in. I'm sure he felt he had sinned. La Divine was unaffected by any notion of wickedness. Her looks and smiles said that she and my father had unexpected joy in the last two days. We were glad for them.

"Fancy a walk son? Ah need tae stretch ma legs."

We strolled for a couple of hundred yards. "How was Edinburgh?"

"Good. Tim, son … Ah…"

"It's OK Dad. Everything's fine. There's no need to explain."

"Ah mean, you and Isobel, yer no' mad at La Divine an' me? Ah thought Steve might be ragin' at me stayin' the night wi' Hugette."

"It's Hugette, Dad, with a soft G. We're all happy about it."

Later that evening, just before bed, La Divine came into the kitchen where Cliesh and I prepared a light supper. "Tim, you meant what you said to your father, didn't you?"

"Of course I did. It was for both of us and for Steve and Catherine too."

La Divine smiled. "What happened with your father; so unexpected … he's a sweet man."

The Armistice Day Parade was over, and the shouts and laughter of soldiers floated up the stairwell from the main entrance.

Had I stayed in Scotland working in Reid's foundry I'd never have set foot in the Officers Mess. I'd be on the ground floor with the soldiers and their women; perhaps I'd have joined the Sergeants and their wives. Now I was a guest on the upper floor with the officers and their ladies.

I'd dressed in Number One Winter Dress uniform, white kid gloves, green tie, and green waistcoat showing in the V of the uniform jacket. I'd polished my shoes to perfection. The gold lanyard arranged on my left shoulder. On my left breast, I'd fastened medal ribbons; and on my right, the coveted silver wings of the parachutist. I wore a black leather belt with gilt medallion and snake clasp, the apple green beret with the winged hand and dagger badge on the right side. I left badges of service and shoulder boards displaying rank in place. Anyone looking would know what I was and where I belonged.

I left the beret on a shelf above the Sam Brownes and Glengarries, and laid the folded white gloves on top. I followed the sound of laughter and tinkling glasses to the Officers Mess where a white-coated orderly presented a silver tray laden with a selection of drinks. I chose a glass of dry sherry and withdrew to a quiet corner. An impressive room: the arrangement of brilliant polished silver serving dishes and a gleaming pyramid of crystal glasses displayed on tables draped in starched white linen. Mess servants waited to serve the buffet lunch.

Pale yellow flames lighted the room, the smokers drawing on cigarettes and exhaling pleasurably. Blue smoke dispersed along the low ceiling. Captains and Majors dressed in khaki bum freezers and McKenzie tartan trews. An Aide de Camp fussed over a Brigadier. A Captain RN accompanied by an aging but still beautiful woman drank steadily. I overheard a Lt. Colonel introduce the socialist Provost of Glasgow, to the Brigadier. They shook hands; thin smiles failed to disguise mutual loathing.

I watched Cliesh surrounded by group of eager subalterns. Her well-cut dress of beige wool was just right for an Armistice Day, and the beautiful apple green silk scarf round her neck, a bright note among the khaki and subdued regimental tartan. I fingered my wedding ring and couldn't take my eyes off her. The dash of freckles on a pale complexion, the well cut chestnut hair, the refined Classical nose suggesting reserves of character.

The subalterns loosened their knot round Cliesh and I had to look at her slender legs made longer by her fine brown, leather shoes with elegant heels. She looked about twenty-five. I couldn't have denied her anything.

Steve came over and steered me in Cliesh's direction. "Right, Tim, the Colonel wants to be introduced."

We stood in front of Lt Col Robertson. A compact man of middle height, a thick red moustache on his upper lip. He was immaculate in khaki bum freezer and tartan trews; his heavy regulation brogue shoes reflected the light. The Butchers Apron was among his medal ribbons; he'd served in the Korean War. The ribbon of the Croix de Guerre, awarded while serving alongside 1REP during the Suez campaign.

"Good afternoon Captain Ronsard. Welcome to the Battalion."

I introduced Cliesh. I thanked him for sending his car to the airport. A mess waiter appeared with a silver tray of drinks. Cliesh had a glass of dry white wine. I had a dry sherry and the Colonel, a gin and tonic.

Lt Colonel Robertson was a man of few words. After a few more pleasantries and saying what we thought of the Battalion's turn out at the parade, he asked about my service, nodded, glancing at my Medaille Militaire. "Awarded when you served in the ranks?"

"Yes, Sir. I was a legionnaire." I won the medal when the Fell killed Aristidies. Had he lived he might have stayed on and won a commission. That would have been something.

"Forgive me talking shop, Madame Ronsard, but it's not everyday I meet a Captain in the Legion." Cliesh smiled and inclined her head. He steered us to the other side of the Mess. "You must meet my wife and my son. He's a Lieutenant with the Regular Battalion."

"The Colonel likes you," Cliesh said. "You've made a good impression."

We relaxed after lunch. Friends gathered to talk and drink, breaking up and moving on.

I separated from Cliesh and saw her with Steve, Catherine, and some young officers enjoying herself. I stood in a quiet corner and caught sight of James Malone speaking to a stout Major. Malone leant forward peering in to the crowd of guests; he didn't see me. The ramrod straight back curved now, dragged forward by his portly torso. James Malone stooped as he walked; his hair, thinner, grey with traces of black, the hairline shooting back from his forehead. He paced through the mess, hands clasped behind his back, a sober figure in a dark grey suit and regimental tie. What brought him to the barracks on Armistice Sunday?

James Malone spotted Cliesh. "Ah, it is Miss Clieshman, is it not?" He extended his right hand to Cliesh. "James Malone, from St. Mary's. You do remember me?"

"Hello, Mr. Malone. Of course, I remember you. How do you do?" They shook hands. "Why are you here?"

"Ah well, I'm one of the old buffers they invite now and then. Some nonsense about a medal. I served in the Regiment at the end of the Great War. I joined the reserves when I attended the University. Later on, I was a Captain."

"We talked about that once, Mr. Malone."

"Yes, yes. You are here alone, Miss Clieshman?"

"No; and you, Mr. Malone?"

"Yes."

Cliesh sipped her dry white wine and James Malone had a good swallow from his glass of whisky and water. "I'm a widower. I visit my son and daughter from time to time."

"Oh Mr Malone, I'm so sorry for your loss. I've lived in Paris for many years, teaching music and playing the piano."

"That's a pity. You're an inspiring teacher, Miss Clieshman. You belong in a school. I remember how well you worked with the boys in Fourth Year."

"Thank you, Mr Malone. I wonder how they turned out. What about that boy, the one who looked after the School Library, you mentioned his name to me. He sang in the choir at the prize giving. What was it Tim, something."

"Tim Ronsard. Married, no doubt and stuck in some miserable job. We shall never know."

'Would you like to meet him and find out?'"

"I would indeed, Miss Clieshman, but surely he cannot be here."

Cliesh waved. "Tim, there's someone who wants to meet you."

My uniform caught his eye. James Malone's bushy eyebrows shot up. He frowned when he saw my scar. James Malone cupped my hand. "Good God! Tim Ronsard; and you're a Captain in the Foreign Legion. This is a most welcome surprise."

It was obvious that Cliesh and I were together. James Malone tried to work out our relationship. "Did you meet again here in the Mess?"

"No, we're both guests of Captain O'Hara, the Adjudant. He's Tim's cousin."

"Ah, you must tell me, Miss Clieshman, what is your connection?"

Cliesh enjoyed teasing James Malone, but I saw that she wanted to tell him about us. I smiled. "Well, Mr. Malone, I'm now Madame Ronsard, but I'd like it if you called me Isobel."

"Only if you agree to address me as James, But for heaven's sake, you are married! When?"

"A few days ago."

James Malone caught the eye of a waiter. "We must drink to your marriage."

The last part of the afternoon flew as we chatted. We wanted to know about the rest of James Malone's teaching career. "I hung on as Depute Headmaster. I waited too long. I declined the offer of a headship of a primary school. It was not what I wanted."

James Malone shrugged his shoulders, and smiled. "I stayed on at St Mary's because I thought I made a difference. Terribly conceited of me; but there you are. My consolation prize, Acting Headmaster for most of the two years before I retired. God alone knows if I made any difference to the school."

We felt James Malone's regret and disappointment. What I liked about him was that he put his ideals before his ambitions; a characteristic of the best officers, who think first of their men. James Malone had thought first about his pupils and the members of staff who cared too. I admired his courage and devotion to service; so would Cliesh.

"Mr. Malone, James. You made a difference," Cliesh said. "The forward looking way you permitted me to teach music. I never had the same scope in the school I went to after St Mary's."

I had to say something. "You inspired me, Mr. Malone; widened my horizons and gave me the confidence to get out of Westburn."

"Thank you Isobel, Tim; most kind of you to say so. However, that's enough of me. I'd like to hear your story."

I told him about my career in the Legion, but James Malone wanted to hear about our marriage.

"Isobel, the few months before you left St Mary's you were happy, radiant, much as you are today. I hoped that you would stay with us. I was sorry to lose you." Cliesh shrugged. "Were you together then?"

"We met from time to time," I said.

We sipped our drinks. Radiant, James Malone said; that was wonderful. I wanted him to leave it there.

"Then you left, Isobel. That must have been hard for both of you."

"Isobel had to go north and you know why."

"How would I know that, Tim?"

I told him that I'd hidden in the kitchen cleaning up after the fight and heard what he said to Cliesh that day in the Library. "I was just a school boy, but I heard your warning."

Cliesh looked into space. James Malone blushed. "I was well out of St Mary's when Isobel went away and it was grim: sick of Scotland, working in Reid's foundry, so I became a soldier. We were apart a long time but we met again and now we're married."

"What I said was not meant as a threat, Tim: I like Isobel; and I like you; though you may not have known it then. I wanted to keep you both from a scandal. There were some nasty people in the school who would have persecuted you and wrecked Isobel's career."

"Its all right, Tim," Cliesh said.

"I'm not going to apologize. You were young, not able to see far enough ahead. The important thing is you're together, and I'm glad."

We grabbed drinks from a passing waiter, and calmed down.

"You must come and have lunch. This afternoon is almost over, and I've only heard a fraction of your story. I live in a rambling apartment. It's much too big for me now, but I like it; I think you would too. What do you say?"

The Armistice Day reception must have taken him back to his days as a soldier, and we reminded him of the time when he ran St. Mary's School. Retirement had stripped James Malone of authority, but he coped with it, and with the loss of his wife; he had bags of guts.

"It would be good if you would accept. I have a fine piano, an upright Petrof with a beautiful tone. My wife played rather well and I can knock out a tune. I keep it in good condition; in memory of her."

"Yes, of course, we'll come." Cliesh said. "Thank you so much."

"Perhaps you might play for us, Isobel."

"I have a Petrof; I'd love to play."

James Malone smiled, rubbing his hands. "You have fought the good fight and have finished the race. You've kept the faith; you have the crown of righteousness. You've travelled far, Isobel, and you, Captain."

"That's so kind of you, James," Cliesh said.

"Oh, just a little adaptation from Timothy, 4: 7-8; no more than the truth."

We travelled to Paris with La Divine, staying one night to pick up some personal things for Cliesh. She would return to wind up her affairs once settled in Calvi.

La Divine was serene. My father had had a powerful effect: how little I knew about him. She sat between us on the plane. La Divine wriggled in her seat; she grasped both our hands resting on the armrests.

"Your father asked if he could come to Paris in the New Year and meet me. He has leave."

"That's wonderful," I said.

"I am so glad," Cliesh said.

La Divine and my father must have felt the muddle akin to my youthful, mercurial, emotional state when I fell in love with Cliesh. But we'd had time in our favour. They had less time for the emotional, and passionate maneouvres of new, young love.

I had no idea where La Divine and my father might end up; they would not hope for too much. We were happy that they'd found each other. Perhaps they would go on.

It had been an amazing leave, and I was so happy returning to Calvi with Cliesh.

Dieter, accompanied by two men from my Company dressed in brown winter uniforms met us at Calvi Airport. They came to attention and saluted; I returned it. I shook hands with Dieter.

"Christ, it's good to see you, Tim."

Dieter grasped Cliesh's hands. "Isobel; it's been far too long. What wonderful news that you're married. I wish I could've been with you but duty called."

He turned to the legionnaires. "They volunteered, Tim. I had many to choose from, said they wanted to help with the luggage."

Curiosity drove them to volunteer; the first and closest look at the Captain, the confirmed bachelor, bringing his new wife to the Regiment. No doubt, a ripple of surprise was discernable among my friends and acquaintances at the news of the marriage.

Cliesh had dressed discreetly, mindful that first impressions are so important. Her make up was understated. She wore a plain, straight navy wool coat, a tasteful, matching hat with an attractive brim framing her face, the navy court shoes and the length of the coat showed off her wonderful legs. I adored her modest conceit.

I wondered what Cliesh made of the two-shaven heads from my Company standing back from Dieter, waiting, as we exchanged greetings. Below the rim of the Kepi Blancs, the backs of their close-cropped skulls shone in the artificial light of the baggage hall. I introduced my two men to Cliesh.

"Legionnaires, Pholmann, and Sante, Madame Isobel Ronsard."

The men saluted and Cliesh stepped forward extending her right hand. They were perplexed. Officer's wives more often pay scant attention to common soldiers. I gave a brief nod of assent. They shook her hand, bowing from the shoulders.

"I'm pleased to meet you, how do you do?" Cliesh murmured.

Pholmann and Sante would report all of this back to the barracks; Cliesh's good manners would go down well.

I was due to report to Camp Raffaelli in two days. Cliesh worried about meeting the officers and my Commanding Officer. The arrangements for the civil marriage, a requirement for all citizens, finding married quarters - all that could wait and we would worry about it in a day or two. After that, we had to think about moving Cliesh's belongings from Paris. I'd find a way for Cliesh to continue with playing and teaching piano. I owned nothing beyond my personal belongings, and lived simply, in Spartan quarters.

I knew by the road Dieter took that we'd be staying in the Cafe-Bar Tizi. Pholmann and Sante were ahead of us in a covered jeep, carrying our luggage. I would have chosen a hotel but Dieter arranged accommodation. He anticipated my worry that a room in the Tizi was unsuitable for Cliesh, glancing in the rear mirror, catching her eye.

"You'll be fine." Dieter turned to Cliesh. "Madame Ouzou, the owner of the Tizi insisted you stay when I told her you two were married."

Pholmann and Sante deposited our luggage in the room, and, after a brief, formal leave taking, they were gone. Then, I introduced Cliesh to Madame Ouzou and after a few pleasantries; she gave us the key to our room.

"What's on?" I said.

"Wait and see; something good, "Dieter said. "Wear your best uniform, OK? You'll be surprised. You're respected, Tim and you're one of us."

I need not have worried. Somehow, Dieter arranged for the decoration of the room with pleasing results. Cliesh liked the plain white walls and the white wool rug on the centre of the mauve tiled floor. The neat double bed with the patterned white counter pane beckoned. I liked the rustic furniture; it was unchanged: two comfortable chairs, wardrobe and dressing table adorned with a vase of beautiful Autumn Crocus with delicate yellow petals. It was warm and I knew the simple bathroom would be spotless.

Cliesh fretted a little about having nothing suitable to wear, but chose a fine, wool dress of red wine colour. She hung it on the front of the wardrobe. I had another, better uniform in my bag and prepared it for the evening.

"Shall we go out and I'll show you Calvi?"

"There'll be many days for that. I'd like to stay here where it's cosy and warm."

"Is the room OK?"

"It's lovely, Tim."

It had just passed two o'clock and there was time to kill. I knew she'd say, "Help me with my shoes, Tim."

Helping Cliesh with her shoes: our sacred ritual, a prelude to our making love. I removed her shoes, as I had many times. I never tired of helping her undress.

My beloved Cliesh was serene once more. Was it our lovemaking, our being in love, and loving so ardently after so many years apart that made her so? She lay against me, curving into my body. That afternoon we moved between tenderness and carnal desire. I dwelt on the hardness of her small tits and I wanted to crush them as the nipples rose under my careful, stroking fingers.

In the light of a late Corsican afternoon, pale winter sunlight shone through the drawn curtains of our room, I saw her cheekbones anew, in softer profile: the merest suggestion, that she had put on a fraction of weight and I had not noticed. She was half asleep, languid after making love. I touched her tits again and they were no longer the small hard tits of moments ago, but delicate, soft breasts, quite lovely to hold. Cliesh sighed with pleasure and I loved that sound of her. She turned facing me and I took in her warm breath and sleep smells. Carnal desire overwhelmed us and I gave in to the delicate touches of her fingers on me.

"You like my fingers, don't you?"

"Jesus, Cliesh."

I was in her arms for a minute or two and we lay together, quiet, the hot rush subsiding. She raised her head, looking down at me.

"Can I tell you something?"

"Yes", I said, drawing her to me.

"I love your fingers on my breasts. My nipples are so hard and ever so sore."

She took my left hand and touched the fingers to her erect, firm nipples.

"Feel the little tubercles. You know what they're for, don't you?"

I shook my head. "Did I hurt you? I'm sorry."

"No, Tim you didn't hurt me. You've been too good to me. It's early yet, but I'm late and I'm never late. It's all your fault, Captain."

"Early, late; late for what, Cliesh? I don't understand."

I must have been half asleep. She quieted me, pressing a forefinger to my lips.

"I think I'm pregnant; just newly, but I'm sure."

A surge of emotion possessed me and I held Cliesh protectively. That was ridiculous of course, for she was in no danger; but I had to hold her this way. I found words that for too long, had not been part of me: excluded from the vocabulary of my solitary life and my calling.

"My love, my love," I said.

Life rushes. Meeting Cliesh again, helping her, making her well, getting it right for once in my life and marrying her: events unfolding at a greater force than the sweep of the surf-like Severn Bore. Cliesh was near forty and in the back of my mind I'd prepared for us not to have children, persuading myself that I did not mind. I'd not have dared hope for the blessing of a child; nor would Cliesh. I thanked a merciful God. I loved her and cherished her so much more in that time when she told me; and then I fell into darkness: "Dear God, please don't let anything happen to her." Did I want a boy, a girl? It did not matter, just as long as they were both well and whole. We had created a new life and, I felt so deeply for the child to be more of Cliesh than of me. Being with her, I was so much more: she had only ever brought good into my life. Perhaps it was too early to think about it, but deep down, I harboured a secret desire and impulsively, I revealed it to Cliesh.

"I want our child to be a girl; like you."

"I'm so happy you said that. But I love you, and I'd adore a son like you."

I held her and prayed once more for God to protect them. "Do you feel OK about it?"

"Well it's something of a shock. I'd not expected it. But I'm so excited and yes, yes, I'm happy. I hope I'm not sick and feel tired too often or have to run to the bathroom in the middle of the night. Then you'll hate me."

"Hate you? Never. Do you know when it happened?"

"Yes, I think so. It was that night in the Old Hotel. I just felt so wonderful that we'd married."

I held Cliesh. "You know how much I love you?"

"Oh, Tim. Yes, oh yes, I know."

I prayed that the unit would not deploy to some God forsaken corner of the globe. If we mobilized, then I must be with my men.

We met Dieter in the bar at seven. His dress was immaculate, in every detail, the complete Adjutant Chief, the most senior NCO. He shook hands with Cliesh, kissing her on both cheeks. Then he shook hands with me.

"Good evening, Captain and Madame Ronsard."

Dieter ushered us in to the private function room to firm applause from the seven NCOs assembled there. I was surprised and gladdened by our reception. As I expected, our marriage pleased Dieter, but I thought it unlikely, that apart from a few officers, anyone else would be interested. The welcome by Dieter was even more of a surprise: the senior NCO, at the right hand of the Commanding Officer. We exchanged salutes and though day-to-day, our paths seldom crossed, I always listened to Dieter's advice. He was well into his forties now, tall hewn from mature oak, a soldier of vast experience, a volunteer in the Fallschirmjaeger.

There were some hard cases in that room. Seven veterans: Corporals and Sergeants, men with chequered backgrounds from as many countries, some, whose ways had not meshed with conventional life at home; all of them, transformed and made good in the Legion. Two served in Algeria. Sobel was there, a Sergeant now; and no, he did not marry Maria. She left Algeria and returned to Colombia with her bankroll to assume her good name. He got over the heartache. Another two served with me in Chad and Djibouti. Men like them shaped me and deep down, a part of me remained with them. They respected the legacies from my days in the ranks: the scar on my face and the tattoo, Legio Patria Nostra, on my left forearm. What did Cliesh make of these men? When Dieter introduced the NCOs, they made a good impression, smiling, shaking her hand, bowing from the shoulder, and murmuring a brief greeting. My comrades helped themselves to drinks, tid bits, and every one relaxed. We sipped at small glasses of Cap Cores, a port-like aperitif and ate black olives marinated in oil and rosemary, sharpening our appetites for dinner as we stood with Dieter.

"Delicious," Cliesh said, turning to Dieter. "I see you're wearing the walking out lanyard, the simple Fourragere with the red colour of the Legion d' Honneur." He nodded, smiling.

She glanced at me. Few outside the Legion knew of the citations and modes of dress.

"Ah, so you learned about us, Isobel."

"Yes. The fascinating stories about the Kepi Blanc and the Christmas celebrations."

"How did you find out?"

"Oh, I was curious. Tim told me a good deal and then I made a point of finding out for myself"

Dieter, an authority on the customs and traditions of the Legion, took great pleasure in Cliesh's remarks. It was marked even more, by her mastery of selected details: the origins of the Legion's colours, red and green, in the Swiss 2nd Battalion in 1885; that Pioneers are bearded, wear buffalo aprons and carry axes on ceremonial parades; the blue waist sash; the green tie, and in 1930, General Rollet's restoration of epaulettes with green shoulder strap and red fringes.

"This is your evening, Isobel and I'm neglecting you talking shop," Dieter said. "But I tell you what, once you're settled, I'll help with anything you want to know about the Legion."

Madame Ouzou waved from the door and Dieter excused himself.

"When did you find out about all of this?" I said.

"Oh now and then, when I thought about you; when we were apart. I had to know what kept you in the Legion. It was hard then for me to understand," she said, turning serious. Then she smiled. "Coming here worried me. I went to the Mitchell Library one afternoon with La Divine to find out everything I could."

"You should have asked me. I'd have helped."

"I know. Anyway, I wanted to surprise you." I squeezed her hand.

Madame Ouzou came in, busy opening two parcels, displaying their contents on a dark oak sideboard with an embroidered linen runner on top. A wedding present: plain, silver mounted, Victorian crystal decanter and a dozen matching wine glasses. Dieter tapped his glass with a spoon for silence.

"Captain and Madame Ronsard,' and then, pursing his lips, "Tim, Isobel, my friends: not every one who wanted to could be here tonight. There are many here in spirit. So, I present you with this gift from your friends and comrades, to celebrate your marriage." That was all he said and it was enough.

A peal of warm applause followed. We left the decanter and glasses displayed on the sideboard and went to table. Dieter sat with Cliesh on his right. A Gabonese Corporal sat on her right. I sat on Dieter's left and Sergeant Sobel sat beside me. Dieter had arranged a round table, so that we faced each other and could talk. The settings were simple and elegant, with the napkin folded triple ripple inside the cutlery. Wine and water glasses twinkled in the soft light. I turned to Dieter.

"Nice room. Beautiful table."

"Thanks, Tim. Madame Ouzou was a great help."

The tone of the room was nautical; the walls hung with pictures of local fishing boats, line drawings of sailing men of war and photographs of contemporary French warships. It was a quiet, discreet room. Madame Ouzou's voice rose above the conversation,

"Dinner is served," and turning to Cliesh said, "My Chef is from a mountain village near Monte Rotondo; local dishes are his specialty. I thought it might be a pleasant change for Isobel if we had a Corsican dinner."

"Thank you, that's so kind," Cliesh said.

It would certainly be popular with the NCOs. The Legion fed us well and kept us fit, but in barracks there was no over abundance of food and we seldom left the table satiated.

We dined on vegetable broth, followed by civet de lapin: rabbit cooked with thyme, laurel, garlic, and the creature's chopped liver, heart, and brain. Corsican specialities of sautéed mushrooms and chestnut bread appeared. We drank a full, smooth red wine. Desert, was ricotta-based cheesecake. A large bowl of Clementine's was on the table to cleanse the palate for the final treat: a salty goat's cheese, infested with asticots, small white worms. Madame Ouzou was proud of the cheese.

"You won't find this in a restaurant. The Chef brought it from his village: it's a special treat."

The live texture and the aroma of the cheese perplexed Cliesh. She ate a little, avoiding the worms and protecting our child.

After the meal, the table and the company mingled. We spent time talking and drinking moderately with the NCOs, thanking each one personally for their generosity. Then Dieter moved me to one side, leaving Cliesh in the care of the handsome Gabonese Corporal.

"Isobel's radiant. What have you been doing to her."

"I listened to you; I'm good to her."

Dieter grunted. He liked the way I waited on Cliesh. I was not conscious of it, but I was pleased when he said that he had never seen anyone so considerate of a woman; nothing too obvious: like the way I walked with Cliesh when we came into the baggage hall, touching her arm, taking care of her. He grinned at me. "There's no empty space in your life now, Tim."

"Cliesh's pregnant, Dieter."

"Christ, Tim, that's wonderful." I waved Cliesh over. "He knows," I said. Dieter embraced us and kissed Isobel. "We'd like you to be Godfather," Cliesh said. "Yes of course. You honour me."

Later, when he thought I was out of earshot, Dieter stood with Cliesh. "Tim's a good man, Isobel and a better one for being with you. Tim's one of us. The present, and what happened here tonight; unusual."

Dieter put on his gruff act, laughing. "Not that I'd tell him, mind you. Several people gave something and not just from the Company. Legionnaires and NCOs, who'd transferred to other Companies, made a point of handing the money to me. Madame Ouzou made all the arrangements."

"Dieter, it's a beautiful present, and a lovely evening," Cliesh said.

"Well, Isobel, I remember the nice things in your apartment in Paris."

We said farewell to the NCOs shaking hands with each one. Dieter was last to leave. "Dieter, thank you so much for everything. It's been really wonderful," Cliesh said.

She took him by the shoulders kissing him on both cheeks. He flushed. "Ach, it's nothing."

He turned to me. "You'll be reporting to the CO the day after tomorrow. I'll see you then."

I nodded and embraced my friend."Good night, Dieter. We need another favour. Will you be witness at the civil ceremony?"

"Of course I will. Thank you for asking me."

Back in our room, we chatted as we readied for bed. Soon, Cliesh would want help with her shoes.

"I worried about coming here," she said.

"I know."

"What I found out helped a little but I didn't know what to expect. Tonight was a lovely surprise."

"You feel better about it now?"

"I feel I'm home, where we'll be together after all our years apart. Oh yes, I'll be happy here."

Later that night, our room bathed in the faint illumination of streetlights, I lay on my side, gazing at Cliesh's profile, listening to the quiet, even breathing of her untroubled sleep. I half rose, leaning on my right arm, careful not to wake Cliesh, and have her find me looking. I loved the just-visible outline of her chestnut hair spread on the pillow framing her face. How lovely she was in the lighted darkness.

Cliesh travelled far on her different, but no less arduous journey than mine, displaying the patience and determination it takes to enter French life; in her quiet unassuming way, Cliesh immersed herself in the hidden world of French music that she loved so much. La Divine and others gave friendship and hospitality when they recognized her talent and loveliness, and strength of character. Cliesh's pupils surely worshipped her.

When I first met Cliesh she was a young woman, a girl finding her way and I adored her. In the months when I visited her rooms, I knew that she loved me, but young and self-centred, I had not understood the purity of her selfless love. Now, I knew that Cliesh's love for me meant that she'd had to leave for the North East coast. I felt the power of her love when we met in Paris. But it was at the end of our long, second separation, when we met in Glasgow, that I understood what I meant to this quiet, beautiful woman and convinced her that I was worthy of her. I held my gaze, unable to turn away from Cliesh, fairest among women.

On the plane from Glasgow to Paris, I had thought about the secret harmonies working on Jake and Fergie and the power shaping the destiny of La Divine and my father. This mysterious source worked on us, establishing our fate, guiding us to mend and renew our love. We'd been apart for so long, but we'd never given up loving each other. I whispered thanks to God.

My hushed offering woke Cliesh and she, reaching up, put her hand behind my neck drawing me to her. My chilled shoulders made her draw breath, but she held on, warming me.

"I like looking at you, Cliesh. You keep me awake."

"I think you love me, Tim Ronsard," Cliesh said, her voice was tender with words from long ago.

Long ago; when I yearned for the Music Room just to see her. Loving Cliesh had unhinged me, sent me to Hell for many years. But I'd kept faith with my dreams of her, and now the days of light had come.

About The Author

Thank you for reading my novel. I write historical novels, the kind I'd read, and hope that my books attract readers who'll spread the word.

I've made a living as a seafarer, production planner, personnel manager, and university lecturer.

I like to write. When not writing I'm reading. Then finding time for Jazz, and travel with my wife, especially New York City.

Contact with me online. http://www.jimellisnovels.com/index.html

Books by the Author

One Summer
The Last Hundred
The Music Room
Westburn Blues

Lightning Source UK Ltd.
Milton Keynes UK
UKHW041055231120
373920UK00001B/100

9 781034 013853